WITCHES' BLOOD

GINN HALE

THE RIFTER

VOLUME 2

WITCHES' BLOOD

GINN HALE

BLIND EYE BOOKS
blindeyebooks.com

Witches' Blood
The Rifter Volume Two
by Ginn Hale

Published by Blind Eye Books
315 Prospect Street #5393
Bellingham WA 98227
www.blindeyebooks.com

Edited by Nicole Kimberling
Copyedit by Audrey Salo
Book Design by Dawn Kimberling
Ebook design by Michael DeLuca
Cover Photo by Rungsan Nantaphum

print ISBN: 978-956422-18-4
ebook ISBN: 978-956422-19-1
Library of Congress Control Number: 2025947001
Printed in the United States of America

Contents

Arc3: Assassins in the Seven Palaces

Chapter 20 9
Chapter 21 21
Chapter 22 32
Chapter 23 42
Chapter 24 44

Arc Four: Amidst the Holy and Profane

Previously 49

Chapter 25 50
Chapter 26 59
Chapter 27 68
Chapter 28 74
Chapter 29 83
Chapter 30 93
Chapter 31...................... 102
Chapter 32 107
Chapter 33 120
Chapter 34 127
Chapter 35 134
Chapter 36 149
Chapter 37 156
Chapter 38 161
Chapter 39 171
Chapter 40 182
Chapter 41 199

Maps .... 6 & 7
Characters ....213 & 215
Ranks and Titles 217
Dictionary 218-219
Grammar 220-221
About the Author 223
Content Warning.................. 225

Black Tower
Ruins
Jath'ibaye's
Glass Palace
Seven Palaces
Bousim
Gaunsho'im
Council Hall
Lisam
Samsira River
Silver Row District
Water Street
Blackbird
Bridge
Domu'lam
Club
Red Brick District
Bousim
Barracks
Gallows
Alidas's Rooms

Nurjima

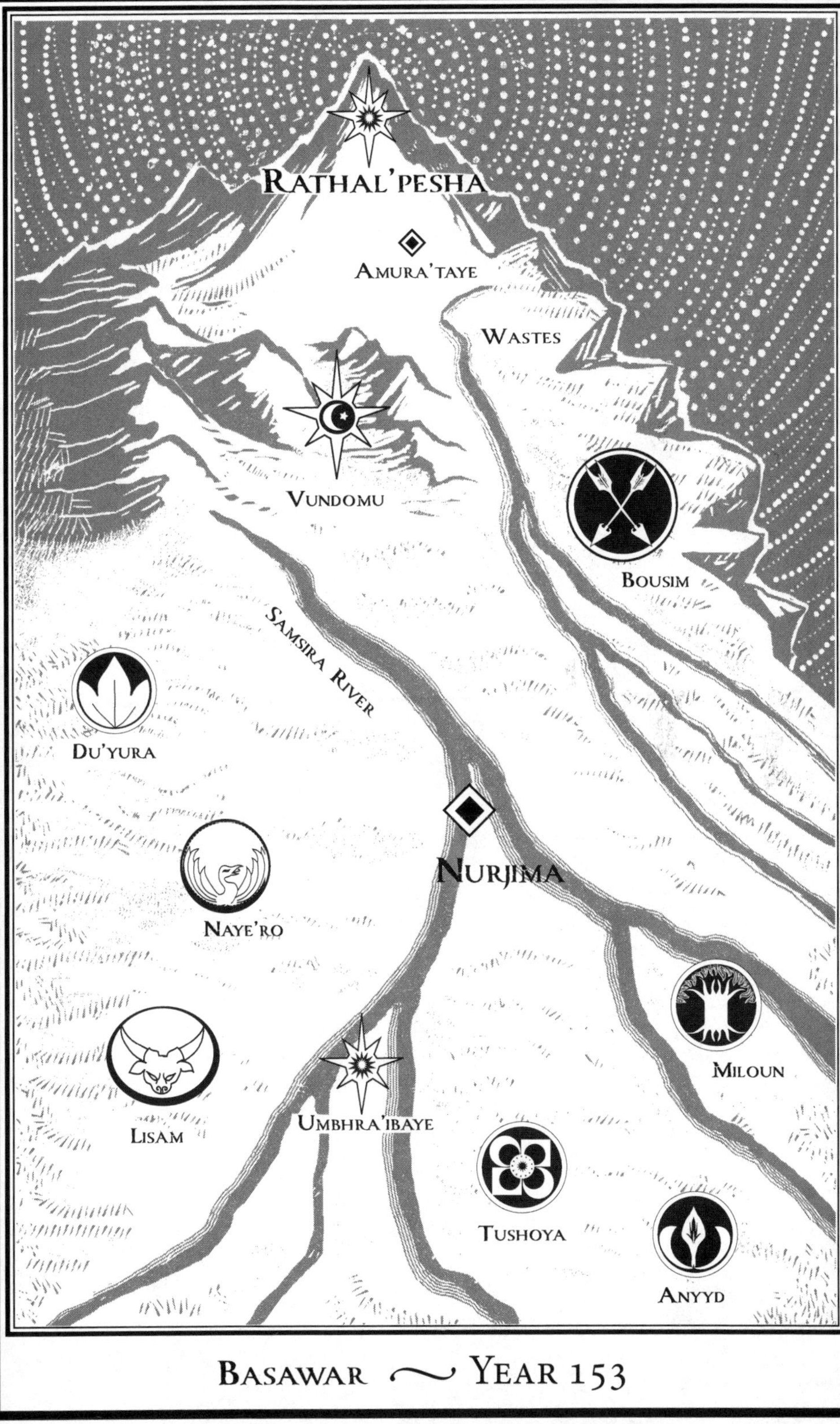

Basawar ~ Year 153

Arc3: Assassins in the Seven Palaces

Chapter Twenty

The panes of Jath'ibaye's Glass Palace reflected the amber glow of the setting sun. At twilight, the glass sheets caught the light so well that they seemed cut from the sky itself, lending the building an ethereal beauty. But the sharp barbs of the surrounding fence stood in stark contrast. Black iron pickets rose above Kahlil in a twisting wall of cast-iron thorns and heavy bars.

Although a number of the palaces were surrounded by fences of ferocious appearance, Kahlil had found most of them easily surmountable. Designs of curving claws and massive teeth often presented perfect handgrips and footholds.

Not that he normally needed to resort to climbing, but still, he couldn't keep himself from reaching out and lightly gripping one of the curving iron projections. It looked strong enough to support a man's weight.

Tiny sharp teeth stung his fingertips. Immediately, Kahlil pulled his hand back. Long, sharp needles encrusted the top side of the iron thorn. Even the tentative pressure of Kahlil's curious touch had been enough to sink them into his flesh. He glanced down at the dark blood beading on his fingertips.

Obviously, Jath'ibaye wasn't fool enough to trust the safety of his palace to any purely ornamental menace. Kahlil supposed he should take some reassurance in that knowledge. Perhaps it meant that Jath'ibaye would be capable of deterring his own assassination.

He had certainly seemed strong and capable enough to do so last night. Kahlil suppressed a shudder of dread at the memory of Jath'ibaye's powerful grip. The previous night's encounter had not been exactly amicable, and he wasn't sure how Jath'ibaye would react to seeing him again. At the same moment, he felt a pulse of excitement. There had been such recognition in Jath'ibaye's face.

The man knew him and Kahlil needed to know how.

He curled his hand into a tight fist, allowing the pressure to staunch the tiny wounds—the last thing he wanted was to stain the white surface of the package he was to deliver—and then he walked his bicycle toward the great iron gate.

Surprisingly, the gates hung open, though two sentries stood posted alongside them. The sentries' tanned and weathered faces made it hard to guess their ages, but neither had gray hair. Their coats were sewn from thick goat hide that might have been dyed bright red at one time but now had faded to dull russet. Their boots were stained and dusty.

They suffered in comparison to the sentries at the Lisam Palace, who wore gold ceremonial swords, and bright badges of rank. These two men gave Kahlil more of the impression of conscripted goat herders than of men in a dress guard.

But their smooth, gleaming rifles shone with the same meticulous care that other dress guards reserved for their buttons.

It wasn't the uniform that made the soldier, he supposed.

"Lisam runner." Kahlil held up Fensal's soapstone seal.

The sentries examined the seal, looked him over, and told him he had to leave his bicycle at the gate. Then one of the sentries escorted him across the open stone courtyard and into the Glass Palace.

The first two floors of the palace weren't built from panes of glass, but from heavy stone. The massive entry doors were solid, black iron. In any gaunsho's palace such doors would have been a foolish extravagance. What iron they could bargain out of Jath'ibaye was always put to use for guns, engines, or new rails. It couldn't be wasted just hanging around as entry doors.

Inside, the sentry handed him over to a muscular auburn-haired man. He looked about Alidas' age, his crow's feet and smile lines lending him an air of experience rather than decline. Unlike the sentries, he wore a new, well-tailored suit.

From his reddish hair and expensive clothes, Kahlil would have guessed that he came from a refined southern family. But his speech destroyed that impression. His words compacted and split in the unmistakable cadence of a northern peasant. Kahlil recognized the accent from countless exchanges with the refugees, thieves, beggars, and whores of the west dock slums.

"I'm Saimura, Jath'ibaye's steward." The man paused, peering at Kahlil closely. "Have we met before?"

Uncertainty shivered through Kahlil. He didn't really know the answer to that question, but he had no intention of saying so.

"No, I don't think so," he replied. "We runners are all over the city. You may have seen me somewhere else."

"True." Saimura nodded. "So, you have a delivery?"

Kahlil took the small box and letter out of his satchel and offered them to the steward. Saimura made no move to accept them.

"They're unmarked," Saimura commented.

"They're meant for Jath'ibaye, but I'm sure it would be fine for me to leave them in your care. You are his house steward, after all." Kahlil gave his best smile.

"That's very trusting of you." Saimura returned his smile but without any enthusiasm. "But I'm afraid that Jath'ibaye insists on proper procedure. You can wait for him in the mist garden. It's relaxing there, and you look quite tired."

"Thank you," Kahlil responded out of habit. He carefully tucked the box and letter back into his satchel and followed Saimura out of the entryway through a wide whitewashed hall.

The darkening rays of orange sunlight poured down from the glass roof two stories above, coloring the walls peach and gold. Kahlil paused and looked up at the sky. At the dull dark center, he could see the faint curve of the crescent moon shining above him like the ghost of a smile.

Saimura glanced back at him and Kahlil hurried to catch the steward. As he walked, he caught voices coming from other rooms. Most of them sounded like Saimura, poor and northern. None of the walls, floors, or ceilings were decorated. Over the doorways, there was only a hand-painted design of two leaves, one red and the other green. The emptiness bordered on monastic.

He didn't know why, but the starkness of the surroundings evoked a weird nostalgia. Out of some forgotten habit, his right hand automatically folded into the Payshmura gesture of peace. When Kahlil noticed, he hid his hands in his coat pockets.

Saimura stopped in front of a door. It, like the others, was black iron, but it had been varnished far more heavily. Its surface gleamed in the fading sunlight.

Saimura asked, "Are you hungry?"

"A little, yes."

"Runners always are." With some effort, Saimura pulled the door open. "Go on in. I'll have some food brought for you. It may be a long wait for Jath'ibaye."

Beyond Saimura, Kahlil saw a profusion of greenery. Walls of ferns and wild ivy sprouted from massive planters lining a huge room whose floor was nothing more than a winding trail between raised beds teeming with lush foliage. He could barely discern the far wall between thick bodies of trees, whose branches reached up past his line of sight.

"There are some benches just down the path," Saimura said.

Kahlil mumbled his thanks, still gaping at the foliage. It seemed like Jath'ibaye had captured a forest and put it inside this one huge room.

Why would anyone, even an Eastern sorcerer, want to keep the outdoors inside?

Rich, scented air rolled over him, bringing to mind the intoxicating air of Nayeshi. He closed his eyes and took in a deep breath so saturated with life that he felt like it could sustain him for hours.

He opened his eyes and noticed Saimura observing him from the door with amusement.

"Breathe as much as you like. It's free," Saimura told him. Then he let the door drop closed. The latch slid into place with a heavy reverberation.

Locked in again. Or, at least, that was what Saimura had intended to do. Kahlil smirked at the thought of common doors and walls restraining him, but he remained. He certainly had no reason yet to disprove Saimura's confidence in the building's security.

He could escape through the Gray Space any time he wanted, but he chose to push ahead into this lush forest.

He strode deeper into the immense chamber.

Overhead, open walkways arched from one side of the second-story mezzanine to the other. A few lamps flickered up there, but otherwise only the last red and violet streaks of the sunset burned against the dark night sky. The white stone floor stood out against the surrounding black soil and deep, shadowy foliage.

Kahlil found the stone bench Saimura had mentioned beside a mound of grayish goatweed, yellow bellflowers, and another scrubby plant he didn't recognize. Two slim chains hung down from the ceiling, supporting unlit lanterns. Kahlil was glad that they weren't burning. The evening darkness seemed to better suit both the surroundings and his mood.

He carefully avoided touching the goatweed, as he knew from experience that it gave him a rash, even if he couldn't remember precisely what that experience had been. It struck him as an odd plant to choose to cultivate, though dimly he recalled that its musky leaves could be used to induce vomiting. The roots, however, contained a deadly poison.

More evidence that Jath'ibaye wasn't exactly helpless.

He sat down to wait.

Somewhere, in one of the trees, birds called to one another.

Just ahead, there came a rustling of dark leaves, then a big yellow dog stepped out from between two bushes. Its hide was faded and graying, but its eyes gleamed clear gold. The dog met his gaze, and Kahlil knew he had seen it before. He stared at the animal with the uneasy feeling of having slipped into a dream: a terribly wrong dream.

A dream in which this dog was his sister.

Her teeth had yellowed with age and her eyes gleamed wild gold. She told him that her true skin had been stripped from her bones and this hide was just a coat to keep her warm. She laughed and he could smell raw meat on her hot breath. Then her brilliant red blood was pouring over his hands.

He couldn't stop staring at it.

After a moment, the dog dropped its gaze from him and rustled back through the undergrowth, disappearing out of sight and hearing.

He put his head in his hands. He had thought he had finally overcome this kind of insane reaction.

The dog was just a dog. The world was full of them. It didn't mean anything. This one had probably escaped the kitchen kennel and was now wandering the household, lost. That was just what dogs did. He couldn't let the sight of one animal throw his mind into disarray. Otherwise, he would end up the same confused, deluded mess he had been before Alidas had found him.

He wished this place weren't so disconcertingly familiar. The leaf designs above the doors, the worn red uniforms, even the smell of the air, everything around him seemed like a fragment of one of his dreams suddenly made real. It awakened shattered bits of memories and nightmare images that he had thought forgotten.

His sister was not a dog. He felt absurd even having to tell himself as much. He didn't even know if he had a sister. Family and history both fell into the realms of conjecture. He didn't really know anything about himself.

But Jath'ibaye did. When Jath'ibaye had looked at him, his hard gaze had been bright with recognition. Last night, Kahlil hadn't dared to stay and see what judgment would come after that first moment of contact. But he couldn't stop thinking about Jath'ibaye's expression—or about the certainty that had flooded him the instant he'd met the other man's stare. They had known each other.

Had they been friends? Had they been enemies? Was Jath'ibaye, like Fikiri, another man who could claim the right to be called a Kahlil?

His gut roiled with a turmoil of questions, but for now he had to bide in patience. There was nothing to do but wait and hope Jath'ibaye would bring the answers.

About twenty minutes later, a young, plump kitchen woman arrived. She lit the lantern above him and then gave him a tray of taye bread, goat cutlets, and steamed blue leaf. Kahlil ate the food and recalled that the Lisam kitchen women had said that coarse, simple food was all that Jath'ibaye ever ate—the kind of thing peasants lived on because they had to. Kahlil couldn't imagine anyone choosing this as their only sustenance. After he finished the meal, he pushed his dishes under the bench.

With every new detail, Jath'ibaye seemed more and more strange and yet more familiar for his oddity. It felt right to Kahlil that Jath'ibaye should choose coarse food. He was suddenly sure that the man drank his daru'sira strong and bitter and that he licked his fingers when he ate pungent goat cheese.

High in the sky, he could see that dim stars had joined the sharp moon. He'd expected that with nightfall the air would grow chilly around him, but it remained warm and sweet. Who knew when Jath'ibaye would arrive? Maybe he wouldn't, and the steward would take the packages after all.

Kahlil smirked at the thought. All this worry, all his fear and hope, just to have the house steward hand him a sweetdrop candy for a tip and thank him for his trouble. That was how this would probably all end up. He guttered the lantern overhead and closed his eyes for a nap.

He didn't sleep, but he stretched his legs out and let his arms lie limp across his stomach. He listened to the sounds around him. Somewhere far off, two men talked in low voices, a strange collision of northern and southern dialects. The words were indistinguishable but the tones rolled over him with soft calm.

As the voices drew closer, Kahlil cracked an eye. On the walkway above him, a lamp gleamed. Two men walked close, but did not touch. He knew them at once: Ourath Lisam and Jath'ibaye.

"You seem distracted this evening." Ourath's voice was tinged with concern. Light from the perfume lamp he carried glowed over his brown velvet jacket.

"It's nothing." Jath'ibaye turned from the lamplight to survey the greenery beneath him. Though his long blond hair was pulled back, it still looked wild, as if it had been restrained in the midst of an escape. He wore clothes like those of his sentries: heavy and simple. But he carried no weapon that Kahlil could see.

"Winter seemed so long this year," Ourath commented.

Jath'ibaye turned back to Ourath but said nothing. Despite his age—Kahlil knew he had to be fifty at the least, older most likely—he appeared as young as Ourath, more powerfully built and much fairer-skinned, but still so young.

Though it struck Kahlil that he should not look so very pale. He seemed almost ill. Then Kahlil recalled the poisoning Fikiri had mentioned.

"It's probably only a whim of the weather," Ourath went on lightly. "I'm sure that it will be warm soon enough."

When Jath'ibaye still made no reply, Ourath began toying with the handle of his perfume lamp. Steadily, he swung it from side to side, causing the chains holding the lamp to spin. The shadows surrounding him jumped and twisted into each other.

"Careful." Jath'ibaye caught the chains and slowly stilled Ourath's lamp. "You don't want to spill burning oil."

Those tiny silver chains had to be hot. They had to burn into Jath'ibaye's palm, but he didn't seem to notice or care. Ourath's full lips spread into a deep smile.

"I'm touched that you are so worried for me." Then he gave a theatrical pout. "Or are you simply afraid that I might burn down your little forest?"

"Whichever you like. Just don't do it again." Jath'ibaye released the chains. His voice conveyed the cold authority of a trainer disciplining a dog. Hardly the manner of the malleable effeminate Ourath had made him out to be during his secret dinner.

"I didn't mean to anger you," Ourath said softly.

"You didn't."

"Really? You seem angry."

Jath'ibaye looked at Ourath as if he were looking through him. "Would it please you if I were? Would it make this easier?"

"Of course it wouldn't." Ourath began to twist the lamp handle again but then stopped himself. "You know I want you to be happy."

Jath'ibaye said nothing. Then again, Kahlil supposed he might become quite taciturn himself had he just been poisoned.

Ourath sighed and said, "You're annoyed because I announced that you would be attending the Bell Dance, aren't you?"

Again, Jath'ibaye didn't respond, and now Kahlil began to wonder if his own questions would be met with the same stony silence Ourath currently enjoyed. He hoped not.

"I'm not asking you to attend because I want you to suffer." Ourath shook his head and his red hair gleamed like polished copper. "And inviting you certainly hasn't done my standing any good. But this is more important than a little social discomfort. If you do come, it will be the first real, meaningful, peaceful gesture since the truce. The Bell Dance is the night we celebrate the alliances of the noble houses. If you attend, I think it would demonstrate to the gaunsho'im that you respect their authority. They need to feel that you aren't just out to destroy them. You say that you want real peace between—"

"I'll go." Jath'ibaye cut him off. "Just don't expect a miracle to come of it."

"Thank you." Ourath gave another handsome smile.

Jath'ibaye simply turned again to stare down at the trees and greenery beneath him. Kahlil squinted up, trying to read his expression. Then he realized that Jath'ibaye returned his gaze. Jath'ibaye stood there, still and silent, looking through the darkness directly at him. A flush of embarrassment flooded Kahlil and he had no idea why.

Jath'ibaye's expression remained as closed as that of a marble statue, his pale eyes luminous in the night.

Kahlil felt his skin flushing hotter, an alarming reaction that he couldn't remember having since his awkward youth. In a sudden panic, Kahlil looked down at his boots as if they had become instantaneously interesting. Slowly, his cheeks cooled.

When he stole a glance back up to the walkway, Jath'ibaye was escorting Ourath across to the eastern side of the building.

"You can see the moon flowers blooming from here," Jath'ibaye said. "They originally grew wild in the southern lands but have died out in the last ten years. I've found them to have a good effect on soils that have been over-farmed."

Jath'ibaye went on describing the properties of weeds and bushes that had apparently died out in the south. The light of Ourath's lamp grew dimmer. Kahlil strained to hear more, but Jath'ibaye and Ourath had moved too far away. He only caught the low rumble of Ourath's voice and then nothing else.

Kahlil stayed put, too shocked by his own reaction to move. It had been inexplicable, unexpected, and humiliating. He'd probably been as red-faced as a bride caught on the chamber pot.

Time passed while Kahlil hunched in the darkness feeling juvenile and self-conscious. Even Alidas had never been able to provoke such a reaction from him. He had to be more exhausted than he had thought. Or perhaps it had been the result of being caught spying on two men in such an obviously private exchange.

Were they really lovers? Last night Ourath had both implied and denied it. Jath'ibaye had seemed cold toward Ourath. Though, in the end, he had given Ourath what he wanted.

Somewhere in the distance of the greenery, Kahlil thought he heard leaves rustling.

"Runner." Saimura's voice broke into his thoughts.

Kahlil jumped up to face the man.

"Yes?"

"I'm sorry to have startled you. I wasn't sure where you were." Saimura squinted through the darkness at him. "I thought that Addya lit a lantern for you."

"She did, but I was feeling tired, so I snuffed it."

"I see," Saimura said. "I came to tell you that Jath'ibaye has retired for the evening."

Kahlil didn't know whether to be relieved or disappointed. He supposed it didn't matter. "You'll want me to leave the package with you, then."

Kahlil reached for his satchel, but before he could dig the package out, Saimura stopped him.

"I won't be taking it."

Kahlil scowled. He wasn't actually going to be asked to come back tomorrow, was he? He wouldn't do it. He'd just throw the damn package away before he went through this again.

"Jath'ibaye requested that you be escorted up to his personal chambers and deliver the package to him there."

☾☾☾

Jath'ibaye's chambers were plain, almost ascetically so. There was a fireplace but no fire. The bare stone floors and walls radiated the night chill. The only light came from an oil lamp on the table, and the room smelled of bitter medicinal herbs.

On the wide bed a roll of bandages lay next to a scalpel. But as Saimura escorted Kahlil into the room, Jath'ibaye snatched both items up and secreted them away in a blackwood box at the bedside.

He stood immediately and welcomed Saimura with a quick smile. His blond hair hung loose, and this close, Kahlil could see how sun and weather had streaked it to white in places. He wore no coat now, just reddish work pants, and his white shirt hung open. Kahlil frowned at the white swath of bandages that encircled Jath'ibaye's broad chest. As if sensing Kahlil's attention, Jath'ibaye turned his back and buttoned his shirt.

"That was certainly fast," Jath'ibaye commented over his shoulder to Saimura.

"I thought sooner would be better than later." Saimura looked to the clay teapot and empty cup on the table. Kahlil recognized the scent of yellowpetal blossoms, so often used by northern physicians to ease pain.

"Should I have Addya bring up more tea?" Saimura asked.

"No." Jath'ibaye turned to face them. He focused his attention on Saimura, hardly glancing at Kahlil. "I'm fine."

Saimura nodded. "Has Ji spoken to you yet?"

"No, but I can wait till tomorrow." Jath'ibaye tied his hair back from his face. As he did, Kahlil noticed that he moved his left arm carefully, guarding himself from pulling a tender spot on the left side of his chest.

"I thought as much," Saimura said. "I couldn't find her anyway."

"She's probably still out digging up the garden." Jath'ibaye smiled slightly.

"Probably true." Saimura shrugged, and then to Kahlil's surprise, he simply walked away.

Kahlil wasn't used to seeing servants, not even house stewards, taking leave of their lords so casually. Jath'ibaye seemed unfazed by Saimura's presumption. He turned back to the blackwood cupboard and opened a drawer.

Kahlil waited, nervously watching Jath'ibaye's back.

His presence dominated the room. Even now, with his back turned, bent over a drawer, Kahlil could focus on nothing else. Physically, he was intimidating, taller than Kahlil, with a sharp, muscular body. Even pale and poisoned, he seemed like he would be a tough man to take on.

But he was more than a physical presence. He had destroyed the Payshmura and held back the armies of the gaunsho'im. As one of the rare few who had altered the world to his will, Jath'ibaye both fascinated and frightened Kahlil. Yet he seemed strong, quiet, and perfectly human. And that made him even stranger. Kahlil expected demons and gods to change the world, not mere men.

"So." Jath'ibaye straightened. Whatever he had been looking for he had either found or given up on. "You have something to give me?"

He turned but didn't look at Kahlil. Instead, he seemed to be taking in the measurements of his room. Again Kahlil noticed how pale and bright his eyes looked. But this time he knew why. It was the brilliance of a fever.

Kahlil dug the letter and box out of his satchel. He offered Fensal's seal, but Jath'ibaye didn't seem to care about it. He yanked the small white box and letter from Kahlil's hands. With angry efficiency, he tore open the envelope and flipped the letter out and read. After a while he crushed the letter and dropped it to the floor. He tossed the box onto his bed, unopened.

"So," Jath'ibaye's voice was almost a growl, "am I supposed to take one look at you, fall to my knees, and hand you the keys to the kingdom? Is that it?"

Kahlil had no idea how to respond.

"I . . . don't know. I didn't read the letter," Kahlil said. What was Jath'ibaye talking about?

"God," Jath'ibaye whispered, "even your voice . . ."

He rounded on Kahlil, his expression cold and disdainful. "Well then, let's play our little drama out, shall we? Shouldn't you tell me your name?"

Kahlil stepped closer to the door. "Kyle'insira."

"Kyle . . . of course!" Jath'ibaye's smile was hardly more than a flash of his white teeth. "Very clever. Go on. You have to have more lines than just that."

Kahlil stood silent. Until this moment, it hadn't occurred to him that when Jath'ibaye had looked at him with recognition, it might have been the crazed expression of familiarity that a fevered man had for his hallucinations.

"Stage fright?" Jath'ibaye demanded. "Or did Fikiri just tell you to stand there and bat your eyelashes?"

"Fikiri?" At last Kahlil had some idea of what to say. "No, I'm not with him. I've been sent to stop him—to save you."

"Nice delivery," Jath'ibaye replied. "Very believable."

"I'm telling you the truth—" Kahlil began, only to be cut off.

"I could kill you for this," Jath'ibaye ground out. "I should."

"But I'm not who—"

"Of course you're not," Jath'ibaye snapped. "You're just an innocent boy who wandered in looking like this and delivered me a bottle of poison." Suddenly Jath'ibaye caught hold of Kahlil's shoulders and pulled him close. His grip was hard and burning hot.

"If they told you I wouldn't hurt you, they lied," Jath'ibaye growled.

He was so close that Kahlil could smell the blood in his bandages. He wasn't about to stay here and find out how Jath'ibaye preferred to punish his enemies. Kindness to Fensal, duty to Alidas, and even his own curiosity weren't worth this. Kahlil jerked his arm back and slammed his fist into Jath'ibaye's wounded left side.

He felt the warm wet of blood soaking up against his knuckles. Jath'ibaye's grip loosened fractionally and Kahlil sprung back from him. With a flick of his hand Kahlil tore open an entry to the Gray Space, but it crumpled closed before he could step in.

Horrified, he looked back to see Jath'ibaye clenching his hand into a fist. Kahlil felt the air shuddering around Jath'ibaye. Somehow, he had closed the Gray Space. True fear surged through Kahlil and his heart pounded like a wild thing kicking in a trap.

He lunged for the door, but Jath'ibaye sprang forward, again blocking his escape. Kahlil stumbled back, evading Jath'ibaye's grasp.

Jath'ibaye stalked slowly after him. Softly, he said, "Didn't they tell you what I am? Didn't they warn you?"

The back of Kahlil's leg struck the bed.

Jath'ibaye dove forward and slammed into Kahlil, hurling him back onto the hard mattress and pinning him against the bed. He caught Kahlil by the throat. His fingers burned like heated irons against Kahlil's skin.

Kahlil fought against Jath'ibaye's grip, but his hands only tightened. He kicked Jath'ibaye's leg as hard as he could, but the other man barely seemed to register it.

Jath'ibaye leaned forward over him. His blue eyes burned like phosphorus. "Didn't they tell you that I am the Rifter?"

Kahlil's arms and legs began to tingle. He clawed at Jath'ibaye's tightening grip. He could put no force behind his kicks now. He gagged and gasped hopelessly.

"Do you understand what I could do to you?" Jath'ibaye whispered over him.

Kahlil's ears rang; his mouth felt numb.

Then, abruptly, Jath'ibaye released him and stepped back from the bed. Kahlil sucked in a desperate breath of air.

"Get out," Jath'ibaye said coldly.

Kahlil had already struggled to his feet. He stumbled toward the door.

"If I ever see you again, I will kill you," Jath'ibaye warned him.

Kahlil didn't stay to hear anything else. His mind burned with just one word, one thought.

Rifter.

Chapter Twenty-one

Kahlil lay curled on the cool surface of the tiled floor. Nausea welled up in him, rolling and rising. His throat ached. Painfully, he swallowed.

The Rifter. After a decade of watching over John, how could he have let his true identity slip from his mind? He had bled himself nearly to death just to pursue the Rifter, just to kill him. How could he have forgotten?

He squeezed his eyes closed and pressed his face against the floor. He remembered the overwhelming feeling of guilt that had enveloped him when he had first tried to find the Black Tower of the Payshmura. Even then, he had known its absence was his fault, his failing. He had allowed the Rifter to escape, and now the Payshmura were no more.

The sacred convent of Umbhra'ibaye and the holy Black Tower had both been lost in an instant, as if devoured by the earth. Rathal'pesha and the city of Amura'taye had been consumed by geysers of molten stone. The entire northland, where he had grown up, rendered a shattered ruin in a day. Whole mountains had fallen, chasms of magma and steaming waters swallowing them. People had died, thousands of them, in the first disaster and then more in the following wars.

It all could have been stopped, but he had failed.

Maybe that's why he'd chosen for so long to forget.

Kahlil pushed himself up to his knees and lurched over the cold porcelain basin. His stomach heaved, bringing up nothing but bile. He coughed. There was nothing left in him to vomit up, but he couldn't stop feeling sick with self-loathing.

He folded back down against the floor.

He had wanted to forget. He had needed to forget.

That very first day when he had arrived in Nurjima he had known, somewhere deep in himself, that he had already been too late.

Now the solace of amnesia had been stripped from him.

He remembered the torn envelope, the letter with its single word: Don't.

Don't fail.

Don't forget.

Don't let him live.

Only one word to obey, and he hadn't managed it.

Dayyid had been right: the taint in his blood, the weakness in his soul went even deeper than Parfir's blessing in his bones. They should have burned him along with his mother.

He'd been sick for hours now, purging everything from his body as if it could somehow empty him of his guilt. He leaned his forehead against the edge of the basin. Strings of his long black hair hung against his damp face.

"Kyle?"

He glanced up to see Fensal, and then hung his head back over the basin, glad of the predawn dimness. No matter how bad he felt, having a witness to his pathetic state made it worse.

"You've been at it all night. Are you dying?"

"I wish," Kahlil managed to croak.

A smaller figure stepped out from behind Fensal. Yu'mir stared at him with wide, worried eyes. Kahlil hung his head in shame, suddenly aware of how badly he stank. Though men in the barrack routinely witnessed each other's wretched states, it seemed somehow wrong to expose a woman to the sight of him.

"You should have called me sooner, Fensal." She crouched down beside Kahlil.

"You shouldn't be here." Kahlil's voice splintered as he tried to speak. His breath tasted of vomit.

"You're hardly in any condition to take me by force," Yu'mir said, misunderstanding his concern. "And I'm not too worried about falling victim to your seductive charms either."

He heard the snort of Fensal's repressed laughter.

"I brought whiteshell tablets." Yu'mir took a small paper packet from the pocket of her apron and placed it in his hand. "Do you think you can keep them down?"

He didn't know what he could keep down, or even if he wanted to keep anything down. A pathetic, tired part of him just wanted to die and have done with it. How hard could it be to simply die?

The moment the thought came to Kahlil, he rejected it.

He had failed. He had ruined the world. No amount of remorse would change that, and he had no right to expect the release of death. He had no right to dream of it, as he did each night. He deserved to feel bad and he deserved to suffer, but he didn't deserve to die yet. He had too many obligations.

Just sagging here, making himself sick like this, was both pathetic and self-indulgent. Only he knew of the world that might have been, of the world that had been lost. To everyone else this was simply life. Fensal and Yu'mir had their own concerns. Alidas had his. They were all present and real. Kahlil's guilt and sickness stemmed from an unalterable past and he needed to pull himself together and see to his present duties.

He opened Yu'mir's paper packet and dumped the chalky whiteshell tablets into his palm. They smelled of salt. Certainly a fresher odor than the one currently clinging to Kahlil. He swallowed them with a gulp of the cool water.

Yu'mir placed the palm of her hand against his forehead.

"I don't think you have a fever. Did you eat something bad?"

"Goatweed, I think." Kahlil took another drink of the water, using it to rinse his mouth out a little. "There was some growing in Jath'ibaye's garden and I was playing with it."

"I've never heard of it." Yu'mir glanced at the cup in Kahlil's hand. "Do you need more water?"

"Yes, thank you."

"It's no trouble." She took the empty cup and handed it back to Fensal. "Get him some more water."

"Me?" Fensal asked.

"Yes, you. You're in his debt," Yu'mir replied firmly.

"So you've told me," Fensal said. "But this is only going to last so long. I'm not going to be serving him hand and foot from now on."

Yu'mir rolled her eyes at Fensal's retreating back. She said, "He can be such an ass sometimes."

"He's not so bad," Kahlil told her, "especially if you ignore everything he says."

Yu'mir smiled. It made her look pretty. Not beautiful, she didn't have that kind of face, but she had a kindness to her expression that could make her quite pretty.

"Feeling any better?" Yu'mir asked.

Kahlil nodded. "I think the worst of it's over."

"So, goatweed?" Yu'mir asked. "What is it, exactly?"

"Just a plant." Kahlil leaned back against a tiled wall.

"I've never heard of it."

"Yes, you said that." Kahlil watched as she straightened her dress around her. He wondered if Fensal had the good sense to find her pretty.

"You look a little dazed," Yu'mir said. "Should you move back closer to the—"

"No." Kahlil shook his head. "I'm just tired. I think the tablets are helping."

"They usually do. If not, then dewroot will," Yu'mir assured him.

"You're quite the physician, aren't you?" Kahlil smiled. Fensal really should marry her, he decided. She'd make a good mother.

"It's mostly herbalism." Yu'mir dropped her voice a little. "That's why I'm curious about your goatweed."

"Oh." As his miserable nausea faded, Kahlil began to realize how exhausted he was. The bruises across his right leg and his throat throbbed with a dull pain in time with his heartbeat.

Yu'mir obviously waited for a better response.

"It's not as though I'm practicing witchcraft," Yu'mir suddenly explained. "Just teas and a few tablets like the ones I gave you. Nothing . . ."

A shadow of worry crossed her face, though he was the last person she needed to fear. Her small concoctions of flowers and leaves were the soul of innocence. They were simple medicines, more cookery to them than power. Kahlil had seen true witchcraft.

"My mother was a witch." Kahlil didn't know why he said it, except that the knowledge had just come to him. "She taught me about goatweed, yellowpetal, and fire vines . . ." He couldn't remember much else about her, except that they had burned her. He'd been young.

He closed his eyes. He didn't want to remember anything more. Not about himself or his life. He just wanted to slip away into the respite of a thoughtless, dreamless darkness.

"Kyle," Yu'mir whispered his name.

He could feel her hands against his forehead again and then touching the pulse at his throat. He must have fallen asleep for a few minutes. The silent dark had been so alluring.

"Kyle," she said again, "are you still awake?"

"I'm sorry. I'm not thinking very clearly." With an effort, he opened his eyes. "Have I told you that I think you'd make a good mother?"

"No." Yu'mir looked a little startled.

"Not for my children." Kahlil smirked at the impossibility of that. "For yours and Fensal's."

Even in the faint light, Kahlil could see the blush that swept across Yu'mir's cheeks.

Then Fensal came through the doorway. For the first time, Kahlil realized that Fensal was only wearing his thin cotton underpants. The skin of his bare chest and arms looked blue in the cold morning light. He must have gone straight from his bed to get Yu'mir.

He had a clay cup in one hand and a pitcher of water in the other. He set the pitcher and cup down, then crouched beside Yu'mir. Next to her, Fensal looked rangy and unkempt. His brown hair stuck up in clumps from where he'd slept on it. Yu'mir's hair was pulled back into a smooth bun at the back of her neck. She'd probably been up for a few hours already, overseeing the morning baking.

"So, he's poisoned?" Fensal asked Yu'mir.

"I'm not sure." Yu'mir poured more water for Kahlil and handed him the cup.

He drank slowly, letting the cool liquid soothe his throat. The bruises Jath'ibaye had left on his throat were probably beginning to darken by now. They'd be black and yellow in a day. He didn't know how he'd explain them. Perhaps he'd be gone by then. Maybe sooner.

"Kyle." Yu'mir lightly touched his hand as he set the empty cup down. "Can you tell me more about the plant you ate? The goatweed?"

"It won't kill me," Kahlil assured her. "I just got some on my hands and forgot about it when I ate dinner. I wasn't thinking."

"I'll say." Fensal frowned at him, then looked to Yu'mir. "So, this goatweed will wear off eventually. It's not going to kill him, is it?"

"Why do you keep asking me?" Yu'mir asked. "I've never even heard of the stuff before now."

"It grows in the north, on scrub hills. Three gray leaves with orange tips," Kahlil said. "If the leaves are eaten, they purge the body. Only goats and sheep can keep it down. It's an unpleasant plant, but the leaves alone won't kill a grown man."

"I'm just going to tell Desh'oun and the others that you're ill. Don't tell anyone else about this weed-eating of yours. It just makes us all look stupid." Fensal paused for a moment and then added, "Particularly you. It makes you look the stupidest."

"I won't do it again." Kahlil couldn't help but find Fensal's terrible bedside manner somewhat endearing.

"Stop lecturing him," Yu'mir said, "and get him to his bed. I have to go before the other runners see me here."

"Go, go." Fensal waved her away. "Thank you for coming."

Yu'mir smiled when Fensal turned his back to her. Then she slipped quietly away.

"Can you walk on your own?" Fensal asked.

"I think so." He stumbled out of the bathroom back into the quiet barrack. The canvas panels were still spread around the other runners' beds, creating an illusion of emptiness. Kahlil went to his own bed. He stripped off his thin, stinking underclothes and lay down naked. The cold sheets smelled clean.

Fensal followed him to the edge of his bed. Kahlil had expected that Fensal would just go back to bed himself, but then he realized that it was too late for that. Thin rays of dawn sunlight were already seeping through the small windows.

"How did the races go?" Kahlil whispered.

Fensal grinned and sat on the edge of Kahlil's bed.

"Good. The only one who came close to me was Nam. He's one of Jath'ibaye's runners. The bastard is a beast on hills. But I know the streets better. I took him at Baker Cross. He pulled off when he saw the trolley coming and I tore right past him."

"I'm sorry I missed it."

"There's always next year." Fensal rose. "I'm getting the rest of the men up now. You stay here and sleep. I want you well tomorrow."

He pulled the canvas panels around Kahlil's bed closed. Kahlil could hear Fensal rousing the other runners. It sounded like he was assaulting them with their pillows this morning. They groaned, coughed, and grumbled. Kahlil watched their blue-toned shadows jump and stretch across the white folds of the canvas panels. Fensal laughed at something. One of the younger runners started singing a song about his morning erection.

Kahlil rolled his eyes at the absurd lyrics.

He had allowed the Rifter to live, but the whole world hadn't been ruined for it. People still laughed and made their livings all across the country. These men didn't even know that their fates were meant to have been different. He wondered who they would have been if things had gone differently. If he had killed the Rifter, would it have changed their lives? Would some of them have become priests or heretics? Would there have been a new war?

There was no way for him to know.

Kahlil heard water running in the bathroom. The shouts and conversations sounded distant and dull. They grew softer and then fell into silence as the runners departed. Kahlil slept.

He dreamed of another room, one with the same strong smell of men, but higher walls and sharp northern light. He was sitting on a large bed, reading a book. A lean blond man sat on the edge of the bed next to him. He smelled like pine and rain. Kahlil could feel heat radiating from his body even through the heavy gray clothes they both wore.

Kahlil said, "You aren't supposed to be here."

The man smiled and said, "You haven't forgotten about the key, have you?"

Kahlil woke suddenly. Instinctively, he grasped Alidas' key, though he now realized that it had never been the key he had wanted it to be. Still, holding it reassured him.

The canvas panels twitched and Yu'mir peeked between them. Seeing that he was awake, she waved. The bright noonday light edged her brown hair in gold. Kahlil secured the blankets around his waist and sat upright.

"Feeling better?" Yu'mir asked.

"Yes."

Though they were alone, she looked nervous. Kahlil glanced down and noticed the folded piece of paper in her hands. She curled her fingers around it, but not enough to crumple it.

"Fensal's bed is to the left of mine." Kahlil pointed in the general direction.

Yu'mir lowered her face as a scarlet blush flooded across her cheeks. "I wasn't . . ."

"The note is for him, isn't it?"

Yu'mir nodded. "I wasn't going to wake you up to ask you, but I thought that if you were already awake . . ."

"I'm awake."

"You don't think I'm being too forward, do you?" Yu'mir asked, and Kahlil knew she didn't mean about waking him.

"Not at all. I left a secret note for someone myself. Yesterday, in fact." It seemed as if it had been weeks ago. "I won't tell anyone that I saw you here."

"Do you promise?"

"I swear," Kahlil assured her.

She rushed to Fensal's bed. Kahlil took advantage of the canvas panel hanging between them to get dressed. His clean pants were cold from hanging against the wall.

"Put it under his pillow," Kahlil advised. "Otherwise the other runners will see it and want to know what it says."

"They should mind their own business." Yu'mir hesitated at the edge of the canvas panels. "Are you getting dressed?"

"Yes, I'm nearly decent." Kahlil dug through the box under his bed for his spare shirt and some socks.

"Was it Wounin'an?"

"What?" Kahlil tucked his shirt in. The sleeves were too short for him, so he rolled the cuffs.

"The woman you sent the note to, was it Wounin'an?"

"Wou—" Kahlil began to ask who she was, but then he remembered the kitchen girl with the freckles. "No. Did she get a note as well?"

"I don't know. You two seem to flirt all the time."

"I don't think she's serious." Kahlil found his belt and threaded it through the loops of his pants.

"Why is it," Yu'mir asked, "that whenever a man isn't serious he says that he thinks the woman isn't?"

"An attempt at delicacy, I don't know. You can come in now. I'm decent."

Yu'mir stepped back through the panels. She frowned when she saw Kahlil lacing up his boots.

"You're not going out, are you?"

"I need to see if there's been any response to my note." Kahlil combed his tangled hair back from his face with his fingers. He probably still looked like hell.

"But you're supposed to be sick."

"I'm fine, thanks to your medicine," Kahlil assured her.

"Was that an attempt at flattery?"

"Did it work?"

Yu'mir sighed. "Fensal will be annoyed if he sees you running around the city. He gave you the day off to recover, not to chase some street girl."

"Street girl?"

"You know what I mean."

"A prostitute?" An undignified image of the fifty-year-old Alidas working a street corner came to his mind and Kahlil almost laughed aloud.

"Just because I'm a decent woman, it doesn't mean I don't know about the other kind." Yu'mir crossed her arms over her chest. "Is she very pretty?"

"No, not particularly," Kahlil answered.

"You're supposed to say that she's the most beautiful woman in the world," Yu'mir told him. "You're not going to get very far telling her she's not particularly pretty."

"That's not what's important between us." Kahlil pulled his coat from its wall peg.

"Is she pregnant?"

"Pregnant? No!" Kahlil gaped at her. He always forgot things like that. Wives, mistresses, children, all the domestic relations of other men's lives fell outside his experience. Pregnancy had a kind of irrelevance to his existence that surpassed even that of abstract math.

"You never know," Yu'mir told him.

"I know," Kahlil insisted. "I have to go if I'm going to get back before Fensal does."

"Fine." Yu'mir turned and started out of the room. "But if the baby's a girl, you better name her after me."

Kahlil waited for her to leave, then stepped into the Gray Space.

A few moments later he let himself into Alidas' rooms.

Because of the weather, they were colder than before. The air felt crisp, despite the sun. He wondered if it would snow again.

"Is anyone home?" Kahlil called out.

No response. The rooms appeared to be the same as when he had left them yesterday, but the notes he had left were gone. He searched all three rooms but found nothing to tell him what response Alidas might have had.

Kahlil knew he shouldn't linger, but still he sat down on the corner of Alidas' bed as he had done the day before. He lay back and stared up at the ceiling.

What was he going to do when he returned to Lisam Palace? Still try to stop the assassination and save the Rifter?

More than a little irony in that.

Should he let Fikiri, Ourath, Nanvess, and Esh'illan all try their best to kill the Rifter? Only the key could truly kill him, and as far as Kahlil knew, Jath'ibaye was the one who had it.

They could all just go on without him while he lay on this soft bed.

He heard the click and groan of the front door opening.

Alidas stood in the doorway. The bright noon light at his back cast his features into deep shadow. Sweeping his eyes across the rooms, he caught sight of Kahlil. Brief surprise registered on his face as he stepped in and closed the door behind him.

"It's cold," Alidas said from the front room. "You should have started a fire in the wood stove."

"I didn't think I'd be here long." Kahlil became suddenly self-conscious about being caught lying in another man's bed. He sat up and joined Alidas in the front room.

"I just came to see if you got my note."

Alidas bent over the wood stove, feeding scraps of paper into the dull, glowing embers.

"I got it last night." He balled up a piece of paper from his pocket and tossed it into the growing flames. "There's a bundle of wood on the step outside the door. Grab it, will you?"

Kahlil found the scrap wood, untied the rope holding the bundle together, and handed Alidas a stick to add to the fire.

Already the first wave of heat radiated out into the room.

Alidas closed the grate and straightened up. "One of Nanvess' men came to the barrack asking about you."

"What did you tell him?"

"I told him that you left last month." Alidas shrugged. "You did."

"Did he say what they wanted me for?"

"To me?" Alidas asked. "They know I'm loyal to the gaunsho. They wouldn't tell me anything, but it wasn't hard to figure out."

"Nanvess wants me dead."

"I know." Alidas glanced to him. "You look pale."

"I was up too late last night." Kahlil watched Alidas' face for some notion of what he would want done tomorrow. Nanvess' involvement in the assassination complicated things.

Alidas observed the fire and after a moment said, "You should sit down."

Kahlil took a chair. As usual, Alidas remained on his feet, leaning against his desk. Kahlil supposed that Alidas only kept chairs for the sake of other people.

"I have a train ticket to Ris'ela. It's southeast in the Tushoya lands." Alidas glanced down at one of the books on his desk. "I know you don't know anyone there, but that might be an advantage. No one there will know you either. You can make a clean start of it."

"You want me to just leave?" Kahlil couldn't credit it. "But what about tomorrow? What—"

"An assassination attempt against Jath'ibaye is dangerous to the Bousim house," Alidas told him, "but division within the house is worse. Gaunsho Bousim is old, and he knows he has lost much of his power to Nanvess' father. For the sake of uniting the entire Bousim house, the gaunsho will appoint Nanvess as his heir."

"But they don't know what they're doing. Jath'ibaye—"

"Kyle," Alidas stepped closer to him. "It isn't your concern anymore. You need to leave."

But Jath'ibaye was his concern, far more than Alidas could know. He looked up to say so just as Alidas reached out and brushed a strand of Kahlil's black hair back from his face, shocking him to silence. It was so unlike Alidas to touch him.

"You should have your own life," Alidas said. "For the last two years you've lived in secrecy, in isolation. You've had no friends, no family. No one."

"I had you, and I didn't need—" Kahlil cut himself off as he realized how pathetic he sounded. "You saved my life; I owed you the work."

Alidas watched the fire. His dark eyes caught its light and glowed like amber.

"I saved you because I knew I could use you," he finally said. "I saw the remains of the man you killed with your bare hands. And I knew that if I could control you, I could bring the men I wanted down. I wasn't moved by kindness or even pity. I wanted your skills."

"And now that you've had them, you want me to leave?"

"I want to give you your life back," Alidas said.

"In Ris'ela?" Scorn crept into Kahlil's voice. "What would a person like me do there?"

"Whatever you liked."

"I don't think I even know how to live like that. I've never—"

"I have orders to kill you," Alidas said flatly. He didn't meet Kahlil's eyes, but only glanced down at the pile of books on his desk.

"From Nanvess?" Kahlil asked, hopeful. Nanvess hadn't been named gaunsho yet. He still had to answer to his uncle's authority.

"From Gaunsho Bousim. The house must remain united." Alidas pulled the grate of the wood stove open. He threw in another scrap of wood, a piece of broken table leg. "That's why I bought the ticket for you. I was going to leave it here and hope that you had the sense to go."

"I see." Kahlil's stomach clenched and for a moment he thought he might be sick again. "So this is my fair warning, then?"

Alidas nodded. "If I see you again, I'll have no choice."

"I understand." Kahlil forced briskness into his tone. "You should probably have your key back."

"Yes, I suppose I should."

Kahlil unclasped the chain around his neck and slid the key off. For a moment he held it in his hand, feeling the warmth it radiated, before he handed it over. Alidas' concerns were matters of house loyalties and political stability. He was an excellent leader to his men and an honorable servant to his gaunsho. He would never involve himself in something he'd been ordered to disregard.

"What will happen tomorrow at the Bell Dance?"

"That depends on the men involved." Alidas dropped the key into his coat pocket. "If they kill Jath'ibaye, then we still have his followers to contend with. If they fail, then it could be easier or worse. It would depend on how forgiving Jath'ibaye is feeling. In any case, it's out of my hands."

Kahlil supposed that this was true. The Rifter was not a matter to force on Alidas. Nothing in Alidas' life or training would have prepared him to take responsibility for Parfir's destroyer incarnation.

"Will you go?" Alidas' question interrupted Kahlil's thoughts. He offered the train ticket.

"I'd be a fool not to." Kahlil managed a cocky smile as he took it.

Alidas said, "I'm sorry that it turned out like this, but perhaps it's for the best. At least your life is your own now."

"Maybe so." Kahlil slid the ticket into his coat pocket. His life was his again. It was like inheriting a burning house. "I should go and pack." Kahlil's voice sounded flat, mechanical. Alidas only gave a nod. They had already said goodbye weeks ago. Doing it all again just seemed pointless.

Kahlil let himself out and closed the black door behind him. It was getting late and dark clouds crawled across the pale blue sky. He flicked his fingers apart and stepped into the silent Gray Space.

Chapter Twenty-Two

After weeks of morning frost and evening sleet, the warmth of the following day was surprising. Balmy winds twisted through the soft blue sky and sunlight poured down.

Street vendors came out in droves. Every corner Kahlil pedaled past burst with the scent of frying dumplings, the brilliance of paper flowers, and the sudden explosion of wings as pigeons took flight before his bicycle. The spring warmth drew crowds of people outdoors. Often, Kahlil had to swerve past some man—a shop clerk, tailor, or banker—who had just stopped to stand with his face lifted to the sky, feeling the sun on his skin.

Clusters of wealthy women, clothed in richly embroidered dresses, emerged from the shelter of their homes as well. They traveled together like schools of fish, younger wives following the lead of the older ones, all of them keeping their children safely between them. Brightly dyed honey candies flashed in the children's hands. Silver wedding rings and fine chains glittered across the women's fingers.

"Know what's new!" a young boy selling newspapers shouted. "Lisam runners menace the streets once again!"

Kahlil glowered at the boy from his bicycle. The boy grinned back at him.

"Jath'ibaye to attend Bell Dance," the boy called out. "Gaunsho Tushoya fears for the safety of his daughters! How safe are yours?"

Kahlil waited for the man ahead of him to lead his wives across the street and then he sped onward. Behind him, Kahlil heard the paperboy shout, "Lisam runners throw streets into chaos! What will be done? Read the paper and find out!"

Fensal had probably already bought the paper and clipped the article to add to his collection. He would have been disappointed to see how politely Kahlil waited at the street crossings, and how cautiously he rode around the potholes and mud puddles in the roads. But today Kahlil couldn't afford to damage the packages bundled up in the basket of his bicycle. He'd spent the entire day collecting each of those little prizes.

He had pedaled back and forth across the Blackbird Bridge twice. He'd searched through dozens of winding narrow streets. He'd ferreted his way through storefronts and into the back rooms of tailors, cobblers, and countless laundry services all over the city. It had taken him hours of hunting, haranguing and no end of lies, but at last he had pieced together one of the uniforms that the servants and musicians would be wearing for this year's Bell Dance.

The shirt, pants, and jacket were all cut from soft white linen. A fine pattern of silver embroidery edged the jacket's cuffs and collar. There were also white gloves, socks, slipper-like shoes, and a set of dull gray cuff links. Kahlil guarded the complete uniform as if it were blown from glass. One tear, one spatter of mud, one missing piece could ruin it.

He waited on a street corner while the trolley rolled by. Noblewomen peered out of windows. Some of the younger ones already wore their hair piled up in the elaborate braids and curls they would wear at the Bell Dance. Most of the noblewomen would be in attendance, as the Bell Dance offered a rare opportunity for unwed girls to assess the men who would one day become their husbands.

Kahlil guessed that for many of them the possibilities of what could happen, both beautiful and humiliating, were far more thrilling than the actual event would be. It was now, in the grip of anticipation, that, flushed with excitement, their imaginations ran wild.

Anticipation meant something entirely different for Kahlil. It was something to suppress, an infection of anxiety that he couldn't allow to take hold. Two years of hunting men through the west dock slums had taught him not to think too far ahead of the moment.

He couldn't trust his past and he couldn't know the future. The present was really the only place for him.

The trolley trundled past, and Kahlil pulled his attention back to the street ahead. His eyes swept over the men there, and then he froze in place.

Nanvess Bousim stood directly across the street from him, chatting with another man. Both of them wore the deep green colors of the Bousim house and their black hair shone in the sun. Nanvess looked up and his gaze fell upon Kahlil without interest or recognition, the same way he might have noted a street sign. Then his attention returned to his companion. Both men stepped off the curb to stroll across the street toward him.

Kahlil swung off his bicycle and walked it across the street. It was hard to find the natural balance between staring fixedly at Nanvess and pointedly avoiding all eye contact. Kahlil focused his gaze on a cage of birds in the shop window directly ahead of him.

Nanvess came close enough for Kahlil to overhear his conversation.

"Would you want your sister to marry him?" Nanvess asked his companion. "I certainly wouldn't."

"But if Jath'ibaye were to marry into a gaun house, then he would have an incentive to protect the rights of the gaun'im," Nanvess' companion replied.

"I think that's assuming quite a bit about the man."

Kahlil was so close that he could smell Nanvess' thick anise cologne. He could have reached out and caught him by the throat. It would be so easy. With just a flick of his fingers and a sweep of his arm, he could drag a sheering edge of Gray Space through Nanvess' neck. Kahlil could almost feel the heat of dark blood gushing across his palm. He'd killed dozens of men the same way, with just a touch.

But killing Nanvess now would only scare his conspirators, forcing them to alter their plans for the assassination. Then he might never find Fikiri again. And Fikiri still had the yasi'halaun. More important than anything else was ensuring that he got the black blade back before Fikiri could use it. Kahlil's only sure opportunity to get it back would be tonight at the Bell Dance.

Kahlil swung back onto his bicycle and sped down the street. The sun was beginning to dip toward the western horizon. Lisam runners would be turning back to the palace for their meals soon. A fellow runner had already zipped past him. Kahlil and the other man exchanged quick waves. Kahlil allowed the other runner to outdistance him.

He coasted along Seven Palaces Road. Parks and stone statues blurred past. He wove between carriages and delivery wagons. In a few hours, the streets would begin to fill with gawkers and newsmen. But for now, there were only subdued clusters of men and women basking in the fading sun and street vendors packing up their wares.

He turned off Seven Palaces Road and raced up the narrow street to the Gaunsho'im Council building. The building itself was only two stories high and comparatively small. There were no vast wings of suites, no private libraries or magnificent treasuries. Even the dark pines and twisting evergreen trees surrounding it were dwarfed. Their topmost branches barely cleared the walls surrounding the grounds.

Despite its diminutive size, it was not a building that could be overlooked, not even among so many palaces. Embossed gold gleamed across the domed roof. Detailed bas-relief wound down the marble walls, giving them the appearance of delicate lace. Bands of gold ringed the carved pillars in front of the massive ivory-inlaid doors. Polished golden tiles flashed from the steps leading up to the entry.

Kahlil rode around the wall, taking in the surrounding land and noting the positions of the armed guards. Their rifles weren't as powerful as the ones Jath'ibaye's sentries had carried, but they still looked lethal. The guards watched him from the stone walls as he pedaled past. He waved. None of them responded with anything but a scowl.

Another three guards were posted at the servants' gate at the back of the grounds. With their rifles and their gleaming gold-and-indigo uniforms they too presented an intimidating appearance. But Kahlil could see that they were more or less hapless in the midst of the intense activity all around them.

Streams of hired men hauled cases of fish, casks of wine, entire racks of roast dog, and bushels of southern fruits from waiting wagons. They grunted and heaved their loads through the gates and past the guards. Delivery boys from city shops darted between them with trays of brilliant candies, vases of cut flowers, and towering silver cakes. Staff from the council building, in blue and gold liveries, scurried from one point to another, shouting directions and attempting to check the deliveries and invoices.

"Lisam runner," Kahlil told a guard. "Deliveries for the steward." He pointed to a tissue-wrapped bundle in the basket of his bicycle. It contained his socks.

The guard just waved him in. Behind him, Kahlil heard tahldi and the creak of wooden wheels. He glanced back to see that several red rented carriages had arrived. Musicians climbed out, most of them cradling or lugging instruments. Some were fully dressed in their white uniforms, but most still wore their street clothes. Immediately, an argument started up as to who was responsible for paying the carriage drivers.

Kahlil caught the guard's momentary expression of tired exasperation. By the end of the night, the guards would certainly have seen enough men pass between them to forget his face.

Kahlil simply drifted through the back courtyard. The unyielding weight of his bicycle protected him from too many bumps and shoves. The air in the courtyard rolled over him as he walked. One moment he grimaced in the grasp of fish odors, then he pushed past a clot of delivery men and found himself plunged into scents of mulled wine and spring blossoms. Men shouted questions and orders all around him. Kahlil didn't think anyone really knew what was directed to whom.

He reached the racks behind the kitchen. He locked his bicycle next to three other delivery bicycles and then wandered into the council building with his clothes in his arms.

The interior of the building didn't pale in comparison to the exterior, not even in the back rooms. The trim over the doors was carved with twining ivy. Scattered between the leaves were gilded coins, each bearing the crest of one of the seven gaun'im houses. The Lisam bull glared down from a corner. Across from it, Kahlil recognized the crossed arrows of the Bousim house. Just faintly, above the ivy, Kahlil could see that there had once been another, larger symbol. He squinted up at the vague shadows and then realized that he was looking at the remnants of a Payshmura sun.

The council building had been constructed before the Payshmura had fallen. Now that Kahlil thought of it, he could see old remnants of their dominance all around him. As he wandered the halls, stepping past flustered staff and deliverymen, he noted the small, incised alcoves where dishes of prayer stones would have been placed. Now they were either filled by bowls of cut flowers or gilded tiles depicting the crests of the seven houses.

"What are you doing?" an older man suddenly demanded of him.

"Delivery," Kahlil answered.

The man rolled his eyes. Obviously most of the men pushing their way through the back rooms and halls had deliveries.

"Who is it for?" the old man demanded.

"A musician," Kahlil said. "I'm supposed to deliver it to his dressing room."

"His dressing room?" The old man scowled. "That's rich. They're all going to be using one room, the light-fingered little thieves." The man suddenly turned to the group of stocky deliverymen slouching next to the wine racks. His wrinkled face seemed to fold in on itself as he glared at them. "If you're done, don't just stand around taking up space! Get out!"

The men quickly retreated back down the hall.

The old man snapped his attention back to Kahlil. "The fourth door on the right."

"Thank you," Kahlil replied.

The old man had already turned away and was stalking toward a cluster of young men milling around two kitchen girls. Kahlil shook his head. He couldn't imagine being a house steward.

He found the room that had been designated for the musicians. Any decoration that could be removed obviously had been. The inlaid walls were bare, and even the flowers had been removed from the alcoves. None of the musicians had arrived yet. Kahlil stripped off his clothes and changed. He doubted that he would have an opportunity to recover his old clothes. Still, he folded them into a neat pile out of habit. He'd miss his coat and boots.

After that, he simply drifted through the council building, randomly carrying out instructions. He decanted a bottle of wine, removed and then returned a vase of lilies to an alcove. He avoided the steward, easily fading into the crowds of other men in white uniforms.

He accustomed himself to the layout of the building. Beyond the small back rooms stood a huge ballroom. There the screens that would hide the musicians had already been spread. Intricately carved chairs and tiny decorative tables had been placed along the left wall. A profusion of fresh flowers was scattered across the tables. The blossoms looked fragile compared to the huge shields and carved wreaths mounted on the walls. The polished floor shone brilliantly as it reflected the blazing gold and silver chandeliers overhead. A staircase on the right wall led to the second floor, but it had been chained off.

Kahlil doubted that Ourath or any of his conspirators would attempt anything here, under so much light and in such an open space.

Kahlil picked up a bouquet of spring buds and stalked purposefully past the other servants out into the gardens. The guards on the walls hardly took note of him.

A path of marble stones wound slowly up a slight hill to the west garden, the one Nanvess had mentioned. At the top, Kahlil found a flickering stone lamp surrounded by dark pines. Yellow and red ivy vines cascaded over trellises. Between the trees, low shrubs hid the bare ground with dark winter-hardy greenery. Here and there tiny patches of red and violet spring flowers pushed through the dark soil.

Kahlil turned slowly around, taking in the deep shadows, the walls of ivy, and the thin, flickering lamplight. He couldn't have chosen a better place for an assassination himself. He was sure it would take place here. But he couldn't just wait around in plain sight. He turned back down the path.

He couldn't know where Fikiri would come from or when he would arrive, but Kahlil did know that one way or another Fikiri would have to get close to Jath'ibaye. So all he had to do was slip back into the council building and wait for Jath'ibaye; then Fikiri would come to him.

When he walked in through the back door, several women looked up at him. They were portioning out cutlets of dog meat into white dishes.

"Where have you been?" an older woman demanded.

"The steward sent me out to get some more flowers." Kahlil held up the bouquet of spring buds he had carried out with him.

"Forget that," the older woman told him. "The ladies are arriving and they aren't half-hungry. Take a tray and get out there."

Kahlil picked up a silver tray and strode out to the ballroom. The musicians had situated themselves behind their blinds and played quietly.

Kahlil followed the other men in white uniforms, serving the exquisitely dressed gaun'im women at the tables.

As more gaun'im arrived, Kahlil's duties changed. He took out trays of drinks for the men and candies for the youngest girls. All of the noblemen came dressed in their house colors and carried at least one long string of fine silver chain. Though the chains were symbols of the wealth that they could offer to their future brides, Kahlil still found them sinister.

Esh'illan Anyyd arrived with several of his brothers and a particularly sturdy set of silver wedding chains. Draped over his silk clad arm, the chains just brushed his knee. No one else seemed to take any note of them. Ourath arrived with his three wives and his young son, all clad in the rich tawny colors of the Lisam house. Ourath's hair looked particularly red, and his low voice seemed to brim with happiness as he spoke. He took a glass of wine from Kahlil without even sparing him a glance.

The music grew louder, competing with the rising hum of conversation. The heat from the lamps and chandeliers swelled with the warmth of so many bodies.

Several members of the Bousim family were announced, but Nanvess was not among them. Then the massive doors swung open again and a boy in blue and gold announced, "Welcome his honor, Jath'ibaye'in'Fai'daum."

Kahlil and every other person in the entire ballroom turned toward the door. Even the musicians seemed to pause a moment to steal glances at Jath'ibaye.

Unlike any of the gaun'im, Jath'ibaye had come alone. His wild blond hair blazed gold under the profusion of light. The blood-red of his clothes declared his Fai'daum loyalty. He hadn't brought a single silver chain.

Kahlil thought he heard an audible sigh of relief from some of the girls near him.

As Jath'ibaye scanned the crowded ballroom, Kahlil bowed his head. He could remember too well how Jath'ibaye had picked him out even in the darkness.

Ourath broke away from his conversation with a Tushoya woman and her unwed daughters. He strode easily through the crowd, lesser gaun'im men quickly making way for him. He greeted Jath'ibaye with a smile and led him into the ballroom. Kahlil stepped back behind a vivid yellow bouquet as Ourath looked around for a server. At last, he stopped a young man in a white uniform and took two drinks. Ourath handed one to Jath'ibaye and offered a toast of some kind.

They drank together and Ourath introduced several other gaun'im to Jath'ibaye. After a few moments, the room seemed to return to normal. More guests arrived. The ancient Bousim gaunsho shuffled through the doors, followed by his dozen wives. Steadily, couples began to fill the middle of the dance floor. Ourath escorted his first wife out for a dance, but afterwards he returned to Jath'ibaye's side.

Kahlil still hadn't spotted Nanvess when he noticed Ourath drawing Jath'ibaye away from the crowd toward the back of the building and the gardens. Kahlil set his tray full of iced fruit down and cut through the kitchen to the west garden.

Once outside, Kahlil raced up the hill, keeping to the side of the path where the deep evergreen leaves hid him. He waited for Ourath and Jath'ibaye. A few moments later they appeared, walking slowly along the path. Far behind them, Kahlil caught sight of Esh'illan.

Suddenly, Jath'ibaye drew to a halt.

"You shouldn't depend upon my affection," Jath'ibaye told Ourath. "It's not my strong point."

"No?" Ourath asked. "What is?"

Jath'ibaye didn't answer right away. Instead, he studied the knots of dark trees and undergrowth ahead of him. Kahlil stood still as a statue, holding his breath. Eventually, Jath'ibaye turned back to Ourath and asked, "Are you sure this is what you want?"

Ourath flushed.

"Absolutely." He smiled at Jath'ibaye and this time the force behind it showed a little. "I know you'll want to see these herbs."

Ourath started forward, but Jath'ibaye caught him by the shoulder.

"I'm not a fool, Ourath. I know you're not planning on showing me any herbs up there." Jath'ibaye's tone was oddly gentle in comparison to his harsh expression.

"Really?" Ourath slid his hand around Jath'ibaye's, twining their fingers together. He lowered his head to brush his lips over Jath'ibaye's wrist.

"So I want to be alone with you." Ourath gazed up at Jath'ibaye. "You can't be disappointed, can you?"

Again, Jath'ibaye glanced to the shadows beneath the pine trees before looking back to Ourath.

"We could stop it here, now." Jath'ibaye spoke so softly that Kahlil hardly caught the words. "I wouldn't hold it against you. People make mistakes."

"What do you mean?"

"You're still so young," Jath'ibaye said. "You can't understand how badly this could end for you."

"How can you still think that I would regret being with you?"

Jath'ibaye just sighed heavily.

"Do you regret being with me?" Ourath suddenly demanded, his voice edged with what sounded like genuine anger.

"I regret using you," Jath'ibaye said at last.

Ourath glared at Jath'ibaye and smiled at the same time. "Well, come. Regret it one more time."

Jath'ibaye allowed Ourath to lead him along the path.

Kahlil rushed ahead of them, cutting through the trellises of ivy, while they took the curving path upward. When Kahlil reached the edge of the clearing at the top of the hill, he came to a halt. There was something different about the place now. Despite the warmth of the evening, a chill emanated from the center of the clearing. The tiny flame in the stone lamp flickered and spat. Kahlil hung back in the shadows.

Ourath and Jath'ibaye rounded the last curve in the path.

"Here." Ourath caught Jath'ibaye's hands and suddenly pulled him forward. It was clear to Kahlil that Jath'ibaye allowed this.

Coming up from behind, Esh'illan made his move. He swung the silver chains and whipped them around Jath'ibaye's throat.

Jath'ibaye shoved Ourath aside, pushing him clear. Then he caught hold of the chains at his throat and jerked Esh'illan off his feet. Esh'illan gave a startled yelp as Jath'ibaye swung him up like he was spinning a child and then hurled him to the ground.

Jath'ibaye's calm speed stunned Kahlil.

Then the scream of rending Gray Space split the air. In an arc of flame and searing cold, Fikiri appeared. Kahlil almost rushed him, but then he realized that Fikiri's hands were empty. The yasi'halaun was nowhere on him.

At the sight of Fikiri, Jath'ibaye's countenance changed utterly. The cold, almost bored expression that he had worn even while Esh'illan attempted to strangle him transformed into raw fury. Jath'ibaye kicked Esh'illan's prone body aside and launched himself toward Fikiri.

Kahlil caught a flicker of a smile from Fikiri as he backed away, drawing Jath'ibaye farther into the clearing.

Then Kahlil saw Nanvess, crouching in the deep shadows of the evergreens and holding the yasi'halaun. His green clothes melted into the surrounding leaves, his black hair dark as the shadows. He lunged for Jath'ibaye.

It was such a simple plan, Kahlil realized. Nanvess would feed the yasi'halaun on Jath'ibaye's blood before Jath'ibaye even registered his presence.

Kahlil threw himself into the Gray Space, passing straight through Jath'ibaye's body. He burst out directly over Nanvess. Instantly, he snapped his fingers apart and punched the razor edge of the Gray Space through Nanvess' throat. Nanvess' hot blood gushed over his hand and splashed up his arm. Nanvess crumpled to the ground.

Initially, Kahlil didn't even feel the yasi'halaun's smooth blade driven deep into his abdomen. Then sharp pain exploded through him. The blade pulsed inside him, tearing through muscle and drinking in his blood. He gripped the hilt with his bloody, slick hands and wrenched the yasi'halaun free.

Fikiri stood, staring at him in abject shock.

Jath'ibaye too stood motionless, blood dribbling from his neck where Esh'illan's chains had cut through his skin. His blue eyes were wide, his expression haunted.

Kahlil felt sickeningly cold. His entire body shook. He fought to remain on his feet.

Only Esh'illan seemed able to move. Kahlil saw him draw his pistol. Fikiri caught the motion as well and a look of fear passed over his face.

"Don't!" Fikiri shouted.

Jath'ibaye spun back just as Esh'illan fired directly into his chest. Jath'ibaye rocked slightly with the impact.

Then the entire earth seemed to shudder beneath them. The stone lamp split. From above them came a sudden tiny white burst of light, like a streak of lightning, and then the entire sky darkened. Pale clouds writhed and blackened as if they were burning.

Jath'ibaye strode forward and gripped Esh'illan by the throat. With a vicious snap he twisted Esh'illan's head back. Esh'illan convulsed and then fell lifelessly to the ground.

Kahlil could see guards running up the path. The gunshot must have brought them. Jath'ibaye didn't seem to notice or care about them. His eyes blazed blue, inhumanly bright. He glanced over his shoulder to the empty space where Fikiri had stood, then he turned his attention to Kahlil.

Thunder crashed above them.

Jath'ibaye simply stood there, watching him as a dirty black rain began to slap down. Three guards came running with lanterns. Other people—curious guests and servants—trailed behind them.

Kahlil brought his hand up.

"Wait," Jath'ibaye whispered.

Kahlil tore open the Gray Space and stumbled into its lifeless depth.

Chapter Twenty-Three

The dark cables and girders of the Blackbird Bridge blurred and wavered in front of Kahlil. Out of reflex, he reached for the railing to steady himself. His hand passed through. He staggered down to his knees.

In the colorless, silent realm of Gray Space, there was neither night nor day, and yet it seemed to be growing darker all around Kahlil. And colder.

He curled his hand over the wound in his belly. In the Gray Space, his blood shone glossy black. It spilled through his fingers and seeped across the entire front of his white jacket and pants. He could feel it soaking into his socks. If he had been outside the Gray Space, it would have been warm. It would have steamed against the night air.

Kahlil pushed himself back up to his feet. He couldn't stop, not here. Not yet. He concentrated. The black mass of the bridge whipped back behind him. Narrow streets blurred past. He moved through walls and gates.

Ranks of rashan'im on tahldi patrolled all streets. Word of the attack at the Bell Dance had doubtless traveled fast. Both Esh'illan Anyyd and Nanvess Bousim murdered. Alidas would be furious. There would be no refuge for Kahlil anywhere in the Bousim district of the city.

No. He needed to go somewhere else. Dim tangled shapes washed past him. Kahlil shuddered. He could hardly recognize the haze of darkness and light all around him. Boats, perhaps. A wave of numb cold pulsed through him.

He should get out of the city. Go somewhere better. Somewhere warm and light. Somewhere like the apple orchards that grew around the convent of Umbhra'ibaye. They'd been beautiful. It would be so nice to go there and see them again. The trees would be blooming.

But he wasn't going anywhere, he realized.

He wasn't even going to be able to stay conscious much longer. Panicked energy burst through him. He had to leave the Gray Space before he was too weak to escape it at all.

He lifted his hand. He'd get out.

And what then?

Again his gaze fell to the black wound in his belly. It gleamed and dripped with a constant flow of black blood. Despite the muting numbness of the Gray Space, Kahlil felt the ache of it tearing through him. Outside the Gray Space it would be agony.

This wasn't a wound that a man recovered from.

Only the Gray Space had allowed him to bear it this long. Now the best of his strength had gone. He could hardly see, hardly move. He was dying.

He squeezed his fingers around the hilt of the yasi'halaun. It had grown heavier, fed by his blood. It almost felt warm against his icy skin. At least he had it again. He had accomplished that much. Neither Fikiri nor his lady would use it to open the Great Gate.

He closed his eyes. There was no point in keeping them open. Only a dull dark haze came to him now.

If he left the Gray Space, it wouldn't save his life. It would only mean that his last moments would be ones filled with the brilliant red of his own blood and shattering pain. He would leave a corpse for someone to stumble across. And the yasi'halaun would be lying there in his hand.

It was better to die here, hiding the yasi'halaun forever.

A tremor of fear still moved through Kahlil. He didn't want to die, but the choice wasn't his. The pain and cold melted into a consuming darkness that engulfed him, surrounding him in soothing emptiness.

Chapter Twenty-Four

A wrenching scream tore through Kahlil's insentience—the sound of Gray Space being torn open. Then blinding, burning light exploded over him. He wanted to flinch back from it, but he couldn't move. A weak rasping cry escaped him as the heat of living hands seared his frigid skin.

He tried to pull himself away. His body remained limp. He couldn't even make his eyes focus. All he saw were faint blurs of color—dirty red, pale yellow—then they were burned away by the sharp, blinding white light that poured down over him.

Reflexively, Kahlil dragged in a desperate breath of the hot air. It tasted of sweat, blood, salt, and animals. It was too much. Kahlil didn't want to take another breath, but his lungs demanded it. Agony flooded over him. It burst up from his abdomen and tore like lightning into his chest. Kahlil's throat tightened around a reflex scream. It came out as a dry hiss.

"He's still breathing." The man's voice was rough and low. Jath'ibaye's voice.

"It's too late." The woman sounded older. She spoke with a careful softness. "I'm sorry, Jahn, but he—"

"No! He won't die. I don't care what sorcery you have to use, Ji. Save him!"

Why would Jath'ibaye want to save him? What did he want? Kahlil tried to clench his hand, to feel for the yasi'halaun. His fingers barely twitched.

"I can't bear his wound. It was made by the yasi'halaun. It would burn me to ash before I could heal him," the woman quietly insisted. "I'm sorry."

"Then let me bear it."

"When the blood transfers, the yasi'halaun will feed—"

"I don't care," Jath'ibaye cut her off. "Just bring him back to me."

"Jahn, he's not—"

"Do it!" Jath'ibaye flatly commanded.

A shadow moved over Kahlil, blotting out the blazing light. A hand touched his cheek lightly. It was still too hot, and yet Kahlil didn't care. Even the terrible pain in his belly seemed somehow distant. Perhaps it was simply unimportant.

The shadow deepened, growing nearly black at the edges of his vision. Steadily, it curled in over him. A dull numbness crept in its wake. It came as a relief after so much burning and hurt.

Low words were muttered over him. Kahlil could not understand them anymore. They were just sounds, whispers and rumbles. It was so much easier to let them drift away.

"No," Jath'ibaye growled, "I won't let you go."

Kahlil wished he could laugh.

He was already slipping away, even within the grasp of Jath'ibaye's hands. It was like a magic trick, like stepping into yet another space, one that carried him out of his own body. It was a perfect escape.

If only he had figured this trick out sooner. It would have saved him so much pain. If only he hadn't been so terrified of this dead darkness. But it was nothing. Not pain, not fear. Nothing.

This, absence and silence, seemed to stretch out forever and through all time. It devoured his future and past, engulfed his present, and absolved all with an endless, soothing darkness.

☾ ☾ ☾

Darkness.

And a slight rocking. But still dark—a soothing, cool dark. Then a creak, almost like the noise of straining wood. Faintly, almost imperceptibly, a scent of river water drifted over him.

He hadn't thought that death would be so much like being on a boat.

Kahlil cracked one eye open and saw polished wood and portholes. Instantly, he realized that he was aboard one of those narrow river clippers. He could tell just from looking at the close angles of the walls and the swift blur of water outside his round windows.

He pulled his other eye open and surveyed the tiny cabin. Apart from the bed that he lay in, it contained a small built-in desk and a chair, which Jath'ibaye occupied. His long, broad body looked absurd slumped in the frail chair. His chin rested on his chest, his wild blond hair fell over his face, and his breath rose and fell with the slow, steady rhythm of deep sleep.

Kahlil tried to sit up as quietly as he could. His muscles ached and resisted. His right hand bumped against something heavy on the bed next to him.

Sheathed, and resting on top of the blankets, lay the yasi'halaun. It had grown to nearly the length of his arm, and its once-black body now shone a lustrous gray. It had tasted the Rifter's blood.

"You're awake." Jath'ibaye's voice sounded rough.

Kahlil eyed him cautiously. The last time he'd been alone with Jath'ibaye, the man had threatened to kill him.

"It's all right. You're safe." Jath'ibaye winced slightly as he straightened in the chair, then offered him a tired smile. His blue eyes were rimmed with red, his mouth almost colorless.

Kahlil arched an eyebrow. "You said you were going to kill me the next time you saw me."

"I never could have . . ." Jath'ibaye's smile faded and his eyes sank to the floor. "The first time I saw you, you were in Fikiri's territory, and then you came to me with that letter and the poison from Ourath. I thought it had to be some trick of Fikiri's. I didn't know how else you could have come back."

Kahlil himself hadn't been sure how he'd come back from Nayeshi; he'd needed to, and he'd been willing to die trying. He supposed that had been enough.

Kahlil pulled himself up a little in the bed. The profusion of pillows on either side of him made the motion awkward. He expected to feel a sharp complaint from the wound in his abdomen, but there was nothing.

"I came back on my own power, but I didn't do a good job of it. I was a mess for a while, and the only work I could find was for the Bousim family." It felt strange and relieving to be able to say this, to tell someone and know that he would understand. "They wanted to avoid the conflict that an attack against you would cause, so they sent me to take a job as a Lisam runner to try and stop your assassination." Kahlil stared at Jath'ibaye, then scowled. "Did you just tell me that you knew Ourath sent you poison and you still accepted his invitation to the Bell Dance?"

Strangely, Jath'ibaye smiled at this. He nodded without looking up from the floor.

"Did you want to be killed?" Kahlil demanded. He suddenly had an insight into how Fensal must have felt about him eating the goatweed.

"I have, from time to time, but no." Jath'ibaye stole a brief glance up at him. "Not now. I was just tired, and it would have offered me an excuse to make a clean break from Ourath. It wasn't as if he could have killed me."

"You let him poison you because you thought it would be easier than breaking up with him? Do you have any idea how stupid that sounds?" Kahlil spoke before he could consider either the intimate nature of the subject or the presumption of his words. Jath'ibaye didn't appear to take any offense at either.

"Saying it out loud just now, I did notice that," Jath'ibaye admitted.

"Maybe you should talk things out a little more often." Kahlil felt oddly at ease with Jath'ibaye at this moment, almost as comfortable as he had felt when they'd shared a house. He could remember that now—their time together in Nayeshi.

He'd been so happy then. He remembered the strong smell of coffee and the absurd simplicity of their domestic troubles—a leaky faucet, no toilet paper, the odd smell the oven gave off when it was preheating. Kahlil recalled the sweet tang of an apple and sitting together in the dark, waiting for the electricity to come back on.

John, or Jath'ibaye as he now called himself, hardly seemed to have changed at all. And yet, Kahlil knew that decades had passed since the Fai'daum leader he was looking at and the graduate student he remembered had been the same person.

"Do you remember our phone number?" Kahlil asked. "It started out 647 . . . didn't it? I can't remember."

"Phone?" Jath'ibaye finally met Kahlil's eyes. "We never had a phone . . . "

"Sure we did. In Nayeshi we had a landline because you didn't like cell phones." Kahlil scanned Jath'ibaye's face for a sign of recollection.

He didn't know why he had expected Jath'ibaye to remember everything from those days. His own memory was hazy—to say the least—and it had only been two years for him. Jath'ibaye had fought wars and destroyed an entire kingdom since then. The seven arbitrary digits of a phone number probably had no meaning at all to him now.

He felt stupid for even bringing it up. There were so many other more important matters that they should have been discussing: the holy key, the yasi'halaun. But Kahlil had just woken up and he wanted to ponder something unimportant, something small and amusing, as was his habit.

Jath'ibaye's expression was a study in blankness, as if he were holding himself back from any reaction at all.

"You followed me from Nayeshi," Jath'ibaye said slowly.

Kahlil couldn't understand why the thought should have such a strong effect upon Jath'ibaye. Maybe it was just the distant memory of Nayeshi. How long had it been since anyone or anything had reminded Jath'ibaye of the life—the whole world he had lost?

"It was hard, but I managed it. Forget about the phone number. It's not important," Kahlil said. Then he didn't know what else to say.

Jath'ibaye pulled himself to his feet. His skin still looked unnaturally pale. Dark bruises ringed his throat and Kahlil could see the uneven, bulky mass of bandages beneath his clothes.

"So, you're still calling yourself Kyle?" Jath'ibaye asked, though he said the name strangely, as if the Nayeshi pronunciation caught in his throat.

"It's easy to remember." Kahlil shrugged, an awkward movement, as his recently healed muscles were still slow to respond.

Jath'ibaye gazed at him so intently that Kahlil felt an embarrassing flush begin to rise across his cheeks. Then Jath'ibaye looked away to the view out the tiny portal. Outside, dark blue-green waters swirled and twisted past.

Kahlil took it all in with a kind of stunned wonder. Even a day ago, he would never have imagined that he could have ended up here. Or with John, again.

"I should go above deck and tell Ji that you're awake," Jath'ibaye said suddenly. "She wasn't sure if you would pull through." He started for the door but then turned back to Kahlil. "Do you think you can eat anything yet?"

"I can try."

"I'll find something easy to start with."

"Thank you," Kahlil responded automatically, but as he studied Jath'ibaye's stark figure and pale face, he did feel genuine gratitude and wonder.

He had come back to Basawar to kill the Rifter and instead the Rifter had saved him. Now the idea of killing John seemed laughably pointless.

He had never wanted to do it in the first place. He had liked John—more than liked him, if he was truly honest. He thought that he might even like Jath'ibaye if he got to know the man.

"Wait," Kahlil called just before Jath'ibaye stepped out the door.

"Yes?" Jath'ibaye asked.

"Thank you for saving my life." The words couldn't convey all of his relief or gratitude, but they were all he could offer at the moment.

"I wish I had." Jath'ibaye gave him another smile. He looked so exhausted and worn that the expression almost seemed sad. "You should thank Ji. She's the one who did the work."

"Oh, I certainly will." He wanted to say something else, something that would make up for reminding Jath'ibaye of the life he had lost. No comforting words came to him, so he settled for a question instead. He said, "Where are we going now?"

"Home."

"Home?" Kahlil echoed the word as though he had just learned it. He had no idea where home was anymore.

"Vundomu," Jath'ibaye clarified. He lingered, halfway out the door.

"I see." Kahlil knew he could have asked another question and kept Jath'ibaye with him, but there was no point in it. It wouldn't accomplish anything. If Jath'ibaye was pained by the memories that Kahlil brought back, then he would want to be alone. He had always guarded his privacy that way.

Kahlil let him go.

Previously in John's Story

After using a key intended for his roommate, John Toffler and his two closest friends—Laurie and Bill—are thrown into the harsh world of Basawar. John and his friends survive the winter wilderness with the aid of a rebellious young priest, Ravishan, and eventually join Basawar society in the city of Amura'taye.

While Laurie and Bill find shelter in the household of the exiled Lady Bousim, John ascends the Thousand Steps to the monastery of Rathal'pesha where he reunites with Ravishan. He hopes that among the mysterious teachings of the Payshmura priesthood he can find a way to return home. After a year of service in the monastery, he has made many discoveries and a few friends, chief among them the aged priest, Samsango. But the way home still eludes John.

Arc Four: Amidst the Holy and Profane

Chapter Twenty-Five

John pushed the hair back from his face and drew in a slow, deep breath.

After two years in Basawar, he had grown used to the thin air and the hungry quality of the soil and stones. It felt comfortable to him. The wet earth moved beneath him, curling around his heels and squeezing between his toes. Pools of yesterday's rain had turned the sparring ground into a wallow. As he moved, the mud slithered and squelched beneath him, but he didn't feel as if he was slipping. Instead, it seemed that the soil accommodated him, shifting and folding to support him.

The priest opposite him charged. John swung to the side. Mud squelched beneath both their feet. John caught the other man's arm in a loose grip and, with the slightest nudge, threw him off balance. The priest flailed out, attempting to catch John and pull him down with him. John stepped back and the priest tumbled down into the mud.

From the sidelines, John heard Samsango's laugh. The old priest sat with several other ancient priests, watching the battle practice and quietly making wagers. Their faded gray robes seemed to melt into the pale stone steps that surrounded the arena. The thin morning sunlight gleamed across his bald head. John guessed, from the collection of polished stones in Samsango's lap, that he had won a fair number of wagers.

John gave him a jaunty wave before turning back to offer his opponent a hand up.

More than a hundred low-ranking ushvun'im, like John himself, were gathered on the steps of the arena. Normally, only the thirty men who shared the same dormitory practiced on the training grounds at the same time. Today, men from all of the dormitories encircled John in a sea of gray robes and black hair.

A year ago, he would have found it intimidating, but now he knew all of them by sight, if not personally. And he knew that most of them cared little about the outcome of these individual tests. They each experienced their share of defeats and conquests. In their dormitory groups they practiced fighting together every day. They were more interested in the opportunity the gathering offered to chat and gamble.

Their subdued conversations produced a low, soft hum. It was a rare, comfortable sound—like distant radio music or birdsong—in the isolating silence of the monastery. It offered John the sense of being surrounded by life while not having to be drawn into it.

Some of the priests had stripped down to just the thin pants they wore beneath their robes. Others were still dressed in their robes and coats, keeping warm while they waited in the shadows of the armory building. A few, like John and his opponent, were spattered and streaked with mud.

John steadied his opponent and watched him slog back to the steps. The other priest simply stripped all his clothes off and tossed them onto a step.

John scraped a dried spatter of mud off his shoulder and waited for the prior to decide who he would fight next.

Normally, with the grounds in such poor condition, the tests would have been called off. But today was special.

Today, they were being watched.

The highest-ranking priests in Rathal'pesha—the ushman'im and ushiri'im—were gathered on the walkways overhead to observe the tests. John easily picked out Ushman Nuritam; his long white braids were swept up in the wind and writhed like ribbons. Beside him stood Ushman Dayyid.

Dayyid's black coat formed a dark column behind Nuritam's frail figure. His thick black braids cascaded down his broad shoulders, too heavy for the breezes to lift. The natural northern softness of his features was undermined by his sharp nose and arched lips.

During the first weeks after John arrived in Rathal'pesha, Dayyid had gone out of his way to come down to the training ground and demonstrate the battle forms, using John as his practice opponent. John hadn't known anything about the handholds or stances, and Dayyid hadn't tried to explain them to him, either. Time and time again, He had hurled John to the ground, twisted his arms back, kicked him in the ribs, and held him down with one foot placed over his throat.

And John knew that Dayyid had done it simply to show John and the other priests that he could.

After a week, John's mouth had been split and too swollen for him to eat without tasting his own blood. Samsango had given him a balm to deaden the pain of his beaten ribs and bruised back. When John asked what he had done to offend Dayyid, Samsango had told John not to take the thrashings personally. Ushman Dayyid always beat new priests as a forewarning against insolence. He'd assured John that if he didn't fight, Dayyid would eventually grow bored.

Samsango had been right. After two days of meeting limp resistance, Dayyid hadn't returned to the ushvun training grounds to abuse him further.

He saw remarkably little of any of the ushman'im or the ushiri'im. They kept to the upper floors of Rathal'pesha, practicing their divine rituals and using the Gray Space to speak to Usho in the Black Tower and the Issusha'im Oracles in Umbra'ibaye thousands of miles away.

Beneath them, the common ushvun'im saw to the day-to-day upkeep of the monastery. As an ushvun, John cleaned goat sheds, tended weasel coops, scrubbed statues, scrubbed floors, scrubbed walls, hauled urns of lamp oil, carried bags of raw taye, prayed until he could barely speak, and stood through icy nights of guard duty. He had worked in the kitchens, the gardens, the laundry, and the bell towers.

At first, the constant labor had left him too tired to think. He had staggered through his first month in an exhausted daze. Once, Samsango had found him passed out with his face nestled into a fetid weasel nest.

He had lapsed into strange fantasies of floor buffers and dishwashers. Memories of spray-on oven cleaner and laundromats had flooded him with deep homesickness.

Steadily, he had adjusted. He had grown used to handling the animals and learned shortcuts through the twisting, maze-like halls of the monastery. He had developed the ability to know which duties were important and which had been assigned to him simply because he was standing there. Most importantly, he had mastered the critical skill of appearing occupied with a duty when the prior was nearby.

Now, the mere sound of the prior's footsteps could wake John from a lazy doze and send him striding down a hall with an intensely focused expression. The prior seemed to judge most of the ushvun by the speed of their movements and the intensity of their expressions. An open frown or scowl would result in a reprimand for a surly attitude, while grins, smiles or any wide-eyed expression of wonder were indicators of too much free time.

John had found that wearing a slight frown, narrowing his eyes, and striding with a fast, deliberate pace down a hall was exactly what the prior liked to see him doing.

Right now, the prior stood at the edge of the practice grounds, scowling. He was a small, plump man and his three honor braids always gleamed with far too much sweet oil. They seemed to slither down his back and often left a slight stain at the nape of his robes. Two silver flail-shaped pins on the shoulders of his robe indicated both his rank and primary pastime.

The prior swung his left hand into the air, calling a new opponent down onto the muddy training ground.

The new priest was a younger man John didn't know well. He scowled as his feet sank into the cold mud. John, in contrast, slid one leg forward slightly, feeling the soil roll across his ankle. He could already sense where the best footing would be found.

His opponent flipped his single black braid back from where it had hung over his shoulder. John's own wild blond hair was pulled back and tied with a strip of leather. Wisps of hair escaped and fell in his face. He tucked them back behind his ears.

He wasn't allowed to wear even a single braid yet. That would come after his initiation this summer. Until then, he was still just an initiate, a man of little importance and the butt of most practical jokes.

Even old, bald priests like Samsango technically wore honor braids. Samsango's were woven from goat hair and sewn to the shoulders of his robes. He had two, which placed him just below the prior in honor. But even without any, John's position was better than that of a priest whose hair had been cut.

For a year after his braids were shorn, a dishonored priest was treated with animosity and utter contempt. He received the most demeaning and dangerous work, often cleaning the latrines or replacing the cracked tiles of the steepest roofs. He ate the coarsest food, wore the roughest clothes, and slept beneath the thinnest blankets. He could be punished for any misfortune and had no right to speak in his own defense.

John knew now that when they had first met, Ravishan's short bristle of black hair had been a symbol of disgrace. Ravishan had been punished for some transgression against the Payshmura creed. John had no idea which one. The ushvun'im rarely spoke of the ushman'im or the ushiri'im. When they did, it was with awe and reverence.

There had only been a few nights, while John had been serving guard duties high on the walls, when Ravishan had managed to visit him. Their time together had been brief and precious. John hadn't wanted to ruin those pleasant few hours by asking questions that could embarrass Ravishan. Instead, they had talked about Nayeshi and shared gossip about their fellow priests.

John wondered if Ravishan was watching from one of the raised walkways. He thought he could see other dark forms on the farthest walkways, but he couldn't make out any faces.

The prior lifted both his tanned plump arms into the air, and John's attention snapped back to the practice grounds and his opponent. The other priest crouched back into a defensive stance. The prior dropped his arms, and John charged forward.

John's opponent shifted to catch John's shoulder, but he moved too slowly. John spun, mud spattering up under his feet. He swung his leg up and hooked the soft back of his opponent's knee. The priest buckled back. John slammed his open hand into the man's chest, and his opponent splashed down into the mud.

Cold spatters smacked across John's bare stomach and chest. It was fast and simple. John found he liked that about the Payshmura battle forms. The fallen priest swore but accepted John's outstretched hand. John helped him back up to his feet. Behind them, John heard another short crow of triumph from Samsango.

"Good form, Jahn," Samsango called out. "Keep on your feet."

John wondered just what Samsango had bet on him. It couldn't have been much. None of the ushvun'im owned anything but their braids, razors, and a few polished prayer stones. Though, they often wagered their duties. It was a sort of gambling where everyone started out laden with obligations and then hoped to come out with none. No one ever struck it rich. Even the greatest winning streak never amounted to more than a day off.

John strode back to the left side of the practice ground.

The prior lifted his arms again. This time, it was John's turn to take the defensive stance.

His mud-caked opponent charged, throwing himself ahead with brutal force. John crouched and, as the priest sprang at him, John lunged into him. The smaller priest was jarred with the force of the impact. John caught him by the hips, then heaved him upward with all his strength. The priest's legs flew out from beneath him as he flipped across John's back and went down into the mud again. John pivoted to face the priest.

Still sprawled in the mud, he shook his head at John. His expression didn't seem so much angry as concerned. John helped him back up to his feet.

"You're too good for your own well-being, Jahn," the priest whispered to him. Then, he glanced up to the walkway above them. John followed his gaze to Ushman Nuritam's thin figure.

John frowned. Ushman Dayyid was no longer there.

The prior lifted his left arm, again pronouncing the test in John's favor. John's opponent wiped the mud from his body. Then he climbed up the stairs and back out of the filthy grounds. John watched him go.

Then, John saw the tall black column of Dayyid's figure advancing down the steps. The soft murmurs and quiet conversations that had hummed across the steps went silent. As John looked out over the steps, he took in row upon row of black braids as all the assembled ushvun'im bowed their heads.

Dayyid spared none of the priests a glance. He stopped beside the prior. The prior bent in half before Dayyid. Dayyid spoke softly over the other man's bowed head. John couldn't hear any of what he said. He only caught murmurs and pauses. The prior bowed slightly lower, his glistening braids spilling down over his face and sweeping against the stone floor. Dayyid turned with mechanical precision and strode back up the stairs.

The prior straightened. His round face was dark red from being bent over for so long. He scowled, seeing John looking at him. John quickly lowered his eyes.

"Practice is done for the day," the prior shouted. "Those of you who have been on the grounds, bathe and then attend your duties. Those who have not been on the grounds, go directly to your duties."

John trudged through the mud and started to pull himself up onto the stairs. His dormitory was in charge of the pine garden this month. With the weather turning warm, the soil would need to be turned and prepared for seeding. It was work that John enjoyed.

The prior held up his hand for John to remain where he was. John waited as the other priests filed out of the arena. Samsango milled on the steps for several minutes after all the rest had gone. The prior gave him a sharp, warning glare. With an apologetic shrug to John, Samsango left too.

Once they were alone, the prior said, "Ushman Dayyid has done you the honor of accepting you for his ushiri'im to practice their battle forms against."

A slightly sick chill slithered through John's stomach. He didn't want Ushman Dayyid practicing anything on him, particularly not battle forms.

"You will wash and then go directly to the golden chamber on the second floor. If Ushman Dayyid finishes with you today, you are to come back to me directly. I won't allow for any distractions or laziness."

John nodded.

The prior scowled. "Well, go! You don't want to keep Ushman Dayyid waiting."

"Of course not." John couldn't manage to force any enthusiastic inflection into his voice. His words came out flat and dull.

He climbed up from the grounds and took the long way around the armory. The baths were a series natural springs, which the priests had sheltered with tall, latticed stone walls. There were carved stone seats where towels and clothes could be left but no roof. Moss and lichen covered the rough stone floor.

John wasn't surprised to find Samsango waiting for him. The old man looked worried.

"You haven't been called up to serve the ushiri'im, have you?" Samsango asked.

John just nodded and stripped off his mud-caked pants.

"But you haven't even been initiated!" Samsango protested. "How can Ushman Dayyid even ask you to walk through the golden doors, much less fight with his ushiri'im?"

"I don't know." John had the feeling that Ushman Dayyid could do just about anything he liked, but he didn't want to say that out loud.

Other priests were in the bath as well, some of them barely bobbing above the water.

A few of them glanced up at John but then looked away. Their expressions were too sober and their voices too low. Normally, one of them would have teased John, or smacked his bare shoulders with a towel. Instead, he received only a few pitying smiles.

"The prior should tell him he's made a mistake," Samsango announced from where he sat cross-legged at the edge of the bath.

"If the prior was going to say anything to Ushman Dayyid, he would have already done it," John replied.

John scrubbed at the dried mud on his legs. Then he dunked beneath the water, washing his face and hair. When he came back up, Samsango continued talking.

"It's not just wrong to do this to you, it does the ushiri'im no good to practice against a novice. Ushman Dayyid should reconsider."

John squeezed the water out of his hair and tied it back away from his face.

"You think that's likely?" John asked.

Samsango didn't answer. His frown deepened. "I wouldn't have encouraged you so much if I had known." Samsango's gaze dropped to his lap. "I would never have thought that you would be chosen. Who would have?"

"It's not your fault," John told him.

"But I feel bad for winning bets on you now," Samsango admitted.

"It's all right," John assured him. "Just tell me what it is exactly that I'm going to be doing."

"You will fight the ushiri'im." The wrinkles lining Samsango's mouth pulled into deep fissures as he scowled. "They use criminals while they're perfecting their open-handed blade work. But after that, they need opponents who are trained in the battle forms, so that they can hone their skills. It's an honor to serve them, but you . . ."

"I'm going to get my ass kicked?" John supplied for Samsango and the old man offered him a grim smile.

"I'm afraid so."

John closed his eyes. Before Dayyid had made it his mission to subdue his insolent spirit, John hadn't known how it felt to truly be beaten. He had thought that he would have to be dying to hurt so much. Black bruises had decorated his flesh like tattoos. His ribs had ached each time he took a breath, his muscles trembled with each motion, and his split lips had cracked and bled when he spoke.

Each day had added injuries and pain. To be hurt that much that often changed a man, he had realized. It made pain the center of his existence, the one constant that he could not escape. Even when Dayyid finished for the day, the pain remained. It became all he felt and all each new day promised. It devoured any pleasure he might have found in his surroundings, leaving him with only dread.

But he had endured it, and it had ended.

His muscles throbbed with the physical memories of those days. He didn't want to go through that again. But his only other choice was to flee.

If he got up right at this moment and abandoned Rathal'pesha, he could avoid it. No one was going to chase a braid-less novice down the steps. But it would mean abandoning his hope of finding a way home. It would mean facing Laurie and Bill and telling them that this world would be where they lived from now on. Sickness would dominate the rest of Bill's life, servitude and repression the rest of Laurie's.

He had brought them here. It had been his foolish mistake. He owed it to them to try and get them home.

"Well," John said, "it can't be much worse than last time."

"It will be much worse," Samsango protested. "This will be blade fighting. The Unseen Edge, the God's Razor, the Silence Knife. You don't even know what these things are! How can you hope to defend yourself against them?"

"With my battle strategy of running, hiding, and crying?" John suggested.

"No," Samsango said suddenly. "I will have to go and tell Ushman Dayyid that this is wrong."

This statement drew a startled gasp from the ushvun'im sitting close enough to overhear.

John said, "Ushman Dayyid has never struck me as a man who is open to criticism."

"No," Samsango admitted. "But someone should . . ."

John could tell that Samsango was frightened. He was old, frail, and of lowly rank. Ushman Dayyid could snap him apart like pieces of kindling. Or worse yet, Ushman Dayyid could pronounce Samsango's criticism a transgression of his holy authority. The two rough braids sewn to Samsango's robe would be stripped away. Then it would be the duty of every ushvun to punish the old man.

Samsango was too old to do much work. Other priests often took his share. They respected the lifetime he had given to the monastery and went out of their way to look after him. He depended on the kindness and generosity of his fellow priests. A year of castigation, abuse, and deprivation would kill him.

"It's all right," John said. "I can do this."

"But—"

"I'm a tough young man." John pulled himself up out of the water. "I'm sure the first sight of me bawling and hiding behind furniture will disgust the ushiri'im so much that they'll just send me away."

Samsango laughed, but then shook his head. "Don't offend them. They carry the god's own bones."

"I won't." John took the clothes that Samsango offered him.

John forced himself to dress quickly. His body seemed to resist him. His legs felt heavy and slow. His hands wanted to become clumsy. He almost dropped his clean pants twice. Finally, with the slow, premeditated gait of a reanimated corpse, John started up the stairs toward the golden chamber.

Chapter Twenty-Six

John had been to the second floor before, but only to scrub the halls. He had never been through one of the ivory-inlaid doors that ran along the left wall of the hall. He recognized a few written Basawar words now, but not many more than those that allowed him to distinguish a cask of wine from a cask of fermenting taye blossoms. Nothing so complex as this writing.

The ivory-inlaid words that arched and curled over the black door panels fascinated him, in part because he couldn't read them. John traced the curving sweep of polished letters with his finger. Beneath them gleamed the emblem of a book. John wondered if the symbols spelled out the word for library.

He knew better than to try to open the door. It would be locked. All of the doors on the upper three floors were always kept locked. There was just one door that he would be allowed through: the door to the golden chamber.

As John continued down the wide gray stone hall, gentle spring breezes drifted in through the windows that ran along the opposite wall. The deep quiet of these upper floors always reminded him of the ruins of an aging, abandoned palace in some forgotten empire.

With its locked towers and inner sanctums that slowly spiraled down and out into nothing but latticed roofless halls and moss-covered stone paths, the monastery seemed as if it were ever so slowly eroding back into the earth.

Only the scent of incense hinted at the presence of the men who inhabited this level.

John followed the hall as it opened into a raised walkway that arched out to another building. At its end stood a heavy black iron door that looked like it had been made to withstand gun blasts and battering rams.

Two silver Payshmura eyes stared down at John from above the doorway. Beneath them, beaten into the door itself, a tight gold script arched over a gold sun and a silver moon. The letters were unusually clipped and square. John didn't think he had seen that style of Basawar script before. Then, as he reached out to the heavy knob, he realized that the gold letters weren't Basawar at all. They were English. A little disfigured, but clearly English.

Through this door to a thousand more.

John read it and frowned. A thousand doors. He remembered the words from a Basawar prayer. Samsango had taught it to him while they had been hiking down the Thousand Steps to Amura'taye to pick up supplies. At the time, John had hardly been paying attention. His thoughts had been more focused on his plans to visit Laurie and Bill in the Bousim house. Now he frowned, attempting to recall the words.

Parfir sleeps behind a golden door

His blessing opens a thousand more

His blood and bone, my sea and stone—

John's thoughts were broken by a sudden shriek.

At first he thought it was a human scream, but it didn't sound right for that. It sounded more metallic and inanimate, like sheet metal rending apart. Then, a faint but familiar smell drifted over him.

It was the same smell his old computer used to produce when it began to overheat: burning ozone. But that couldn't be possible, not here. It had to be something else.

A moment later, the scent was lost in the breeze rolling across the walkways. John supposed he would find out what the smell was soon enough. Or he might find himself in such pain that he wouldn't care. Either way, he had wasted too much time already.

He pulled the heavy latch and swung the door open. A stronger wave of the ozone smell wafted over him. As John stepped from the outdoor glow back into a darker interior, he found himself momentarily blinded. The door fell shut behind him while he waited for his eyes to adjust. When they did, John realized that he stood in a dark hallway only a few feet from two black-coated ushiri'im.

Payshmura emblems of silver suns glinted on their high, straight collars. Both men were older than John. Their faces showed that strange, worn texture that John had noticed in many ushiri'im. They weren't tanned, wrinkled, or chaffed like the ushvun'im. These men's skins were pale and too fine, almost as if their features had been eroded to an unnatural smoothness. Eight black honor braids cascaded down their backs. They were each only one braid short of being first-rank ushman'im.

John immediately bowed before them. "Ushman Dayyid sent for me."

"So he said," one of the ushiri'im replied. "It certainly took you long enough to get here."

"I'm sorry." John bowed again. "I was instructed to bathe."

"You'll be dirty again soon enough." The other ushiri smiled, but not kindly. "Come along. You've already kept the ushman waiting longer than he likes."

The first ushiri gestured for John to precede him down the hall.

The oil lamps gave a yellow glow to the inlaid writing on the doors they passed. John lowered his eyes. More and more of the words were in English. He had never realized just how difficult it was not to read words written in his native language. Just glancing at a few letters sent the words ringing through his mind instantly.

Holy . . . Forbidden . . . Sacred . . . Eternal . . . Divine.

He read the words with the same reflexive quickness that his lungs drew in breath. Only keeping his eyes squarely lowered to the floor allowed him to maintain the appearance of ignorant awe that any other ushvun would have possessed. Maybe later, under better circumstances, he would dare to read the doors, but for now, he couldn't afford to act out of his place.

The ushiri ahead of John stopped in front of a door. John pulled to a halt behind him. Despite himself, John stole a glance to the letters on the door.

Golden Chamber, Burn and Shine.

The ushiri lifted his finger to his lips and John heard the hiss of the Gray Space tearing open. A chill seeped through the air.

The ushiri's mouth moved, his lips pressing words against his raised fingers. John couldn't hear anything, not even a faint whisper of breath. It was like watching television with the mute on. The ushiri's voice slipped into the Gray Space to be heard by someone else.

Then Dayyid's low voice split the air above them. "Bring him to me, and we will see."

Again, John thought he smelled searing ozone, but this time he was more disturbed to note a tiny flash of flame shudder through the air. It died in an instant, and John might have thought he hadn't seen it at all, if that burning scent hadn't lingered after it.

The door opened and the ushiri led John through.

The golden chamber was neither gold nor a chamber. It was a long, white training hall. The polished stone floor was covered with heavy stuffed mats. Intense light poured in from windows cut in the upper third of the high walls. Lower on the walls there were iron racks holding spears, swords, axes, and other weapons John didn't even know the names for. There was even a locked gun rack displaying a vast collection of rifles and pistols.

Directly ahead of John on a raised dais rose a huge iron statue of Parfir. John didn't think he had ever seen the god's face carved into such a proud expression. The only hint of his usual smile was a cruel upturn at the corners of his mouth. Two rows of ten ushiri'im, dressed only in their gray pants, stood with their backs to John. They had the builds of young men in their late teens and twenties. None of them wore more than seven braids. Most only possessed six.

Only Dayyid, standing at Parfir's feet, faced him.

The room felt weirdly cold and the smell of ozone caught in John's throat.

"And, at last, here he is." Dayyid gestured to John.

At once the gathered ushiri'im turned to face John. They moved with a tight militaristic precision that unnerved him. He almost stepped back from them, but he forced himself to hold his ground. He didn't want their first impression of him to be that of a cowering giant.

He straightened slightly and returned the uniformly cold stare the group gave him. For an instant, his eyes caught on Ravishan's face. His hair had grown out some, but not enough yet to braid. It hung around his face in silky strands. He'd grown since John had last seen him. The boyish softness had gone from his cheeks, and now even a hint of dark stubble shadowed his jaw.

Ravishan's dark eyes widened at the sight of him and John looked quickly past. As far as anyone here could know, this was the first time they had met. It was safer for him to meet Fikiri's surprised eyes.

Fikiri too had grown, but not so markedly. There was certainly a lot more meat on him now, but his proportions remained those of a boy, his feet and hands a size too large for his body. His dark blond hair was pulled back into five braids, and his right arm was swathed in white bandages. John gave Fikiri a brief smile and the young boy returned it, only for an instant, before schooling his expression back into the hard stare of an ushiri.

As Ushman Dayyid stepped down from the dais, the ushiri'im parted before him, then immediately closed ranks again. Dayyid stopped just out of John's reach. He turned slightly to address the ushiri'im behind him while keeping his eyes on John.

"This is Ushvun Jahn. He will be serving as our welter-body for today."

John couldn't help but steal a glance at Ravishan. He had no idea what a welter-body was, but the way that Ravishan's face went slightly pale assured John that it couldn't be good. Samsango had said that the ushiri would be training against him with blades. John's eyes drifted across the racks of spears, swords, and knives. They didn't just look painful. They looked deadly.

"We will begin with a demonstration." Dayyid held his right hand up. It was empty. A momentary relief filled John, but he didn't trust it. Samsango had been too upset for John to even hope that he would get out of the golden chamber without suffering.

"The Unseen Edge." Dayyid snapped his fingers apart and John heard the hiss of Gray Space tearing. "This is only the edge of the space. It is not open and does not lead to any destination, but it may still have a use."

Dayyid stepped closer. John frowned at him, unsure of what he should be doing. Then Dayyid swung his hand out toward John's shoulder.

Frigid, tearing pain slashed through John's flesh. He jerked back. A weird nausea pulsed through his whole body. He clamped his hand over his wounded shoulder to staunch the hot blood spilling down his sleeve. But the injury didn't alarm John as much as the sense of utter revulsion—a physical sickness—that came from touching the edge of the Gray Space.

Dayyid's dark eyes twinkled. He smiled at John as if he were just on the verge of laughter. To the ushiri'im, he said, "A long, thin cut is produced. It often hurts more than it harms."

Dayyid held up his right hand again. This time he flicked his first two fingers up and folded the rest down against his palm. Again, John heard the hiss and felt the chill of Gray Space shredding open.

Dayyid said, "The Silence Knife."

Animal panic shot through John. He suddenly wanted to run for the door. But he forced himself to stand his ground as Dayyid turned on him.

Dayyid jabbed his right hand at John's chest. Automatically, John blocked with his left arm and jabbed his right fist at Dayyid's throat. Sick agony tore through his left forearm, as if Dayyid had driven a stiletto of ice through the muscle. John jerked back out of Dayyid's reach. Blood poured from a deep puncture just above his elbow.

This time Dayyid wasn't smiling. His left hand was lightly pressed to his throat, where John's knuckles had grazed his flesh.

If he hadn't jerked away from the pain, John realized, he could have brought Dayyid down. The thought sent a warm rush through John's body.

If only he had held his ground.

Then what? Would he really have killed Dayyid? He couldn't do something like that. He wouldn't. It was just the rage of so much pain boiling up in him. John forced himself to lower his gaze.

To get through this day he would have to let his anger go.

John kept his eyes down. Dark rivulets of blood slipped down his trembling fingers and spattered across the white mat.

Dayyid began again, "The God's Razor—"

"Don't!"

John, and every other man in the room, instantly looked to Fikiri. Dayyid scowled at him.

"He's a good man." Fikiri's voice trembled and he dropped his gaze submissively to his own feet. "You shouldn't be hurting him."

To John's surprise, Dayyid's voice was soft, almost kind. "Fikiri, I am not punishing Ushvun Jahn. This is an honor for him. And I am not hurting him much. Certainly not more than he can endure." Dayyid glanced back at John. "Just a scratch and a pinch. Demonstrations always look far worse than they are. Isn't that right, Ushvun?"

John forced himself to smile. The last thing he wanted was to cause Fikiri trouble. He just had to get through this, he reminded himself. Just take what Dayyid dished out. It would be over soon enough.

He said, "I'm fine."

Dayyid continued, "It requires determination and great will to perfect your blade work, but it will be necessary if any one of you is to become Kahlil. I know this, and Ushvun Jahn knows this. For the sake of your education, Ushvun Jahn has offered himself to assist you all to learn. Now, it does him and you no good to refrain from practicing the forms of the sacred blades because you might spill a few drops of his blood. That is why he is here and why you are here. Do you understand, Fikiri?"

Fikiri nodded glumly.

"Very good." Dayyid smiled. It was a professional expression, one that conveyed pleasure in mastery more than any warmth. "Now, let us return to our lesson. The God's Razor is an extension of the Unseen Edge. It is formed when two or more ushiri'im or ushman'im create a field of Unseen Edges. I will need an assistant for this." Dayyid glanced over the gathered ushiri'im. For an instant, Dayyid paused on Ravishan.

If Ravishan felt any hesitation at the thought of slicing through John's flesh, it didn't show. He kept his expression as cold as the rest of the ushiri'im. He met Dayyid's eyes defiantly.

Dayyid moved on to Fikiri.

Fikiri tried to control his expression, but his mouth was obviously pressed closed too hard and his pale brows crunched together in misery.

"Fikiri," Dayyid said, "this will be an excellent opportunity for you to better your skills."

"But I don't know how—"

"It's simple." Dayyid beckoned him forward. Then he said to John, "Since Fikiri isn't experienced, you should probably hold as still as you can while we practice."

For a few minutes John watched with a growing feeling of dread and sickness while Dayyid tutored Fikiri in opening an Unseen Edge. The rest of the ushiri'im watched Dayyid's instructions with rapt interest.

Except for Ravishan. His eyes seemed to be focused on John's bloody right hand. When he looked up to John's face, he seemed startled to find

John looking back at him and a faint red blush spread across his face. John returned his attention to the lesson in progress.

"Very good." Dayyid nodded as Fikiri snapped his fingers apart and the Gray Space wrenched open with a shriek. John felt the air around Fikiri's hands writhing as if it were in agony. The sensation sent a shudder through him.

"Now, push the edge outward." Dayyid extended his hand and snapped another edge of Gray Space open next to Fikiri's. "Push and allow the God's Razor to spread."

Fikiri emulated Dayyid, but the action didn't seem easy for him. Sweat beaded his forehead and chest. Fikiri's arm trembled as he extended the edge of Gray Space. A noise like nails being dragged across sheet metal filled the room.

John found himself hoping that Fikiri would succeed, and at the same time, deeply worried about what would happen if he did.

Dayyid held his own broad, tanned hand out over Fikiri's and then lowered it, so that his palm just touched the back of Fikiri's hand. He spread his fingers over Fikiri's, and a thin horizontal line of flames suddenly burst up midair. The thick smell of searing ozone washed over John.

Instinctively, John's arms came up, protecting his face and chest. Then the edge of the Gray Space hit him, ripping into the muscle just above his elbows. A choked gasp of pain escaped him. He wanted to scream, but he could hardly draw a breath. Nothing in his life had hurt like this. The edge ground through his skin and muscle like a saw blade.

It had to stop. Now.

John could see the thin, trembling edge of the God's Razor. It blurred into a pale line, turning pink as his blood spattered along its surface. It looked absurdly small, like a tiny fissure in the air. Like a thread that he could just grab and snap if he wanted to.

John wondered if he was in shock from the pain.

He watched, feeling almost like a distant observer, as his right arm dropped down and grabbed the God's Razor. He felt the jagged grinding edge of Gray Space bite into his palm, but the pain seemed muted and dull. His blood spattered up in a fine mist as he clenched his fist around the opening of Gray Space. He crushed it closed.

Fikiri staggered back. Dayyid gaped in abject disbelief.

John's entire body shook. He felt hot and strange. He swayed on his feet and barely caught himself from falling. Every single ushiri stared at him in shock.

Even Ravishan.

He shouldn't have done that. Whatever it was that he had done.

John turned his hand to look at his palm. It glistened like ground beef. Nausea welled up. John looked away from his ruined hand to the men in front of him. They all stood perfectly still, as if paralyzed. Then Ravishan bolted forward. He placed a hand against John's back.

"Sit down," Ravishan said. "You should sit down."

John sat on the ugly, blood-spattered mat.

He wondered why his hand and arms didn't seem to hurt so much now. Shock, he supposed. He tried to remember first aid procedures. Treat the wounds. Keep the victim warm and hydrated.

"It's just shock," John mumbled. His words sounded strange and garbled. He started to say that he thought he needed stitches.

Ravishan scowled at him and whispered, "Be quiet!"

Then John realized that he had spoken to Ravishan in English and clenched his jaw shut. He had to be careful.

A moment later, Dayyid crouched down opposite Ravishan, scowling.

"You were a fool to grasp the God's Razor. Your hand should have been severed."

John scowled back at Dayyid, not trusting himself to speak yet.

"His injuries need to be treated," Ravishan said.

Dayyid narrowed his eyes at Ravishan. "I know what needs to be done and what does not," Dayyid replied curtly.

"Then you know that he needs to be tended to." Ravishan stared straight into Dayyid's face.

John had the distinct feeling that the struggle between them could have been about anything. Effectively, treating his injuries had become secondary to the crisis of their opposing wills.

For the first time, it struck John how much Ravishan and Dayyid resembled one another, not just physically, but in their mannerisms. The inflections of their voices and their expressions mirrored each other. No wonder Dayyid became so infuriated when Ravishan turned a commanding glower on him. It was Dayyid's own glare.

The pain in John's arms grew duller and he wondered if Dayyid had been telling the truth when he had said that the demonstrations looked worse than they were.

He glanced down and noted that both sleeves of his robe were dripping out little droplets of red. In the cupped curve of his aching right hand, a dark pool of his blood steadily welled up. He could feel tiny streams escaping between his fingers and slipping down the back of his hand. The color was brilliant against the white mats and the dull gray of John's robe.

"Please," Ravishan barely whispered the words, lowering his head as he spoke, "please call for Hann'yu to treat his wounds."

Dayyid nodded and then stood. "Fikiri, go fetch Ushman Hann'yu."

John tried to stand and follow Fikiri, but Ravishan held him back. "Don't try to move too much. It isn't just your hand. You touched Gray Space. You could be hurt inside."

"I'm not. I'm fine." John was pleased to note that his voice sounded stronger and the Basawar words came to him easily. He gave Ravishan a reassuring smile. Then, without warning, his vision went white and he crumpled down to the mat.

Chapter Twenty-Seven

John didn't open his eyes. He lay still, hardly awake but listening. The softness of the mattress beneath him tempted him to return to sleep. An antiseptic smell hung in the air, reminiscent of a hospital emergency room but not quite right. Some botanical note, a hint of pine, instantly told John he was not in a hospital. Not anywhere close to home, but in some bed in Rathal'pesha.

He heard the rustle of robes nearby. There was another man in the room with him. John considered opening his eyes and stealing a glance to see who it was, but the movement seemed like an immense exertion. Maybe in a few minutes he'd wake up enough to do it.

A warm hand touched his forehead and then very gently pushed the hair back from his face. An instant later the hand was withdrawn.

John caught the distinct sound of a door opening and then the snap of boot heels striking the stone floor.

"Hann'yu."

John instantly recognized Dayyid's voice. He forced his eyes open just a crack.

He lay in a large room with tall, narrow windows. He counted five other beds, but only one seemed to be occupied and John didn't recognize the man in it. He appeared badly injured, his body forming the wrong curves and hollows beneath his blankets. A leg and part of his arm seemed to be missing, but John couldn't be sure. The indistinctness of the body, blankets, and pillows disturbed him.

He turned his attention back to the other men in the room. Dayyid stood to the right of John's bed with the painted red door behind him. Ravishan and another ushman stood a little closer to John on his left.

"So, will he live, Hann'yu?" Dayyid asked.

The priest standing beside Ravishan nodded. Like Dayyid, he looked to be in his mid-forties. His hair was walnut-brown and pulled back into eight braids. His gentle features reminded John of Samsango's. His skin was much darker than either Ravishan's or Dayyid's.

"He may wake up tomorrow or the next day." Hann'yu smiled at Dayyid. "He's surprisingly strong."

John wondered how they could not have noticed that he was, in fact, already awake and watching them.

"Can you rouse him sooner?" Dayyid asked.

"I don't see why I should. Is there some emergency?"

"Ushman Nuritam wishes to test his bones," Dayyid replied.

"Really?" Hann'yu's grin was positively gleeful. "So, you nearly killed an ushiri candidate?"

"We can hope. But I doubt he'll pass the test." Dayyid stepped closer to John's bedside and gazed down over him. "He looks more like the tainted remnant of some Eastern bloodline."

"Well, who knows." Hann'yu shrugged. "They say that even the sun started out as a blond boy from the east."

"Who says that?" Dayyid asked. His tone was harsh but his expression struck John as almost playful.

"Storybooks. Didn't you ever read any when you were a child?"

"Of course not," Dayyid replied. "I read only the holiest of the holy. My thoughts were never polluted by heresy or trash."

"Well, there's no point in being bitter now," Hann'yu responded. "I'm sure that your parents didn't mean to deprive you."

Ravishan, who had until this moment remained silent enough to be overlooked, coughed to cover a little laugh. When he raised his hand to his mouth, John noticed the edges of white bandages poking out from beneath Ravishan's sleeves. Dayyid glared at him and Ravishan bowed his head in quick supplication. When Dayyid turned back to Hann'yu, the lightness in his expression had completely gone.

"Can you wake this one, or not?"

Hann'yu shook his head. "Not so soon. Perhaps tomorrow. Right now I think he's lucky to have a pulse. We should let him sleep as long as he needs."

How could they still not have noticed that he was looking at them? John frowned, and then realized that he couldn't actually feel the muscles of his mouth move. He'd just thought of frowning, but his body had not responded.

Dayyid asked, "Will you be keeping Ravishan as well?"

"I might need him to bear another wound."

"What about Ashid?" Dayyid's tone softened. John followed Dayyid's gaze to the misshapen body in the other bed.

Hann'yu's gentle smile faded. Dayyid closed his eyes, head bowed.

"Does he know? Is he suffering?" Dayyid asked quietly.

Hann'yu shook his head. "No, he won't wake. Tomorrow he'll be in better hands than mine."

Dayyid remained still and silent, gazing at the white blankets. Then he turned back to John.

"See if you can get him on his feet soon."

"I will," Hann'yu replied, "but next time don't knock him off his feet so hard."

"I know." Dayyid started for the door. "But they have to learn somehow. The Fai'daum certainly aren't going to show them any greater compassion." He pulled the door open and disappeared into the dark hall outside. The door fell shut behind him.

John wanted to sit up and say something, but he couldn't seem to do it. He wasn't even sure that his eyes were really open now. When he concentrated intently, he could feel his lids pressed closed. He had to be dreaming then. It wasn't the first time that he had slipped into a dream that seemed so deeply real. Still, he found it strange that he would dream of this. Maybe he was catching snippets of some conversation around him and building these images. Even as he thought about it, the dream continued just as the real world would have.

Hann'yu drifted past the row of beds to a heavy, carved table laden with dozens of smoked glass jars. Farther back, John thought he saw a wide shelf stacked with even more jars as well as several leather-bound books. Hann'yu took a pen and started writing something.

"Do you think Jahn's bones will pass?" Ravishan glanced back when he spoke to Hann'yu, but remained at John's bedside.

"I don't think it matters." Hann'yu didn't look up from his work. "It's not as if he could take your place. I think Fikiri's the one you have to worry about."

"Fikiri's too scared to even walk through the Gray Space."

"He broke a prophecy." Hann'yu opened two of the jars and poured dark powders from them into a mortar. "Even the Issusha'im Oracles don't know how he did it. You shouldn't underestimate him."

Ravishan nodded, and Hann'yu seemed to take this as the end of their conversation. He dropped some wilted clumps of leaves into his mortar.

"Maybe," Ravishan whispered, "it wasn't Fikiri who broke it." Ravishan's warm hand brushed John's forehead again. His fingers swept John's hair back from his face. Then Ravishan lifted his hand away.

The touch hadn't been more than a moment of contact, but somehow it soothed John. It eased him to know that Ravishan watched over him. John slid into a deeper rest. His vision dulled to shadow, and for a time, he simply drifted in a mist of sleep.

The next time an image opened up before him, John knew he was dreaming right away. He was moving up a white stone staircase, floating through heavy gilded doors and passing deep into forbidden chambers.

The air around him roiled with the smell of burning ozone. Plumes of pale blue-toned smoke hung like the suspended letters of a script he couldn't read. They twisted around him and broke apart as he swept through them. As he took in a breath, he felt an electrical sensation prickle his lungs.

It drew him, though he felt a little afraid of it. He passed through the final door and stepped into a vast, circular room. The air inside crackled. Thick clouds of bluish smoke hid the ceiling. All along the curve of the walls were gold arches. They looked like doorways but only opened to flat expanses of solid wall. Though they appeared to be nothing more than decorative details, the doorways revolted him. He couldn't bring himself to approach them.

Overhead, bolts of white light burst through the cloudy blue smoke. John caught the silhouette of something huge hanging just above him: a long spiral of human vertebrae strung together on red copper wires.

Dislocated arm bones jutted out, extending their fingers to other skeletal bodies. Ribs arched open, holding hipbones and femurs. There had to be hundreds of bodies woven together, flickering with tongues of electricity. Suddenly, the spinal column directly above John twisted and a yellow skull peered down. The jaws gaped over him.

"We smells its blood," the skull whispered. The finger bones began to tremble and clatter against each other. They twitched and tugged at the wires holding them as if struggling to pull free.

John jerked back, falling through the door behind him into a sudden darkness.

He bolted upright.

"It's all right." Ravishan gently caught his shoulders. He was still in bed at the infirmary. It was darker now, almost nightfall.

"Lie back down," Ravishan told him. "You're not well enough to be up yet."

"I'm fine," John answered, but he let himself be pushed back into the comfort of the pillows. He felt cold and slightly sickened. Ravishan smoothed the blanket over him.

John said, "Have you been sitting beside me all day?"

"No, I was standing most of the time, but then Hann'yu left and I took his chair. One of the ushvun'im came to see you."

"An old man?"

Ravishan nodded. "Bald, with two honor braids. Very few teeth. I don't think he told me his name."

"Samsango," John supplied.

"I told him that you wouldn't be up for another day." Ravishan leaned back in the chair. "You really shouldn't be awake, you know."

"I don't think I'm as badly hurt as you think I am. The cut in my palm was pretty deep but nothing life-threatening." He felt a little embarrassed now, remembering how he had fainted from the injury.

"It's not the cuts that I'm talking about." Ravishan's dark eyes narrowed as he gazed at John. "Don't you know what you did?"

"I know I passed out. I think it must have been shock. But I'm fine now."

"You collapsed the God's Razor." Ravishan lowered his voice slightly. "You overpowered Dayyid and Fikiri."

"It could as easily have been something Fikiri did wrong." John didn't know why, but the speculation that he harbored some kind of strange power within him made him uncomfortable.

Ravishan scowled.

"It wasn't Fikiri," Ravishan said. "He can hardly open his own Gray Space, much less crush Dayyid's."

"So maybe it was someone else."

"Who?" Ravishan asked. "We all saw you do it."

"I don't know." John sighed, feeling tired again.

"It was you." Ravishan smiled at him. "Now Ushman Nuritam wants to test your bones to see if you are an ushiri candidate."

John didn't see any point in arguing about it. And he suspected that he didn't know enough about the Gray Space to win the argument anyway.

"So, what will this test entail?" John asked. He closed his eyes.

"Nothing much," Ravishan said. "A few prayers. You drink tea, open the Gray Space . . . take off your clothes and dance—"

"What?" John opened one eye, and seeing Ravishan's grin, whispered, "It's not nice to tease the man from another planet."

"You have my deepest apologies." Ravishan stretched in the chair and yawned.

"Tired?" John asked.

"Tired and sore." He lifted his arms slightly so that the sleeves of his robes fell back, exposing his bandaged arms. He smiled proudly. "Hann'yu asked me to bear your wounds."

"What does that mean?"

"I give my blood in place of yours." Ravishan lowered his arms. "It lessens the extent of your injuries."

Like donating blood, John imagined. But there seemed to be far more bandages than a transfusion would have warranted.

John asked, "Does it hurt?"

"Not much." Ravishan shrugged. "You?"

"A little pinch in my palm, but that's about it." It was something of a lie, but John didn't feel like complaining.

"You should sleep," Ravishan told him.

"You as well," John replied.

"I'll be right behind you. Don't worry."

"Don't take too long," John said. "I'll be waiting."

Ravishan gave a soft murmur. His eyes were closed and his arms hung limply across his lap. Steadily, his breath slowed and deepened. John smiled, realizing that Ravishan had already gone ahead of him.

Chapter Twenty-Eight

The simple, bell-shaped cup in John's hand looked as though it could have been carved from alabaster or limestone, but it felt lighter than either. No mineral created that finely grained surface. Delicate ridges marked where a ligament had once attached, where the force of muscles had once flexed and strained. The cup had to be bone.

Heat from the tea inside lent a living warmth. John took a quick drink of the greenish tea, expecting the bite of daru'sira. Instead, a weak, floral fragrance hung in his mouth. There was almost no taste, just a light scent after he swallowed.

A year ago, he wouldn't have tasted anything at all, but he had somewhat adapted to the faint flavors in this world. He supposed that when he got back home everything would be too strong for a while. He tried to imagine what his favorite salsa would taste like now. For a moment, he drifted back to sharp, searing tangs of lime and lemon suffusing earthy-sweet cherry tomatoes, fresh cilantro clinging to chopped red onion, and slivers of jalapeno pepper all bursting up like fireworks between the soothing, cool bites of cucumber.

He took another sip of the tea, hardly tasted it at all, then glanced up to see how the men around him were enjoying theirs.

Rows of ushiri'im and ushman'im knelt on either side of him, forming a neat corridor between him and the raised gilded dais at the front of the room where Ushman Nuritam sat. It was easy to find Ravishan's shorter locks in the sameness of bowed heads and long black braids. Fikiri, too, stood out with his dark blond hair. Both knelt directly behind Dayyid at the edge of the dais.

Ushman Nuritam sipped slowly from his own white cup. His long white braids fell around him like cascading streams.

This room was small compared to the massive scale of the rest of Rathal'pesha, but still it seemed almost empty with few more than fifty men filling it. Sharp morning light diffused into a soft glow as it fell through the hundreds of sheet mica windowpanes. Carved vines climbed the stone pillars and twisted over each of the steps leading up to the dais. Behind Ushman Nuritam rose the huge figure of Parfir.

John studied the statue. As always, Parfir's body rose up in an amalgam of trees, leaves, flowers, and animal forms. His raised hands extended to the ceiling. His fingers became arched supports. His hair had been sculpted into waves with marble fish and water lilies braiding through them. The light barely reached the heights from which Parfir stared down over his assembled priests.

John squinted up into the dimness. The god seemed to offer him the faintest smile.

Ushman Nuritam lowered his cup and set it to his right. Not knowing what else to do, John emulated him. Ushman Nuritam nodded just a little. John hoped that it was a sign of his approval and not that the priest was drifting off to sleep. The old man almost always seemed to have a distant point of focus, and often he seemed utterly unaware of his surroundings.

Ushman Nuritam's voice was not loud, but it carried easily throughout the absolute stillness of the chamber. "Parfir bless us, for we are your loyal sons. And forgive us, for we are not so wise as you. Help us know your purpose for our brother Jahn. Help us so that we may serve you more perfectly. Help us so that we may defend your holiness."

"Bless us!" The words rose in a loud unison from all of the priests surrounding John. John only managed to come in on the end, calling out "us."

Dayyid rose, strode to John, and then crouched down in front of him. His expression conveyed nothing.

He opened his black coat to reveal a leather vest reminiscent of a gun holster. From this, Dayyid drew out two sheathed knives. The hilts of both were black. They looked just like the knives that Ravishan and the other ushiri'im carried. Dayyid placed both in front of John.

"Choose one," Dayyid whispered to him.

John regarded the identical knives. John frowned, realizing that he should have kept Ravishan up, asking him more about this test. He wanted to peer out at the ushiri'im and ushman'im to see if he could catch a clue from Ravishan. But there was no chance of that. Dayyid was watching him too closely.

There was no point in dragging this out. He simply reached for the knife on the right. Immediately he pulled his hand back. There was something wrong with that knife. The air around it shivered with a cold, electric sensation.

"Why didn't you take it?" Dayyid asked.

"I don't know," John replied. He didn't want to tell Dayyid more than he absolutely had to.

"Is there something wrong with it?" Dayyid asked.

"I don't know."

"There must be a reason you drew back." Dayyid leaned closer to John. "It is important that you tell us."

"This knife just feels . . ." John paused, searching for a word that didn't betray his revulsion but still conveyed the sensation that radiated from the knife. "Powerful and strange."

Dayyid nodded slightly. "And the other blade?"

John reached out more tentatively this time. He picked the sheathed knife up and held it for a moment. It was carved from bone.

John said, "I don't feel anything from this one."

Dayyid stood and addressed Ushman Nuritam. "Ushvun Jahn did not choose the blade bearing the curse."

"And yet he knew it?" Ushman Nuritam replied softly. "He felt it?"

"Yes."

"Then, let us continue," Ushman Nuritam decided.

Dayyid carefully collected the knife and carried it to Ushman Nuritam, who slipped it into his robes. He wondered what exactly had been so disconcerting about that particular blade. He recalled a similar but much more intense revulsion when he had come across the remains of the Great Gate at Wolf Rock two years ago. Were there certain elements in the world of Basawar that were so integrally foreign to him, to his entire world, that they were inherently repulsive?

John examined the sheathed knife that he had chosen. What about it had differed from the other so greatly? His fingers slid across the clasp that kept it sheathed, but he stopped himself from drawing it. He had no idea how an action like that would be taken in the context of the test. He wasn't even sure how his last action had been interpreted. He seemed to have chosen the wrong knife, and yet Nuritam insisted that he go on.

John set the knife down beside his small white cup.

Dayyid strode back down from the dais. With a flick of his hand, he swept his long, glossy black braids back over his shoulder. "Stand and approach," Dayyid told him.

John stood, though not as gracefully as he would have liked. His left foot had gone numb from sitting cross-legged on the stone floor for so long. As he limped forward, John thought he caught a brief smile from Dayyid. It was gone before John could be sure it had been there, much less guess why. Perhaps it was simply an acknowledgment of the universal experience, which all priests in Rathal'pesha had, of having a foot go numb.

Dayyid said, "Close your eyes."

John's instincts rebelled at the thought of closing his eyes with Dayyid standing so near him. He lowered his lids but still peered through the shadow of his lashes. Again, Dayyid gave him a brief, amused smile. John realized that Dayyid knew he was peeking.

"Now turn your back to me," Dayyid told him.

With great reluctance, John did as he was told.

From behind him came the nearly inaudible hiss of the Gray Space opening. John almost bolted back around as he felt the chill. In an instant, it snapped closed again and another space opened. John held perfectly still, eyes pressed closed. He desperately didn't want the Gray Space to touch him again. But he could do nothing but stand here and wish.

John found himself willing away the Gray Space with the same intense concentration that he had called upon as a young child to destroy the monsters he imagined awaiting him beneath his bed. It was all he could do, and he hated it.

One space after another opened and closed beside and behind him. Each time, John felt the air writhe. Even after the spaces closed, a wounded feeling remained etched in his mind like the gashes a skate left in ice. The air seemed to be growing thinner and torn. It felt rough, almost ragged, as John drew a breath into his lungs.

Behind him, he could hear Dayyid drawing in deep breaths, as if he were winded. John wondered if the grainy, broken texture of the air bothered him as well.

John waited for another space to open, but none did. All he heard was Dayyid taking in one deep breath after another. John opened his eyes a little wider. Rows of unfamiliar ushiri'im and ushman'im stared at John. John stole a quick glance to Ravishan, but his head was bowed, hiding his expression. Fikiri's eyes were wide, his mouth slightly open in surprise. He turned back to Dayyid.

Instantly, the Gray Space arched up over John like a mouth about to swallow him. A flare of repulsion, fear, and anger rushed through John in a wave of heat.

"No!" John shouted. His breath burned as it rushed from his mouth. Dayyid shuddered. Flames seared along the edges of the Gray Space above John. Then, it snapped shut. John swayed on his feet, feeling dizzy.

Dayyid stood before John, breathing heavily, his pale skin beaded with sweat.

"Parfir has blessed you with strength, Brother Jahn," Ushman Nuritam said at last.

"Or there's witch's blood in your veins," Dayyid whispered.

John felt the blood draining from his face. He had been here long enough to know what the Payshmura did to witches. They flayed them alive or burned them on the Holy Road along with Fai'daum traitors.

"The test has not been as conclusive as we could have wished. We must discuss your candidacy," Nuritam declared from the dais. "Dayyid, Hann'yu, you will attend."

Dayyid nodded.

"All rise," Dayyid called out to the gathered ushiri'im and ushman'im. All fifty men in attendance stood.

"See to your duties," Dayyid ordered. "Hann'yu, please remain to attend Ushman Nuritam."

The other priests filed out. John watched them, wondering if he, too, should leave. Dayyid clamped a hand on his shoulder.

"I am sure you will want to stay to hear this out, Ushvun Jahn."

It was only a matter of moments before the chamber emptied. Dayyid led John up the steps of the dais. Hann'yu followed them. All three of them sat down on the broad step just below Ushman Nuritam.

Up close, Ushman Nuritam's skin looked like a veil of fine silk. John thought he could see the man's bones just beneath the surface. His gaze drifted past John and seemed to settle on the distant wall.

Hann'yu offered John a quick smile—nothing like the hard flash of teeth John so often caught from Dayyid. Hann'yu appeared genuinely friendly. He stretched his legs and massaged his ankles.

"Jahn, don't you think we should have cushions? They have them at the Black Tower in Nurjima and so do our sisters at Umbhra'ibaye. I don't see why we shouldn't. We're not fanatics like the Kahlirash'im in Vundomu, you know."

"I have spoken to the Usho." Ushman Nuritam nodded seriously. "He has approved the purchase of 400 cushions."

"Then we could add them to the supply list for next month." Hann'yu's smile widened almost comically. "My butt will be so happy."

Ushman Nuritam returned Hann'yu's smile in a wide grin that almost startled John. He had grown used to seeing the ushman'im with dour and distant expressions. At just this moment, Hann'yu and Nuritam seemed suddenly very human and approachable. It was a relieving sight after being attacked, cut, and put through an incomprehensible test. It offered John some small hope of being able to appeal to either of the two men.

Then John glanced to Dayyid. His expression remained cold, almost grim. And for the first time, John noticed that the insignias on Dayyid's collar and the style of his braids were different from Hann'yu's. Hann'yu wore emblems of suns on his collar where Dayyid wore a both a sun and a small crescent moon. Hann'yu's braids hung forward where Dayyid's were pulled back close to his skull and fell behind his shoulders.

"I believe we can discuss provisions later," Dayyid stated. "Right now, there is the matter of Ushvun Jahn's placement."

Again, Ushman Nuritam nodded. "This is a difficult matter." He shifted slightly and looked at John. "You obviously are of an Eastern bloodline."

John nodded. He had no way of contesting the statement. He certainly wasn't going to tell them that he was from the bloodline of an entirely different world.

"So, it is not so surprising that you felt the power of the curse blade." Nuritam patted his robe, where he had tucked the knife away. "But you also seem to have some sense of the Gray Space. That would indicate that your bones may be blessed by the god Parfir."

"Or, it may simply be that he comes from a strong line of witches," Dayyid said. "An Eastern taint can remain strong through generations. Witch's blood is not the same as the god's bones."

"True." Ushman Nuritam nodded and gazed out at the panes of mica that filled the tall windows. "It is hard to know what should be done."

"Even if his power arises from an Eastern ancestor, that doesn't mean it can't serve the god." Hann'yu glanced to the small tray beside Ushman Nuritam. "Do we have any more tea?"

"No," Dayyid stated flatly.

"We should have made more." Hann'yu glanced to John. "Are you thirsty?"

It was a simple question, and yet John wasn't sure of what to make of it. His life was being discussed. Whether he was thirsty or not seemed like an utterly insignificant and unrelated question.

Hann'yu nodded, despite the fact that John had said nothing. "Dayyid," Hann'yu said, "have someone bring us more tea. I can tell that Ushvun Jahn is thirsty and confused. He doesn't even know what we're talking about."

"Of course he knows," Dayyid replied. "He's not an idiot."

"Well, perhaps we should let him have a little more say in the decision, then," Hann'yu remarked.

Dayyid shook his head but then glanced over to John. "Tell me, have you ever dreamed in another place? Have you ever felt that you have slipped through walls or doors into places you have never been before?"

"You mean, in a dream?" John asked.

"It would seem like a dream," Dayyid replied.

"I don't remember most of my dreams too well." John didn't want to tell too much. "But I may have had one like that."

"You may have." Dayyid shook his head. "There are already too many young men struggling as ushiri'im. I don't need another."

"Of course you do. Someone should take Ashid's place," Hann'yu answered.

"And follow him to his grave?" Dayyid demanded. "It does no good to have a hundred ushiri'im if they are all torn apart by the Gray Space.

A taint of witch's blood simply isn't strong enough to protect them in the Gray Space. They must have Parfir's blessings. They must carry it in their bones."

Hann'yu shook his head. "You see, this is why we need some tea. It would give us a chance to pause and think over each other's points."

Dayyid scowled. "I won't train him. The signs aren't sure enough. If he only has witch's blood, then the first time he enters the Gray Space, it will chew him to pieces."

"But if his bones are truly blessed and you don't train him, you may have passed over the Kahlil," Hann'yu replied.

Listening to the two of them, John suddenly realized he wanted Dayyid to win this argument. He didn't seem to be accusing John of being a witch, as John had feared. Instead, Dayyid seemed to be arguing that he couldn't withstand the Gray Space. A sick shiver wriggled through John's stomach as he recalled feeling the edge of the Gray Space against his flesh. He knew he never wanted to be inside one.

And suddenly, he remembered where he had heard the name Ashid before. He had been the mutilated ushiri in the bed a little way from John's.

"Ravishan will be the one," Dayyid said. "His flesh may be sinful and his will wayward, but I know his bones are the god's own. He will be Kahlil."

"What of Fikiri?" Hann'yu suggested. "His bones broke a prophecy. He crossed death itself to be delivered to us."

"Perhaps, but it's too early in his training." Dayyid's assured expression wavered slightly.

"You see, you don't know," Hann'yu went on quickly. "Not one of us knows. The Kahlil could be a heretic's son or a gaun'im's by-blow. We can't afford to cast even one possibility aside."

"Ushvun Jahn is not even a possibility," Dayyid stated. "It would be a waste of my time and his life."

Hann'yu's smile flattened. "He has power. You couldn't even touch him in the test. How can you let such potential go untrained?"

"Moving through the spaces is not just a matter of power. There is a . . ." Dayyid scowled as he tried to find the word. His fingers moved as if trying to pull the word from the empty air. "There is a particular character that a man must have. And Ushvun Jahn does not have it."

"How can you say?" Hann'yu asked. "You hardly know him."

"When he first came, I practiced against him on the ushvun'im grounds. He has no passion. No fury. He will take beating after beating without question. To walk between the worlds, a man must fight. He must struggle even when he may be beaten. That is not Ushvun Jahn's nature. If the Gray Space closes on him, he would simply allow it to devour him."

A small, egotistical part of John wanted to tell Dayyid that he had no idea what he was talking about. But John kept his mouth shut. If Ushman Dayyid thought he was weak-willed, so be it.

"With all respect," Hann'yu replied, "you're only describing men who share your own nature, Dayyid. But you, yourself, could not become Kahlil. Despite your devotion and your fearless nature, you failed that test. So, it could be argued that you do not know what qualities are required for a man to become Kahlil."

As Hann'yu spoke, John could see a dark flush spreading across Dayyid's tanned face. Ushman Nuritam shook his head.

"I have heard enough," Ushman Nuritam said softly. "Thank you both for arguing the matter before me."

Both Hann'yu and Dayyid bowed their heads.

Ushman Nuritam turned to John. "It seems that you have great potential, Ushvun, but perhaps not among the ushiri'im. I am sorry."

A wave of relief rolled over John. He didn't think he could have stood another assault from Dayyid, much less having to train under the man every day. John noticed Dayyid's slight smile and Hann'yu's sigh.

"If I may make a request." Hann'yu kept his head lowered.

"Go ahead," Ushman Nuritam said.

"At least allow Ushvun Jahn to be trained under me. I could use him to bear wounds, if nothing else."

Ushman Nuritam nodded. "Of course. Ushvun Jahn, you will be given the honor of serving Ushman Hann'yu in the infirmary."

"Thank you." John lowered his head to the stone step. A queasy feeling was already seeping through him. Bearing wounds. He wondered if he had just gotten a better, or worse, appointment.

"So, now we should have our tea," Hann'yu suggested.

Ushman Nuritam nodded slowly and somberly.

"If you could excuse me," Dayyid said, "I must return to the ushiri'im. We will have to break in a new welter-body."

"Of course. You are excused, Ushman Dayyid." Ushman Nuritam smiled at him. "May Parfir walk with you."

"And with you," Dayyid replied. He bowed to both Ushman Nuritam and Hann'yu, then quit the chamber.

John remained on the step, apparently forgotten, while tea was sent for and then brought. Ushman Nuritam discussed the division of tithes and how much would be allotted to Rathal'pesha as opposed to the holy fortress of Vundomu. As Hann'yu nodded and listened, he passed John a cup of tea with the ingrained politeness of the Basawar nobility.

The irrelevant conversation felt restful to John after so much intense focus on himself and his training. He relaxed on the lower step, only half-listening to the discussion concerning southern nobility and rumors of their secret funding of the Fai'daum. Then the conversation turned to the vague prophesies surrounding the Rifter. It was good to hear about things that had nothing to do with him for a while.

Chapter Twenty-Nine

A month later, John had learned his way through the twisting halls of the higher floors. These days he spent most of his free hours in the library attempting to reclaim the prowess literacy offered.

This morning, the yellowed panes of sheet mica in the skylights turned the harsh light soft and golden. The heavy hand-bound books filling the shelves and lining the walls added insulation against the cold that would have otherwise crept up through the stones. The books themselves all seemed infused with a scent of incense, and perhaps in a few volumes, just the hint of fires. It made him feel drawn into autumn.

Paging through a strange-smelling old book under the warm light reminded John of returning to school after the summer break. But of course, here in Basawar, all his associations were wrong. It was spring, and there were no summer vacations or post-graduate classes. Here, no one had even heard of ecology, much less an ecology degree, and John was far from a scholar. He could hardly read.

Ravishan rocked his stool back onto two legs and peered over John's shoulder.

"Par. Fir. Ati. Hyy. An. Pahr." Ravishan gave the sound for each of the letters as he pointed to them. "Parfir'ati hyy'an pahr."

Parfir brought rain. John understood the spoken sentence perfectly.

John traced his fingers beneath lines of faded brown symbols. One after another, they flowed and arced together into the long sentences that filled page after page of the aged book in front of him. He knew most of the letters now. Hann'yu had insisted that he learn them and John had been happy to. But it was frustrating to have to go so slowly, sounding the words out like a child.

"It's boring stuff," Ravishan commented. "Parfir creates earth and air and water and then gives them all life by pouring pieces of himself into each of them. His blood, his skin, his flesh, and his tears. All that, until the world is alive and he's just . . . I don't remember exactly. An eyeball, finger bones, and some ribs, and I think some teeth."

John glanced down at the page. He thought he recognized the word for eye. It even looked a little like an eye, with a circle and a single dot in the center.

"Then the first empire of demons arises and Parfir creates the first Rifter from what remains of his body, except one finger bone, which got lost." Ravishan tapped the small brown illustration at the bottom of the page. "The Rifter slaughters them all."

It was of a woman with long, wild blond hair and wide staring eyes. The ground buckled and split beneath her feet and bolts of lightning cut the air above her head. She vaguely resembled Laurie.

"But the Rifter, the sacred destroyer, was made too well, made too strong, and Parfir's own body shuddered as she walked across his back." Ravishan shrugged. "The same story everyone knows."

"I don't know it."

"Really?" Ravishan sat all four legs of the stool firmly on the ground.

"Really."

"They don't speak of Parfir's sacrifice in Nayeshi?" Ravishan asked.

"They don't even know about Parfir in Nayeshi."

"Such a strange place." Ravishan leaned closer and studied the picture. "I can't imagine what that would be like."

"When you become Kahlil, you'll see it for yourself," John told him.

Ravishan radiated pleasure at John's words.

It struck John that Ravishan had a disarmingly handsome smile, and then John recalled that he had thought the same thing the last time Ravishan had flashed him that charming grin. He supposed it wouldn't have had such a strong effect back at home, where dental care and toothpaste were common. Here it was different.

Ravishan's white teeth shone like pearls in contrast to his tanned skin. His eyes caught the afternoon light, glowing gold.

"When I am Kahlil," Ravishan whispered. "I like the way that sounds."

John smiled. When Ravishan was Kahlil, hopefully he would help John, Laurie, and Bill get back home. But that was probably still years away. John returned to learning his letters, but found himself distracted by the illustration of the first Rifter.

She reminded him of Laurie more each time he looked at her. The small mouth, the thin body—it resembled her in that simple but clear way that some police sketches seemed to exactly capture a suspect.

"So, my guess would be that Parfir has to destroy the Rifter." John skimmed the page, picking out words that he recognized and skipping those he didn't.

"Parfir can't destroy the Rifter. They're made of the same body, just as the living world is. They are all one divinity." Ravishan smiled. "That's why the Payshmura were created. One holy man found Parfir's single finger bone, and it guided him. He created a poison to calm the Rifter, and when she slept, he cut off her leg, then used her own hungry bone to bleed her until she couldn't fight."

Ravishan leaned close to John and ran his finger under a line of gold script. "From Parfir's single remaining finger bone, the first priest forged a golden key that could open the Rifter's death. And from the Rifter's own blood-soaked thigh bone, he carved the first yasi'halaun."

John studied the words, sounding them out under his breath as Ravishan read.

"The yasi'halaun?" John asked. "It looks like one of the knives I was offered at the test."

"Yes. All our curse blades are carved to resemble the yasi'halaun. But the divine blade must be carved by the Kahlil from one of the Rifter's bones. Right now, the Holy Kahlirash'im guard the sacred bone at their temple in Vundomu. When I become Kahlil, I will bring the bone back to Rathal'pesha." Ravishan flipped ahead in the book, then stopped on an ornately decorated illustration of two black knives and one long gray sword. Golden words were written in minuscule script around all three.

"This is just a curse blade." Ravishan tapped the first black knife in the picture. "They're made from bone like the yasi'halaun but just animal bones, so they aren't all that powerful. Really, any blade made from bone can be made into a curse blade. All the ushiri'im have them. Even you carry one, though yours doesn't carry a curse."

"The knife I chose in the test?" John asked and Ravishan nodded. John was glad that his knife wasn't cursed. It now hung in its sheath from his belt. He had grown accustomed to the way it swung against his thigh when he walked.

Ravishan briefly drew his own black blade from its sheath. "You can place any kind of curse on a blade. 'Burn the blood, silence the cries. Sear the flesh, blind the eyes.' Then when you use the blade on an enemy, the curse infests them."

"Infests them?" John asked.

"Well, it kills them." Ravishan shrugged. He slid his knife back into its sheath.

"You're sure the wound doesn't do that?" John asked.

"I'm sure it doesn't hurt. But the wound doesn't need to be fatal. If you can cast a curse, then all you need is to draw blood. Your enemy won't be able to escape it."

John didn't respond. He wasn't inclined to believe in curses, but he also wasn't inclined to believe in gateways to other worlds or men who traveled through the Gray Space. He'd been living around too many things that he wasn't inclined to believe in to feel completely secure in his skepticism.

"And this second black knife is the yasi'halaun?" John thought he now recognized the symbols that made up the name.

"Yes." Ravishan smiled at the drawing. "The Kahlil carries both a curse blade and the yasi'halaun."

John nodded. He remembered the knives that Kyle had carried. He glanced down at the drawing again. This time he studied the long gray sword. Kyle had carried one like it as well.

"Nayeshi'hala," John sounded the name out, recognizing the words as he heard them. The key to Nayeshi. John looked to Ravishan. "The key to my world?"

Ravishan nodded, as if this were common knowledge. And John guessed it was, here in the libraries of Rathal'pesha.

"When the yasi'halaun drinks the blood of the Rifter, it grows into the Nayeshi'hala. That, too, is carried by the Kahlil." Ravishan beamed at the picture.

"It drinks the Rifter's blood and is made from her bones?" John asked.

Ravishan nodded. "Exactly."

"And the Rifter is . . . who?"

Ravishan frowned at him as if the question didn't make sense. "The Rifter is the Rifter, the destroying aspect of the divine Parfir."

"But . . ." John tried to think of another way to get his answer. "How does the Rifter end up having her bones carved up and her blood drained?"

"First, the Rifter must be poisoned. Then the blood is fed to the yasi'halaun. Then the golden key opens the Rifter's death. Once the Rifter is dead, the bones are taken and another yasi'halaun is carved."

Ravishan's description sounded like some kind of terrible ritual sacrifice. And it still didn't tell him what he wanted to know.

"They don't just pick some woman to be the Rifter, do they?" John asked at last.

Again Ravishan paused a few moments, looking at him as if he had asked something completely bizarre, almost incomprehensible.

"No, the Rifter is Parfir's own flesh, not just someone who can be appointed. If the Payshmura could just choose a Rifter, then they would be rid of the Fai'daum already."

"Oh." John frowned. There was something he failed to understand about the Rifter, something that made his questions seem absurd to Ravishan. John flipped back to try and find his place in the book.

He turned page after page, scanning the black, brown, and gold illustrations for a familiar image. Absently, he wondered if numbering pages had just never occurred as an idea or if somehow the Payshmura had deemed it sinful. So far John hadn't encountered a single page number in any of the massive texts he'd thumbed through.

Ravishan too apparently had other things on his mind. He asked, "Is Hann'yu sending you down to Amura'taye for supplies?"

"Yes, I'm going down with the other ushvun'im tomorrow."

"Do you know where Candle Alley is?" Ravishan lowered his voice to a whisper. John stopped scanning the book.

"I could find it. Do you want me to bring something back for you?" John lowered his voice as well as a reflex.

"No, I want to meet you there tomorrow night."

"Why?" John asked.

"There are things we can't talk about here." Ravishan glanced over the two empty tables behind them and then studied the rows of shelved books. John followed his gaze. There didn't seem to be anyone else in the small room with them, but John couldn't know for sure. There was always the possibility of some ushiri watching from the Gray Space.

John wondered what it was that Ravishan needed to tell him in strict privacy. Was it about Nayeshi? Something Ravishan had overheard Dayyid mention? Or perhaps it had to do with the nun at Umbhra'ibaye who Ravishan secretly spoke to.

Ravishan whispered, "After seven bells. There's a stone wall at the end of the alley."

"I'll be there," John agreed.

Ravishan smiled.

"You won't get into trouble, will you?" John asked quietly.

"Not if I don't get caught," Ravishan replied easily.

John thought of cautioning Ravishan, but he heard the soft whisper of the door opening behind the two of them. Ravishan instantly spun around to see who had entered. John restrained himself. He kept his eyes glued to the book in front of him. Nothing seemed more conspiratorial than two people simultaneously looking up in sudden, startled silence.

"So, this is how Rathal'pesha is written?" John ran his finger over the sweeping script.

"Uh—" It took Ravishan a moment to refocus on the book. "Yes, that's it."

"The reading is going well, then?" Hann'yu asked from behind them.

John turned back, as if he had just realized that Hann'yu had entered the room. "Not as well as I would like, but I think I'm improving."

"Good." Hann'yu walked to their table. To Ravishan, he said, "Ushman Dayyid must be expecting you at practice, don't you think?"

"I just stopped in to have Ushvun Jahn look at my arm." Ravishan pulled himself off the stool. "It's been hurting lately."

"Yes, I've noticed you've had a sudden rash of injuries." Hann'yu nodded, barely concealing his amusement. "You've been in to see Ushvun Jahn almost every day for the last three weeks. I hope you aren't dying."

Ravishan flushed. "No, I just . . ."

"Yes, yes." Hann'yu waved aside anything else Ravishan might have said. "You really should get to practice."

"Of course." Ravishan bowed deeply to Hann'yu and gave John a slight nod. "Thank you for your time and skills." Then he quickly slipped out of the room.

Hann'yu watched him go and then addressed John.

"I hope you won't take this the wrong way, but he likes you quite a bit."

A wave of guilty dread rolled over John. He didn't want this to be the moment when Hann'yu warned him against getting too close, being too friendly. His skin suddenly felt slightly too hot and his palms went clammy. It was a guilty reaction, and he knew it. He said nothing and simply continued to gaze at Hann'yu as if the comment had been no more than a mention of the weather.

"It's good to see," Hann'yu continued. "I don't think he's ever made friends with any of the other ushiri'im. He's so much better at controlling the Gray Space than most of them and too proud of himself for any of them to like him."

"He's not a bad kid." John shrugged, hesitant to be drawn out any further.

"He's hardly a kid at all anymore," Hann'yu said. "When I was first sent here five years ago, he was scrawny, awkward, and so brittle. You wouldn't have recognized him. I used to worry that he'd just come apart one day."

"But he's gotten better?"

Hann'yu sighed. "I think having a friend has helped him greatly. It's brought a value to his life other than becoming Kahlil. I was worried for a while that if he failed it would kill him. When Fikiri came . . ." Hann'yu shook his head. "I suppose I'm just trying to thank you for befriending him. I hope it isn't too much of an annoyance to you."

"No, not at all." John knew it was as important to conceal his pleasure as it was to hide his earlier alarm. Yet he couldn't help but feel happy to know that he had bettered Ravishan's life. "It's nothing, really."

John flipped through the book and found that he was once again looking at the drawing of the first Rifter. Her wide eyes and tiny pinprick pupils stared out in an expression that struck John as more horrified than wrathful. She appeared to be shocked that the world was crumbling beneath her feet.

Hann'yu glanced to the book and rolled his eyes. "Dull, isn't it?"

"It's not too bad," John replied.

"There must be something better here." Hann'yu studied the spines of the books on each of the shelves. "If we were in Nurjima, we could just walk down the street to a bookshop. Have you ever been there?"

"No. I've heard about it."

"A den of sin and revolutionaries." Hann'yu smiled as he spoke. "It's a beautiful place."

"Sounds like you miss it."

"I do, but politics won't allow me back," Hann'yu answered.

"I see." John returned to the book. He sounded out the words under his breath, slowly piecing together sentences as if he were reassembling the splintered remains of an ancient fossil.

"Parfir is the water, the air, and the land," John mouthed to himself. "He smiles, and the rain is gentle, the sun shines, and the fields prosper. But his rage is the Rifter bringing floods, fires, and chasms."

"You don't ask many questions, do you?" Hann'yu asked.

"Pardon?" John glanced up in confusion, his thoughts still occupied by the Rifter.

"It's nothing," Hann'yu answered. "I am simply surprised that you didn't ask me more about it. I think every other priest in the entire monastery has pulled me aside at one point or another to ask why I was sent from the Black Tower. Most of them seem to think I'm reporting back to the Usho."

"I guess that might follow." John knew that the Usho was the highest-ranking ushman in the Payshmura church. Their Pope, he supposed. But that was about all John knew of the subject.

Hann'yu smiled. "You couldn't seem to care less."

"Should I care?"

"No," Hann'yu replied. "I'm just not accustomed to such honest indifference."

"Well," John offered, "you can tell me all about it if it would make you feel more comfortable."

Hann'yu chuckled. "You're too amusing of a man to have to read that tired old rag. Let me see if I can't find something more diverting."

Hann'yu wandered back between two rows of towering shelves. John heard him climbing the rolling ladder that offered access to those books shelved up against the ceiling.

"You know," Hann'yu called back to him, "looking at the books here, you'd think that there was no such thing as literature at all. Holy text, holy text, appendix to a holy text. And . . . oh. Well, this isn't too bad. *A History of the Practitioners of the Forbidden.* Ah, and this as well. Not as bad as I thought. Oh, this doesn't belong here at all!"

John heard Hann'yu rustling through the books.

"Jahn," Hann'yu called him, "come here and take these. I can't carry them and get down the ladder at the same time."

John put his own book aside and took the small stack of books that Hann'yu handed down. Two were the heavy leather-bound volumes that John had expected. Brass clasps held them shut, and silverwork had been inlaid across their covers and spines. The third volume was startlingly different.

John stared at it in disbelief. The cover was glossy, the binding supple and cheap. The title, *Dan the Milkman,* was written in the cheery typestyle of so many American children's books. There were deep gouges in the cover, and as John opened it, he could see that the pages had faded badly. He could hardly read the name printed on the flap. John squinted at the awkward pencil marks.

This book belongs to Kyle Harris. Please return if lost.

Kyle's book was beyond lost, John thought.

"Strange, isn't it?" Hann'yu asked. John almost jumped at the sudden intrusion into his fascination.

"Yes," John answered. "What is it?"

"A thing most rare." Hann'yu smiled. "It's a text from the world of Nayeshi."

John didn't know how to react. It was a children's storybook, probably printed sometime around World War II, judging from the look of the illustrations.

"I've seen copies of it," Hann'yu said. "But I never imagined that the original would just be filed with the rest of the books here." Hann'yu gazed down at the book with a warm, nostalgic expression. "I learned my first holy words from this book."

Carefully, almost tenderly, Hann'yu turned the pages of the book.

"His name is Dan." Hann'yu said the English name with a mechanical exactness. Then he smiled at John. "The book tells the story of how every morning, before anyone else rises, Dan visits the houses of good children, leaving gifts of sweet milk and cream."

It was an entirely different impression of a milkman than John had ever had. He sounded more like a kind of Santa Claus than a distributor of dairy products. But it did offer him a hint as to why all the ushiri'im were taught to claim they were milkmen. And also why Kyle had claimed his name was Kyle. For a brief moment, John wondered what would have happened if the book had been something like *Don't Let the Pigeon Drive the Bus* or *Heather Has Two Mommies.*

Hann'yu closed the book gently. "I'm sure it was put here by mistake. It should be up in the holy cases." He gazed at the beaten cover a moment longer and then glanced up at John. "It looks like nothing but scribbles to you, doesn't it?"

"Pretty much," John replied.

"Maybe someday you'll learn to read it. For now, let's stick to simpler things." Hann'yu picked up one of the leather-bound Basawar volumes and handed it to John. "*Practitioners of the Forbidden.* Don't let Dayyid catch you reading it."

"I won't." John took the book with a feeling of slight dubiousness as to its contents. He didn't imagine that any of the "practitioners of the forbidden" managed to live happily ever after.

"And speaking of reading." Hann'yu reached into the folds of his robe and produced a scrap of paper. "These are the herbs that I'll need you buy when you go down to Amura'taye. Can you read all this?"

John slowly sounded out the names of the plants.

"Good." Hann'yu handed him the list. "Then I'll leave you to it."

Hann'yu picked up the other two books. John thought he glimpsed the words "Tales of Tempting Women." Hann'yu grinned at him and said, "I may have to watch out for Dayyid myself."

After Hann'yu had gone, John pushed *Practitioners of the Forbidden* aside and returned to his original study. He flipped through the heavy pages, catching whiffs of incense, until an illustration caught his attention.

John knew it had to be the Kahlil. The dark-haired man glared out from the page with a ferocious intensity. The black tattoos above his eyes seemed to glare as well. He held a short black knife in one hand and the hilt of a gray sword could be seen rising from over his left shoulder. Ragged white bandages waved from his right arm like banners.

John leaned closer to read the minuscule gold letters that surrounded the figure.

Kahlil. He who crosses the worlds. He who hunts the Rifter. He who receives the golden key. He who unleashes the Rifter. He who spills the sacred blood. He who slays the Rifter. Blessed three times. Flesh, blood, and bones.

John read the words two more times, slowly absorbing them. Everything he had been reading, the conversations he had overheard, the images he had seen, they all clicked into place.

His roommate Kyle had been the last Kahlil, and he had been on Nayeshi hunting for a Rifter. The memory of how intensely Kyle had stared at Laurie washed over John. Kyle had asked her if she was a witch. He had felt that she had power, real power, while John had just thought her deluded.

Anxious tension gnawed through John's muscles.

Kyle had to have recognized Laurie as a Rifter that first morning when they'd met. He had even managed to send her back to Basawar. But something had gone wrong. John guessed it had to do with the key he had taken from Kyle. Guilt still nagged at John for the theft. Now, it seemed a far worse transgression. Kyle, the last Kahlil, had ended up torn to pieces in the space between worlds—the White Space.

Now, the priests at Rathal'pesha were desperately attempting to train another Kahlil to find a Rifter to destroy the Fai'daum. And completely unbeknownst to them, their Rifter was already here, living at the very foot of their monastery.

John didn't want to think about what the Payshmura would do if they found her. But he had read the words. He had seen the images. They would use her to destroy their enemies and then they would poison her, bleed her, and murder her. Then they would retrieve her bones to carve another yasi'halaun, find another woman, and do the whole thing again.

John laid his head down against the cool surface of the table. He wanted to be wrong. But it all made too much sense. He would have to tell Bill and Laurie as soon as he got to Amura'taye. They needed to be warned.

Ironically, he remembered arguing with Laurie about the reason for the three of them being transported to Basawar. He had said that it was a mistake. She had insisted that there was a purpose behind it. Now, John knew that Laurie had been right. And as much as she liked being right, John doubted that she would take much consolation in this particular victory.

What an awful thing to have to tell someone: you're the Rifter, the living incarnation of destruction, desolation, and death. He couldn't even imagine how much worse it would be to be told such a thing.

Chapter Thirty

Laurie leaned onto her elbows, resting her chin on her cupped hands. The bands of silver rings and fine chains that linked her fingers gleamed in the afternoon light. Her long, pale hair had been drawn up from her face in twisting braids. Silver beads, like those Lady Bousim and her maids wore, decorated her hair.

"The Rifter," Laurie whispered. She laid her hand on Bill's arm.

Bill's black hair shot out around his face like an ink spill. His skin was the color of wax. He said nothing, just frowned, and took a deep drink of his tea. The last two years had altered Bill deeply. He had recovered some of his strength and could move without struggling for breath, but he was still weak. John rarely saw him laugh or joke in public. He was only slowly drawn out by these quiet, private conversations.

"That sucks," Bill said at last.

John nodded.

Outside, he could hear a kitchen woman shouting at a Bousim rashan for stealing a taste of the evening meal before it was finished. He picked out the sound of children's voices as well, loud and high-pitched but farther away. These were sounds that John never heard in Rathal'pesha. Even the season seemed different here. Protected from the harshest winds by the mountain, a gentle warmth hung over Amura'taye. The scents of blossoms filled the air, while up in Rathal'pesha frost still came at night and the wind remained frigid.

A breeze curled through the open window, brushing aside the thin green curtains. Two stories below, red and yellow spring blossoms colored the garden. Bright green ivy wound up the wall enclosing the Bousim house and grounds.

Most of the buildings of Amura'taye were yard-less stone structures, hunched close together along narrow lanes and alleys that wound crookedly through town. John watched as a herd of tiny black goats hurried up the muddy street outside the Bousim compound, darting between wagons and among the bicyclists who pedaled along the rutted streets.

"Are you sure?" Laurie still hadn't lifted her hands away from her small mouth.

"I don't know, but it seems very likely." John absently swirled his tea, feeling the liquid within the cup curl into a tiny vortex.

"Destroyer of worlds?" Laurie's eyes widened. "Does that sound at all like me?"

John sighed. He wished someone else could be telling her this. He was already tired from the early morning trek down from Rathal'pesha. He didn't know if he had the strength to argue.

"I thought it was a myth, like some kind of personification of an earthquake or something," Bill said.

"I thought the same thing at first, but training with the ushiri'im convinced me otherwise. These men aren't crossing through Gray Space and tearing themselves apart in pursuit of some philosophical concept. They are hunting a living person. The Rifter is real."

"And a guy," Laurie suddenly broke in. "The Rifter is supposed to be a man, right? Lady Bousim said as much."

"The one who destroyed the Kingdom of the East was a man, but there isn't just one Rifter," John replied. "As far as I've read, there have been five Rifters, two men and three women. Each of them were brought from Nayeshi by a Kahlil."

"But then it could be any one of the three of us, couldn't it?" Laurie glanced to Bill, again plainly seeking his arbitration, as she often did.

"Maybe, but if it was John, then why wouldn't Kyle have brought him back right away? He wouldn't have shacked up with his destroyer-god for months just to hang out with him, would he? And as for me, behold my awesome might." He gave a brief, dry cough. "I'm not shattering this world anytime soon."

"You're the one who has power here, Laurie," John said.

"But I'm not evil." Laurie glared at her clay cup. A wisp of steam rose off it and John wondered whether the intensity of her emotion had caused it.

"I don't think any of the Rifters were," John replied soothingly.

Laurie turned her glare on him. "They tore apart whole kingdoms!"

"But I don't think they did it on purpose. The Payshmura used them. They set them off somehow."

"Like bombs?" Bill asked.

"Not literally. They didn't explode," John replied. "But two of the pictures I found showed the Rifters wounded, and all of them looked scared." John shook his head. "I don't know. I'm piecing all this together from what I can read and some drawings. I could be completely wrong. But I thought you should know. You should be careful and not light any more fires or do anything else like that."

Laurie and Bill shared a cagey glance that sent a thrill of alarm through John.

He said, "You haven't been doing anything, have you?"

"No," Laurie said quickly.

"Yes," Bill admitted.

Laurie shot him a reproachful look, and Bill shrugged.

"They've been practicing witchcraft," Bill whispered, leaning in close. "Laurie, Lady Bousim, and Ohbi."

"But nothing that would blow up the world," Laurie insisted. "Just healing spells for Bill and small things like that."

"At the foot of Rathal'pesha, you're practicing witchcraft?" John shook his head in astonishment at their recklessness.

"We're careful," Laurie assured him.

"You'd better be. You know what they do to witches here?"

Laurie leaned back and crossed her arms over her chest. "It's not as though Bill and I have been drifting along in dreamland while you've been figuring everything out. There's a chance that I could find a way home for us through my spells. Have you thought of that?"

"If you did, it would be great." John wasn't about to be drawn into an argument over what Laurie was or was not allowed to do. "Just don't get yourself killed trying."

"I won't," Laurie said flatly.

John nodded. He'd told her what she needed to know. He wasn't going to get any further when it came to warning Laurie. She'd just think he was being highhanded and resist his advice. He knew her well enough to recognize that set expression she wore.

Living in Basawar had only made her resent being told what to do even more than she normally had. John couldn't blame her. As a woman, the culture didn't afford her much respect. Even with her relatively elevated status as Lady Bousim's attendant, Laurie didn't have the right to venture outside the Bousim grounds without a male escort. She couldn't carry her own money and she couldn't be out past six bells when the sun began to set.

John sipped his tea. It was a refined drink, like the best served in Rathal'pesha, and so didn't have much taste at all. The same held true for most elite foods. He could hardly taste them. Rough taye and the game meats, considered the coarsest peasant fare, were the foods he liked best. They had the strongest flavors.

He drank a little more tea anyway, just to fill the time and allow Laurie to relax.

"How have things been with Rasho Tashtu?" John asked finally. The last time he'd spoken with Laurie and Bill, they had been having problems with the commander of the rashan'im.

John only vaguely remembered Tashtu. His broken nose and black beard had dominated his face. His body had seemed heavy with both hard muscle and fat. Apparently, he had taken offense to the fact that Laurie had chosen to marry Bill, whom Tashtu deemed a sickly weakling, and decided that a course of harassment would convince her to take up with him instead.

John had spoken to Pivan about it, but there wasn't much Pivan could do to curb the commander's comments or leers. Though Pivan had assured John that he would never allow Tashtu to act on either.

"He's been better lately," Bill answered. "He's still a huge asshole. But now that I can walk, he's had to really cut back on calling me a worthless cripple."

"I wanted to curse him, but Lady Bousim thought it would be too obvious." Laurie sighed. "I still think most of the women in this town would be relieved if the man fell off a cliff."

"Most of the world would be relieved, but it's not something you should get involved in," Bill said. "Dropping the bastard off a cliff is a just something we have to hope the drunk fuck will do to himself. Maybe we could shove him a little, but no more than that. One little shove . . . maybe throw a rock down after him . . . but that is absolutely all."

Laurie caught Bill's hand and gently squeezed it. "You say the nicest things."

"I just want to share your beautiful dream."

John looked past them out the window as they kissed. He was glad that they had each other. It seemed to keep them both safe and sane, but moments like this brought his own solitude to the fore. It had been two years . . . no, even longer. Nearly three years since he'd been with anyone.

The little black goats were back, scampering across the busy street. John wondered if anyone owned them. Were they just feral things, like alley cats, being adopted or abandoned according to the whims of children and lonely old women?

Bill said, "Forget Tashtu. It's that sweet talker, Fikiri, who I'm more worried about."

Laurie laughed in that odd, silent way that Lady Bousim and her maids laughed. It was like seeing the image of pleasure without the sound.

John had only been half-listening, not quite sure if the words were meant for him or Laurie alone. But that name caught his attention.

"Fikiri?" John asked.

"Lady Bousim's son," Bill said, as if he would need to explain that to John.

"He has a little crush on me." Laurie smiled. "It's pretty harmless. He sneaks down from time to time to visit his mother. He always brings me a cookie or something."

"Last time, I taught him a couple dirty jokes to ease those lonely nights up on the mountain," Bill added.

"How does that exactly help?" Laurie asked.

Bill shrugged.

There was no way Fikiri could just walk down from Rathal'pesha without being missed. The trip down lasted hours, and getting back up took nearly a full day. He had to be moving through Gray Space, which meant he had been hiding that ability from Dayyid.

"He's a nice kid," Laurie went on. "He's got a lot of potential."

John just nodded. He saw nothing wrong with what Fikiri was doing. But if Dayyid discovered it, John imagined, he'd be furious.

"He can do incredible spells with water." Laurie poured more tea for Bill and glanced to John's cup.

"He's practicing witchcraft with you?" John felt a rush of horror at the thought. He could see Fikiri creating a direct route for Dayyid to discover all of Laurie's transgressions against Basawar law.

Laurie frowned at him. "Is there something wrong with that?"

"He's a teenage boy—" John began.

"It's not like we're corrupting him," Laurie snapped. "What do you think we do, dance naked and hold orgies?"

"I'm not accusing you of anything like that," John replied. "I was going to say that Fikiri might not be the most reliable confidant, if you want to keep all this secret. Boys like to brag, and they make mistakes. If he gets found out, then all of you could be discovered."

"It was only once." Laurie glared at him, as if expecting him to challenge her. Bill just shook his head weakly.

John's cup was nearly empty. He drained the last of it and then shook his head. "I'm not saying anything right today. I just want you both to be safe."

A week ago, he had been looking forward to seeing his friends. He'd thought of all the things they could talk about that none of them could mention to anyone else: washing machines, television shows, Band-Aids, popcorn. He'd remembered earlier times, when they would all three laugh and joke together. They had been relaxed in each other's company.

But that had been an entirely different world, and it had been years ago. Basawar had changed all three of them. With everything she was and everything she did being wrong here, Laurie had grown to expect condemnation and offhanded dismissal. She had become angrier than she ever would have been and more defensive.

Weakness and illness had drained Bill to a mere impression of the brash man he had once been.

It was harder for John to recognize the changes in himself, but he knew they were there—signified, or maybe even caused, by the nightmares that haunted him. He dreamed of the dark chambers high in the monastery, where doorways led nowhere. He saw a room full of mutilated bodies, skinned, but still struggling. Their slick bones writhed against bindings of red wire while they whispered threats into his sleep.

These certainly weren't dreams he'd had before this.

Outside, the town bells rang out low and loud. Five bells. It would be getting dark soon.

"I should get going soon," John said at last. "I have an entire list of medicinal herbs to purchase for Hann'yu."

"You just got here," Bill said.

"I'm sorry, but—"

"Did he tell you where to buy the herbs?" Laurie asked.

"No," John replied. He couldn't imagine why it would matter.

"Dahl'ami sells the best herbs." Laurie leaned forward slightly "She and her husband live close by. You could stay a little longer . . . "

"I would, but I have to find a place called Candle Alley as well. It might take me a while."

"Bati'kohl knows the entire city. He could take you there." Laurie refilled his cup.

"Candle Alley?" Bill raised an eyebrow. "Why?"

John didn't know why, but he hesitated in answering the question. It wasn't as if Bill or Laurie were going to inform Dayyid. "I promised Ravishan that I'd meet him there."

"Now who's taking chances?" Laurie asked.

John scowled at her. "It's nothing like that. He has something he needs to tell me privately."

"What do you think that's going to be?" Laurie asked. Bill let out a weak snicker.

John said, "If I knew, I wouldn't need to be meeting with him to find out, would I?"

"It's going to be David Lewis all over again," Laurie pronounced.

For several moments, John had no memory of anyone named David Lewis. Then, with sinking dread, he remembered. It amazed him that Laurie could so quickly recall an incident that had taken place in the third grade. He didn't think that he would have remembered David Lewis without her prompting, and he'd been the one who had been caught kissing the boy.

"I'm serious," Laurie went on. "Ravishan likes you way too much."

"He's just lonely," John assured her.

"Lonely, handsome, and completely infatuated with you," Laurie replied. "You're a total sucker for that kind of thing."

"I am not." John felt his face flushing.

"You are," Bill concurred.

Laurie pressed on. "What about that other guy . . . Anthony Salazar. That was the same thing."

"Anthony Salazar?" John didn't have to dredge the archives for that name. He had broken two bones in his right hand by punching Anthony Salazar in the mouth. Anthony had lost a tooth and sported a lip the color of an eggplant for a month.

"The one who got expelled for trying to burn down the school," Laurie prompted.

"Hey, I remember him." Bill narrowed his eyes at John. "You and him?"

"Are you kidding? No," John said firmly. "He was getting girls pregnant in the fifth grade."

"Maybe I've got the name wrong." Laurie frowned. "But there was some kid that almost got you thrown out of school . . . "

"That was Anthony Salazar," John said. "We were both suspended for fighting. We weren't boyfriends."

Laurie studied him intently over the edge of her cup. "Are you sure?"

"Positive."

"I don't know if I believe you. There was always this weird tension between the two of you," Laurie said.

"That was seething hatred, utterly free of homoerotic underpinnings."

Laurie scowled, though not with any real anger. John could see that she was enjoying needling him. "Yeah, but what about David Lewis?"

"What about him?" John said.

"You totally got caught." Laurie jabbed a delicate finger at him. The silver chains on her rings tinkled against each other. "Full on, sucking face with David Lewis in the tunnel slide."

"Yes. All right, I admit that I got caught with David Lewis." How could this incident still embarrass him almost two decades later?

Laurie grinned.

"Wait." Bill suddenly straightened up. "That wasn't the same David Lewis from high school, was it? The guy who stuffed me in my locker?"

"Yeah, that was him."

"Talk about overcompensating," Bill said. "He didn't even have a neck. Tell me he had a neck when you kissed him."

John laughed. "In third grade, he had a neck."

"Good. I mean, it's none of my business, but I'd hate to think of anyone I knew dating no-necks."

"Have no fear," John assured him. "I have no intentions of dating the neckless."

"No, you're going to end up dating teen-priest." Laurie smiled and threw back her tea like it was a shot of whiskey. John imagined that she rarely had an occasion to tease anyone anymore.

"So, how old is Ravishan now?" Laurie asked. "Sixteen, seventeen?"

"Nineteen," John supplied flatly.

"Nineteen," Laurie repeated. She looked meaningfully at Bill. Lewd jokes were normally his specialty, but this time he passed.

Bill said, "I know this is off topic, but when we get back home, what are we going to tell everyone? I mean, we've been gone two years now."

"I don't know." John hadn't dared to think that far ahead.

"Alien abduction," Laurie whispered. "We could make millions on talk shows."

Bill smiled. "Hey, yeah, we could sell the rights to HBO or some place and have one of those cheesy docudramas made about us. I'm kinda seeing myself played by a buff male model, running in slow motion. Then a silver-suited ninja-alien leaps out. We fight. More ninja-aliens materialize all around me. I go into this super-powered spinning kick and knock off all of their heads. As their decapitated bodies slump to the ground, I growl, 'Probe my ass, will ya?!'"

John just stared at Bill for a few, stunned seconds. Then he said, "You really have a rich fantasy life, don't you?"

"You have no idea."

"Do you think a Black actress would play me?" Laurie asked.

It was the kind of question he would have expected from the Laurie he had known two years ago: simple and at the same time completely out of the blue.

"Color-blind casting is cool," Laurie explained. "It could bring more depth to our characters and dialogue."

"You mean dialogue like, 'Probe my ass, will ya?'" John asked, deadpan.

"Hey, that line has plenty of depth," Bill objected.

"It would definitely get you a date with David Lewis," John replied.

"Laugh all you want," Bill continued. "Just wait until it's splashed all over McDonald's collectible toys and cups. Children, women, and men all around the world will be asking for the 'Probe My Ass, Will Ya' special."

"I can just see the relish with which employees will ask, 'Can I supersize that for you?'" John replied.

Laurie laughed out loud and then clapped her hands over her mouth. John smiled. It was good to hear her really laugh, even for a few seconds.

Bill went on, building larger and more absurd fantasies on the theme of their disappearance and return home. None of the stories touched on the ugliness of their real lives. Laurie's repression, Bill's illness, and John's isolation were all outside the realm of their new fantastic adventures.

Instead, they were played by beautiful movie stars, made millions, and received Nobel Peace Prizes. They took over several tropical islands, were inducted into a secret ninja clan, learned to fly and to communicate with dolphins. Laurie became a goddess with millions of followers. Bill usurped leadership of the ninja clan, and John had a brief but beautiful relationship with a brave super-intelligent dolphin.

When six bells rang out across the city, it all came to an end. Reality washed back in over them. The sky was going dark, and John couldn't stay any longer. He drank the last of his tea, glad he hadn't left earlier and disappointed that he had to leave now.

When he stood, Laurie hugged him fiercely.

"Be careful," Bill said quickly.

John nodded. "You too. Take care of each other."

He hated saying goodbye, and he hated leaving. It always felt like it could be forever.

Chapter Thirty-One

Rough stone walls pressed close and rose up over John's head. He could only see a thin strip of night sky directly above him. Everything else was compressed into a jumble of dark shadows that briefly burned away before John's lamp, then closed in behind him.

Within the tight confines of the winding alley, his senses narrowed to the feel of old thatching beneath his feet and the smells of urine and soured human sweat that emanated from the humid alcoves. When his lamp revealed the half-naked forms of couples, John averted his gaze and hurried past.

Bati'kohl had given him directions to Candle Alley but refused to go there himself. It wasn't the kind of place a young boy from a good house went.

A lone girl looked up at him as his lamplight fell across her. Her black hair hung in strings over her emaciated arms and small, bare breasts. With a listless wave, she beckoned him to enter the dank alcove where she lay. John could see dark stains on the blanket beneath her. The girl's head dropped back to the ground. She seemed hardly awake as she mumbled, "Come on in."

She spread her legs.

John walked on quickly.

Other men wandered through the narrow lane. Some carried lamps. Most had only cheap tallow candles. There seemed to be an unspoken order to their pacing. None of them walked close enough that the lights they carried illuminated another man's features. When they passed going opposite directions, each averted his eyes and said nothing.

Only once, as John passed by, did another man reach out and brush his hand across John's hip in clear invitation. John offered no response, and an instant later, the other man was swallowed by the darkness as he disappeared into one of the alcoves.

John didn't like to think of Ravishan even being in a place like this, let alone cruising here. He thought that it might even come as a relief to discover that he'd gone to the wrong location entirely.

He reached the wall that sealed the narrow lane off. No one waited for him. John lifted his lamp to scan the partially collapsed wall. Stones had fallen, or been pulled from their mortar, creating a gap that a slim man could squeeze through. John stepped closer to the crumbling space.

"Up here." Ravishan's voice sounded in the darkness. "You should put out the lamp."

John blew out the flame and waited for his sight to adjust.

It was always remarkable to him how much he could see in the dark here. With the lamp lit, his eyes never adjusted and so the shadows remained impenetrable. But as his pupils widened, he realized that he could make out the wall quite well.

Higher up, the wall was thick and wide, and the broken spaces where the stones had fallen away formed rough steps leading to the very top. Spindly saplings had taken root on several of the steps, and they created even darker shadows than the night offered. Small pale flowers drooped from several branches.

Ravishan lounged against the slender trunk of one of the saplings near the top. His dark hair looked wet, and John guessed that he had just washed it.

John started climbing. The air was cooler beneath the young trees. The flowers gave off a faint honey-like scent. It almost masked the dank, humid odors that emanated from the alley below.

"I thought you might not come," Ravishan said.

"I told you I would."

"I know." Ravishan smiled briefly at John, then glanced anxiously away. John wondered what was making him so nervous. Obviously not something that was easy to talk about, otherwise he would have come out with it already.

John frowned as Ravishan pulled several weeds out from between the stones of the wall.

"Their roots break the mortar apart." Ravishan gazed intently at the small plant in his hand. Then he threw it aside. "I suppose the trees do worse."

John could have told him that it was the smaller plants that made the first inroads through which the trees' roots would spread, but he knew it wasn't important. They weren't here to talk about mortar erosion.

"There was something you wanted to tell me," John said.

"There was." Ravishan leaned back, letting the young tree take his full weight. He stared upward. John followed his line of sight up between the spindly branches of the tree to the dim stars.

"But now that you're here . . ." Ravishan shook his head just a little. "I'm not sure."

John frowned but didn't say anything. He wondered if Ravishan was trying to tell him goodbye. The awkwardness of the exchange reminded him of the uneasy farewell he'd exchanged with his brother when he'd come to visit John against their father's wishes. It had been the last time they'd ever spoken to each other.

Had Ravishan finally decided to escape from Rathal'pesha? John dropped his gaze down to his hands. He didn't want Ravishan to leave.

"When you think of someone in your mind," Ravishan said softly, "they are exactly as you think they are. You think they're kind, and in your mind, they are kind. But then you encounter them in the flesh, and you realize that perhaps they could be different." Ravishan looked at John for a quiet moment before going on. "Right now, you and I exist in each other's minds. Perhaps you have an idea of me, and I have an idea of you, but we haven't tested those ideas. Do you know what I mean?"

"I think so." John nodded. He just wasn't sure where Ravishan was going with the conversation. He wondered if Ravishan was simply trying to avoid saying anything.

"Right now, I think you like me." Ravishan quickly looked back up at the stars. "And I don't want you to change your mind. So I don't want to tell you something that will make you think I'm not the person you like."

"So, you've changed your mind and you don't want to tell me?" John asked.

"No." Ravishan sighed. "I want to tell you. And at the same time, I don't want you to know."

"Well, that's a quandary," John said. "It's going to have to be one or the other."

"I know," Ravishan said.

"I suppose it all depends on how much you trust me," John said.

Ravishan gazed up at him from beneath heavy lashes. "I trust you."

"Then you should tell me."

Ravishan straightened. John could see the pulse hammering along the curve of Ravishan's throat. His hands shook and his dark eyes went wide. Suddenly, he looked away from John down to his feet.

"I can't say it when you're watching me." Ravishan flushed. John could clearly see the dark color spreading across his cheeks.

John realized that Laurie had been right and he was a complete idiot. And if this truly was David Lewis all over again, John knew exactly what would happen next. Ravishan would ask him to close his eyes and then kiss him.

"Ravishan." John's voice felt suddenly rough in his throat. His skin felt hot. "You know that this isn't safe for either of us."

"I know," Ravishan whispered.

John could smell faint hints of sweat and incense on Ravishan's skin. A deep, primal part of him longed to draw in more of Ravishan's scent, to taste him.

"Close your eyes," John told him.

Ravishan hesitated for a moment, then obeyed, his head tilted back just slightly, his lips barely parted.

As he leaned close, John whispered, "Just this once." He felt the heat of Ravishan's breath. Then, very gently, John kissed him.

Ravishan's lips parted beneath his and John automatically deepened the kiss. Ravishan's mouth tasted sweet and felt burning hot. Hungry desire throbbed through John's body. He hadn't expected Ravishan to give himself so well.

John's hands instinctively slid down the curve of Ravishan's back and around the stiff leather edge of his belt until his fingers touched the cool metal of Ravishan's belt buckle.

Ravishan trembled against him and arched into John's hands, his skin radiating heat even through his heavy clothes. The scent of him, the taste of him, the feel of his strong body—it was everything John had been deprived of for years. The intensity of his own arousal alarmed him.

They were courting death doing this.

John pulled away. If he didn't stop now, he wouldn't stop at all. He knew that much about himself.

Ravishan started after him, but John placed a restraining hand against his chest.

"We can't." John's voice sounded hoarse even to himself.

"But you said this once." Ravishan's hands slid along John's arm, stroking the tender skin of his wrist and elbow. Shivers of pleasure whispered through the muscles of his arm and spread through his chest.

"I meant just one kiss." John could hardly catch his breath. His entire body burned and he ached to pull Ravishan against him again.

"Couldn't we be . . . together just once—"

"It's never just once." John knew better than to hear out any argument, since he already wanted to give in. He stepped out of Ravishan's reach. "Neither of us can afford to start this. Not here. Not now."

"But you liked it." Ravishan pursued him, pressing close enough for John to feel his breath tickle his ear.

"Of course I liked it. That's the problem." John dropped his voice to a soft whisper. "I like it. I like you. If we got started, I wouldn't want to stop. And that could get us both killed."

"I would be willing to die, if I could be with you," Ravishan whispered.

John knew the words were meant to be arousing, to show John how deeply Ravishan longed to be with him, but they only revealed the innocent arrogance of his youth. He wasn't considering actual death.

Ravishan plainly envisioned himself as a character in some ancient, tragic love poem. But John could too easily imagine a real execution, so

Ravishan's words sent a spike of cold dread down his spine. The thought of Ravishan bound and burning on the Holy Road destroyed John's desire in a moment.

"I will not put you in that kind of danger," John said flatly.

"I don't care," Ravishan insisted.

"I do!" The words came out harsh and angry. John didn't mean them to, but he needed Ravishan to stop tempting him. "You don't endanger the life of a man you care about just so you can get laid. How selfish can you be?"

Ravishan recoiled as if he had been physically struck. The color drained from his cheeks and mouth. His hands dropped to his sides.

"I'm sorry," John said. "I shouldn't have ever kissed you."

"I wanted you to." Ravishan hung his head.

John wanted to comfort him, but he couldn't afford to do that right now. He said, "I'll see you tomorrow at Rathal'pesha."

Ravishan only nodded.

John turned and climbed down the broken wall. He wanted to look back to see if Ravishan still stood there watching or if he had already gone, but he didn't. He kept his eyes on the muddy, torn ground ahead of him, steadily retracing his path back out of Candle Alley as if by finding his exact footsteps he could take the entire night back.

CHAPTER THIRTY-TWO

Bright beams of morning light streamed through the windows and warmed the infirmary as if spring had at last reached the mountains. But outside, snow still lay across the monastery grounds and deep drifts blanketed the surrounding peaks.

In the midst of so much snow and ice, the pungent scents of fresh herbs seemed strange, out of place, and too much of a reminder of things John did not want to think about.

He glowered at the bright emerald herbs filling his mortar and then pounded the pestle into them with unnecessary force. Thick stems and glossy leaves rapidly dissolved into a frothy green pulp under his ministrations. He took what satisfaction he could in that.

"Good spirit, Jahn, but I think you may have gone past paste to liquid." Hann'yu offered the criticism without much concern as he leaned across the long wooden table and peered into the mortar. He appeared somewhat amused by John's overly enthusiastic preparation of the herbs. "Something isn't bothering you, is it?"

"No," John replied, though he couldn't bring himself to meet Hann'yu's speculative gaze. Despite his unconcerned manner, Hann'yu could be a very insightful man.

In truth, John had spent most of last night attempting to purge his mind of the memory of Ravishan's warm body pressed against him—the taste of his mouth and the longing in his handsome smile. John had tried to concentrate on anything else, and yet the tempting sensations of Ravishan's bare skin, his willing lips, and his strong hands had suffused John's dreams with both desire and terrifying visions of persecution. He'd woken sweating, frustrated, and lonely for Ravishan's company.

But the monastery of Rathal'pesha was the last place to indulge himself. Or Ravishan, for that matter. So John had chosen instead to put his energy to use in the infirmary.

"I suppose I'm just a little nervous about preparing all these medicines correctly," John told Hann'yu.

John looked meaningfully at the heaps of fresh and dried herbs that engulfed most of the table and lay bundled in parchment on the windowsill. He'd bought them in Amura'taye less than an hour before he'd met with Ravishan in Candle Alley. Yellow pollen from several of the blossoms still clung to his gray cassock. He wondered how much of it had brushed onto Ravishan's black coat during their one brief kiss.

"You'll do fine." Hann'yu offered him a charming smile; the expression betrayed more of his cosmopolitan, southern background than did his dark skin and delicate features. "Just go a little more gently with the fresh herbs. Treat them more like you would ladies."

John glanced between the phallic-looking pestle in his hand and Hann'yu's lascivious grin.

"You mean pounding them?" John lowered his voice, despite the fact that all of the infirmary beds were currently empty. Someone might be listening from the common sickroom on the floor below them.

Hann'yu simply laughed at John's expression. Then he schooled his features into something close to contrition.

"I'm sorry, Jahn," Hann'yu said. "I shouldn't tease you."

"You shouldn't," John agreed, though he suspected that wouldn't stop Hann'yu.

And despite Hann'yu's occasional lewd joke, John found the work and conversation relaxing. He passed most of the morning grinding, pounding, and mixing the plants into various pungent concoctions, while Hann'yu observed from across the wooden table.

The sunlight grew stronger and the infirmary warmed. Now and then, Hann'yu offered John instructions or made a face at the smell of a particularly rank herb. After hours of work, the entire infirmary smelled of strange medicines. The sharp, astringent scent of the herbs clung to John's hands and only one last bundle remained on Hann'yu's table.

It was nearly noon, and he still hadn't seen Ravishan. After weeks of regular visits, John found himself routinely glancing up, expecting to see him at the door or standing silently among the rows of beds. The long hall of the infirmary seemed oddly abandoned without him.

John unwound the kidskin vellum that held the last bundle. The tannic scent of leather evaporated as he spread the vellum and exposed the dark knots of dried gray leaves and thick roots. An earthy, almost living aroma rose from the clumps of gnarled root, reminding John of both the musky weasel nests and the acrid tang of sweat.

"Don't touch that one with your hands." Hann'yu nudged a black-glazed clay jar toward him. "Use the vellum to funnel it into this."

"What is it?" John carefully slid the leaves and roots into the jar. A fine dust wafted up and John held his breath until it settled.

"Not much in itself. Eastern physicians used to call it goatweed. Eat some, and it will be right back up with you in a few minutes. If you get some of the sap into your blood, though . . . " Hann'yu shook his head. "It could well be the end of you."

"It's poison?"

Hann'yu nodded. "You should close the lid and wash your hands well."

John frowned. The tips of his fingers where he had touched the vellum felt hot and tender. There was quite a bit of fine residue left on his skin.

Then Hann'yu burst into laughter. "You'll be fine. It has to be specially prepared to be deadly. Whole and dried it won't affect anyone but a witch."

The definite tingling in John's fingertips and knuckles continued. He suppressed the guilty urge to hide his reddening hands behind his back.

Hann'yu went on, "You should wash up before you touch any of the ushiri'im, though. They're sensitive to it as well."

"Witches and ushiri'im?" John went immediately to the washbasin. He poured water from the pitcher and then soaped up his hands and rinsed them. The water felt bitingly cold, yet soothing. He emptied the basin out the window, poured more water and plunged his hands into it.

"Witches and ushiri'im." Hann'yu gazed at him evenly. "Odd, isn't it?"

"Is it?" John eyed Hann'yu back, wondering if Hann'yu was making an oblique reference to something he should have known about or if this was more of the intellectual sedition that had gotten Hann'yu exiled to Rathal'pesha in the first place. From Hann'yu's expression, John guessed it was the latter.

"A man who didn't know better might make some connection between the two that could get him exiled or worse." Hann'yu drifted to John's side, in the way that he always did when he seemed to feel the subversive urge to educate John.

"But you wouldn't be that man?"

"Oh, no." Hann'yu lowered his voice. "That man was a colleague of mine who now has a price on his head. He joined the Fai'daum."

John raised his brows at such a frank admission of familiarity with a member of the revolutionary group.

Hann'yu simply peered down at John's hands. Beneath the water, they looked deathly white, except the tips and knuckles, which were bright red. John glanced to Hann'yu, trying to read his expression. He didn't appear alarmed, only curious.

"Often in backwaters like Amura'taye, town chiefs pay exorbitant sums for powders made from the scrapings of goatweed roots. They call it whores-torch. Usually it's used to ferret out a suspected witch. They could as easily be finding ushiri candidates. But they don't know that, of course.

Church secret." Hann'yu kept his circumspect gaze on John's hands as he casually said, "I won't have you handle goatweed again. It affects you worse than it does me."

"Thank you for that."

Gradually, the burning sensation receded. John watched the redness fade from his knuckles, wondering if it had been some kind of allergic reaction or possibly a sensitivity to the fungus that formed the mycorrhizae sheathing the plant's roots.

"Where you grew up—" Hann'yu began.

"Shun'sira," John supplied quickly. Years ago, he and Ravishan had decided on Shun'sira as the safest district for John to claim for a homeland. It was a remote district at the ragged edge of the Bousim tithing lands and was populated mostly by subsistence hunters who lived distant, scattered lives in the rugged hills and bogs. John had memorized the names of the few settlements that dotted the otherwise-barren map of the area in a single afternoon.

"Did they have many witch burnings there?" Hann'yu inquired, still passively inspecting the progress of John's inflamed knuckles.

"They didn't have much of anything there." John kept his answer deliberately vague.

"The town chiefs preferred to skin the witches for their bones, then?"

"I don't know . . . probably. My family lived in the hills. We didn't see too many other people, unless it was on market days." John didn't want to talk about burning or flaying anyone. Just the thought of witches' bones and how they were acquired revolted him utterly.

Months ago, John had read about the sacred bones in the holy texts. Bled and skinned, the still-living remains of certain women were bound together with copper wires and used in divination rituals. Apparently, in the southern convent at Umbhra'ibaye, the remains of thousands of women had been assembled into something called the Issusha'im Oracles. The text had contained a small drawing, and since then, the image had worked itself into the worst of his nightmares.

Now it was too easy for John to picture their white teeth and hollow eye sockets; readily he conjured the stale, rotted scent of them and heard the clatter of their thin arm bones against their ribs as they twisted amidst the red wires restraining them.

A cool breeze drifted through the open window and John shuddered. Hann'yu cast him an oddly mournful look.

"Did you know that, once, it was only the holiest of women who were allowed to sacrifice themselves and become Issusha'im Oracles?"

"No," John replied flatly.

Hann'yu plainly wanted him to understand something about the connection between the Issusha'im and goatweed, but John didn't know exactly what. Though he now spoke Basawar fluently, there were many aspects of the language and the culture that John suspected only a native understood innately. All he could do was drift along in the conversation and hope that, eventually, he would perceive the implications.

"Before the war with the Eastern Kingdom, there were no witches. Women with witches' powers were considered Parfir's holy brides, equal to the Kahlil in the depth of the god's blessings upon them. Look back through the books for yourself. You won't find a mention of a witch until after the first siege at Ganaa." Hann'yu glanced up at him. "Am I scandalizing you?"

"No." John lifted his hands from the water experimentally. His fingers felt slightly stiff, but the burning was gone. "Were you hoping to?"

"A little," Hann'yu replied. He tossed John a cloth to dry his hands.

John smiled tiredly, sad to see Hann'yu disappointed, but there was nothing he could do. He couldn't be surprised by heretical disclosures when he lacked the instinctive knowledge of what was normal and what was profane here in Basawar.

"You just don't believe me, do you?" Hann'yu asked.

"I believe you," John assured him, and he did. "Even holy doctrine is bound to be altered by wars. A church can't remove itself from the society in which it exists." John dried his hands. His skin felt tender against the rough cloth.

Hann'yu studied him. "You're a strange man, Jahn."

"How so?"

"You seem so unconcerned sometimes, as if even the most startling revelation means nothing to you. It makes a man want to surprise you."

"You could just jump out from a dark room," John suggested. It was something of a shame that the provocative social impact of Hann'yu's conversation was so wasted on him.

"Jumping out of closets might be just a little beneath my station," Hann'yu replied. "I may just have to stop trying to shock you. Parfir only knows what I might end up saying."

John shrugged. "So long as you don't confess to a burning passion for me, we'll be fine."

Hann'yu's dark eyes went wide with shock. His face drained of all color.

John instantly recognized the expression of horror, but the words were already out of his mouth. He had unintentionally struck upon a subject far more profane to Basawar society than either immolating women or skinning them alive. Backtracking would only get him in worse trouble, so he pushed on. "You're not in love with me, are you?"

"No." Hann'yu coughed. "My god, what a thing to say."

"I haven't scandalized you, have I?" John asked in a deadpan voice. He gazed levelly at Hann'yu with a slight, sardonic smile.

Hann'yu stared at him for a moment, and then laughed. It was loud, relieved laughter.

"I see your point, Jahn. It is a little cruel of me to just say things to you in hopes of getting a startled reaction." Hann'yu shook his head and then lowered his voice. "But you truly must take care, as far as such desires are concerned. Before you came here there was an . . . incident . . . " Hann'yu looked a little sick, and John felt afraid to ask what the outcome had been. "A young man was put to death," Hann'yu said at last. "Now Dayyid will not tolerate the mention of such abominations, not even in jest."

"Not to fear. Dayyid and I don't share many jokes." John forced a smile.

Hann'yu nodded, but his expression was bleak. He stepped back to the table and picked up the sealed jar of goatweed roots. He studied it for a moment and then placed it back among the smoked glass jars and dark bottles on one of the tall shelves behind him.

John watched him and wondered what would be done with the poisonous knotted roots. As if sensing his curiosity, Hann'yu said, "The goatweed will be distilled into a poison, potent enough to lay even a god low. Though for now it is nothing but an ugly irritant." He sighed heavily and turned back to John. "You know, I don't just say things to you to see if I can disgust you—"

"You didn't disgust me," John assured him. "It's just that sometimes I don't know why you tell me these things. I know it isn't just to shock me. There are obviously simpler ways."

"Yes, obviously," Hann'yu agreed. He offered John a half-smile. "It's not easy to be alone, not even when it's just in knowledge. A man wants someone else he can talk to. In Nurjima, there were dozens of us who would gather at teahouses and discuss these things. The conversations could go on for hours, and sometimes people got angry. We'd argue and rant, but I always came away from the discussions feeling alive with thoughts. But here, no one wants to know more than they have to. No one wants to ask questions. You'd think knowledge was a poison." Hann'yu glanced briefly to the dark jar of goatweed, then returned his attention to John. "You don't seem like the other men here. You're not afraid to learn new things. You pursue knowledge. I suppose it makes me nostalgic, talking to you like this."

John nodded. "I know what you mean."

"Do you?" Hann'yu smiled at the idea. "There was a large intellectual circle in Shun'sira?"

"No, but I understand isolation—" The rest of John's words were cut off by a loud pounding on the infirmary door. John strode across the room quickly and pulled the door open. Fikiri and another ushiri stumbled in. Their arms, chests, and faces were crisscrossed with long, narrow gashes.

John led them both to beds and had them sit down. He had now seen enough of the ushiri'im's injuries to be unsurprised by the profusion of blood. These kinds of long, narrow slices weren't usually lethal. They bled a great deal and were obviously very painful. But it was the deep, organ-piercing punctures and bone-shattering impacts that killed most ushiri'im.

Those internal injuries could be easy to miss at first glance. Often, the shocked ushiri'im weren't even aware of the extent of the damage to their bodies.

Hann'yu walked quickly to them. "All right, let's get a look at the two of you."

While Hann'yu undressed the other ushiri, John swiftly and efficiently removed Fikiri's clothes. The heavy wool of Fikiri's coat was still cold from the Gray Space. Jagged rents marred the coat's front and back. The leather vest Fikiri wore beneath his coat had fared better. Only one cut punched all the way through it. A single, tiny scratch marked Fikiri's thin chest, and that had already stopped bleeding. His legs, too, were unharmed. His worst injuries seemed to be a deep cut along his right arm and a gash across his chin.

From the next bed, John heard a quiet hiss escape from Hann'yu. John glanced up to see Hann'yu tossing aside the other ushiri's blood-soaked underpants. The ushiri's face was white and he shook violently. His hands were folded over his groin.

"It looks worse than it is," Hann'yu assured the ushiri. "A few stitches will patch everything up good as new." Hann'yu glanced to John. "How's Fikiri?"

"Two superficial cuts. He'll need stitches in his arm and maybe his chin. Otherwise just bandages." John studied Fikiri for a moment. There was a dark bump on the side of his temple. "Did you hit your head?"

"In combat practice two days ago," Fikiri said. "Ravishan did it."

John nodded. Nothing life-threatening, then.

Hann'yu moved swiftly, gathering his needles and stitching thread. "Get Fikiri's cuts cleaned up and bandaged. I'll start sewing up Thuum."

"Will you need my help with him?" If the wound was very bad, Hann'yu would want John to bear it for Thuum. John didn't relish the thought, but if absorbing some of the ushiri's injuries would save Thuum's life, then John would do it.

"No." Hann'yu gave him a quick smile. "This will just require stitches. It would be most helpful if you could prepare Fikiri."

John nodded, relieved. As Hann'yu pulled the canvas panels shut around the bed where Thuum lay, John turned back to Fikiri.

"Is he going to live?" Fikiri asked.

"He'll be fine." John didn't know if that was completely true, but it was what Fikiri and Thuum both needed to hear right now.

John filled the washbasin with water and brought bandages and towels over to Fikiri's bedside. He sat down on the stool next to the bed and kicked Fikiri's discarded clothes out of his way. Bright red splotches of blood spattered the sheets all around Fikiri. The boy looked scared. He held his right arm close to his body and pressed his left hand over his slashed chin.

John tore a strip off one of the towels, folded it into a pad, and held it out to Fikiri. "Hold this against your chin."

Fikiri obediently did as John told him.

Gently, John cleaned and bandaged Fikiri's injured arm and then the deep gash in his chin. Then, John turned his attention to the smaller scratches that slashed across the skin of his arms, neck, and face. Fikiri looked like he'd gone a few rounds with a gang of angry cats. After John was done with him, he resembled a poorly wrapped mummy. Tufts of his blond hair had come loose from his tight braids and now hung like wisps of smoke around his pale face. John found the blood-stained sheets beneath his skinny body and the heap of torn, bloody clothes at the foot of the bed too depressing to look at. A fifteen-year-old boy shouldn't have to endure this kind of life.

"Come on, let's get you into a clean bed." John easily lifted Fikiri's thin body and carried him to the next bed. Fikiri lay back into the pillows and pulled the blankets over himself. John thought the boy might just go to sleep, but instead Fikiri looked up at him with a strange, yearning expression.

"Do you want me to get you something for the pain?" John asked.

Fikiri nodded, and John brought a cup of yellowpetal water. Fikiri took the small clay cup with his left hand and sipped the liquid. After taking several more drinks, he set the cup aside on a small medical tray that stood beside the bed.

"When we were on the Thousand Steps . . . " Fikiri's voice was just a whisper. John stepped closer to the bedside and knelt down to hear him.

"What about it?" John asked.

"We could have turned around," Fikiri murmured. "You could have let me turn around, and we could have gone back to Nurjima."

John didn't say anything in response. He didn't even move.

Fikiri continued to fix him with that intense look. "Why didn't you let me turn around?" His voice wasn't angry, but soft and confused.

John stood and retrieved the empty cup. He didn't want to look at Fikiri. Seeing the boy's pain and knowing that he was complicit in it made him sick with himself.

"I'll get you another drink," John said.

"My mother promised to take you and your family with us," Fikiri persisted in a whisper. "Didn't you believe her?"

"I had to bring you, Fikiri—" John cut himself short, knowing he couldn't explain himself to Fikiri. He turned, found more yellowpetal water, and refilled the cup. Without looking at Fikiri, he set it down on the bedside tray.

"I have duties in the common sickroom." John forced the words out with a mechanical flatness. "You should rest. Hann'yu will be with you soon."

"Why can't you tell me?" Fikiri persisted in a whisper. "Even Behr and Loshai don't know why you did it."

"I'm sorry," John said. Then he turned and walked away.

☾ ☾ ☾

The common sickroom was located outside the infirmary down a flight of wide stairs. It was a larger, open chamber with more beds arranged in close rows. The shelves that lined the back wall were not packed with medicines but with bedding, canvas panels, and bedpans. Hann'yu rarely sent John down to the common sickroom to work. He seemed to think that it was in some way beneath John.

John surveyed the few men who occupied the beds. Most were older and sleeping. Two gray-haired ushvun'im stood near the large windows that opened to the gardens. They held buckets and scrub brushes, but seemed lost in conversation. Neither of them took note of John, which suited him.

There were several baskets of clean sheets and beds that needed to be remade. John needed to do something. So he started with that.

He didn't want to think about what he had done to Fikiri. At the time, he hadn't really known what would be expected of the boy. But even if he had, John knew he would have forced Fikiri up those steps anyway. He would have done it because Rathal'pesha was the key to his return home.

He could offer himself the excuse that Laurie and Bill were both depending on him. He could tell himself that it was only a matter of numbers—the needs of three to those of one. He could say that Fikiri wouldn't have been alive at all if it hadn't been for him. John had simply made the best of the options he had been given. He had done what needed to be done. He wanted to take some consolation in the truth of all that, and yet none of it made him feel good or just. It made him feel sick with himself and with the world that surrounded him.

Sometimes his life seemed like nothing but a series of ugly choices. Putting his dog down or having it live on in crippling pain, lying to his family about his life or losing them for the sake of honesty. There never seemed to be a painless option, only degrees of what he could live with and what he could not bear.

John made the beds quickly, with focused intensity. Crisp, tight corners came to him easily, as did high polish on boots and miles of silent marching. His father would have been proud of that, at least. These were beds the old man could have flipped a quarter on.

John stopped, staring at the basket of sheets. He didn't know why he was suddenly thinking of his father. That was pointless. Even if John did ever get back home, his father wouldn't spare him a word.

It was regret, John supposed. Another right choice that he had made that hadn't been much better than the wrong choice. And what for? So that he could end up here, in this stronghold of repression, lying awake at night fantasizing about Ravishan and praying that he didn't get them both killed. What consolation was he supposed to take in knowing that his father, an entire world away, knew he was gay?

Pointless, John thought. Sometimes life was simply pointless. He supposed that this entire silent rant of his was much the same. No matter how bad he felt, there was nothing to be done about it. He had made hard and even cruel choices, but in the end they were the ones he knew were right. There was no use in regretting them.

John made another bed, more slowly this time. He wondered, not for the first time today, where Ravishan was and what he was doing. He was probably training, taking his frustration out on some undeserving opponent—or possibly taking it out on Dayyid.

The thought of that, at least, brought a slight smile to John's lips.

He supposed he should go back upstairs and see if Hann'yu needed him. He picked up two sets of new, clean sheets and folded them to take with him. He'd need to change the beds Fikiri and Thuum had used.

When he reached the infirmary, he found Thuum tucked into a clean bed and lying in a sedated sleep. The canvas panels were drawn closed around the bed that John had left Fikiri in. John poked his head in. Hann'yu glanced up from where he sat on the stool next to the bed. His delicate needles, his spool of fine black thread, and a bottle of astringent sat on the tray beside him. Fikiri stretched across the bed in an unconscious sprawl. A fine track of black stitches arced over his chin. Hann'yu continued his work over Fikiri's arm, stitching Fikiri's flesh as if he were sewing nothing more than a shirtsleeve.

"He'll be fine," Hann'yu assured John. "It was good you gave him the yellowpetal water. He was beginning to babble."

"I didn't mean to knock him out."

"Oh, you didn't. I did that myself." Hann'yu bent back over Fikiri's arm. "He was going to end up saying something that would embarrass him later, so I gave him a little prick of something. It ensures better stitches anyway. No tossing and twitching."

"What was he saying?" John asked. He hoped it wasn't more about Lady Bousim's offers to him.

"He hates it here. He hates all of us. He wants to go home. He wants his mother. The kind of thing that boys say when they're hurt and scared." Hann'yu tied off one stitch and started another. "I suppose you heard a lot of the same when you brought him up the Thousand Steps."

"Not much," John replied. Though he vividly remembered Fikiri curled up and sobbing on the frigid steps, it wasn't something he needed to share with Hann'yu.

"Two years ago, this behavior might have been acceptable, but now he's getting a little too old for it."

"He's only fifteen," John argued, though he didn't know why except that it seemed that someone should defend the boy.

"He's an ushiri. A couple of cuts like these are the least of his problems, and calling for his mother isn't going to do him any good."

John guessed that Hann'yu was right. Still, what harm did it do anyone when Fikiri cried or complained? It didn't hurt Fikiri.

But John was beginning to realize that Fikiri's obvious misery pained the men around him. It pricked at their guilt, knowing that they put these demands upon a child. It would be so much easier if he were strong and silent, if he shrugged off his injuries the way Ravishan did. It would have allowed them all to think that the ushiri'im were made of tougher stuff than other men, that they didn't feel the hurt as deeply and weren't terrified in the face of their own agonizing deaths.

John frowned down at Fikiri's pale face. He really was just a boy. John found that he had to look away. Like the rest of them, he couldn't stand to think about it.

After a moment, John asked, "Do you need me for anything?"

"You could clean up the beds."

"I thought the same thing." John lifted the clean sheets slightly and Hann'yu offered him an absent nod.

John turned aside and let the canvas panel fall back into place. He stripped the stained bedding off one of the beds and quickly spread and tucked in the new sheet. John had just started towards the next bed when he felt that slight shudder of air and that whisper of a chill behind him. Though he disliked the sensation of the Gray Space opening, John also associated it strongly with Ravishan's arrival.

He turned, expecting to greet Ravishan, only to find himself smiling inanely into Dayyid's glowering face.

"Is he with you?" Dayyid demanded.

"What?" John was too startled by Dayyid's unexpected presence to reply properly. "Who?"

"Ravishan?" Dayyid almost growled the name.

"No." Then a worrying thought came to him. "Is he missing?"

"He's been gone since last night." Dayyid's scowl deepened the lines of his weathered face. "Even when he is disobedient, he doesn't stay away for a whole day."

"Maybe he's lost," John suggested. Though he thought that Ravishan was just avoiding him. This was probably wise for both their sakes . . . though it seemed somehow very unlike Ravishan.

"He doesn't get lost," Dayyid stated flatly.

"I'm sure he gets lost sometimes." John remembered Ravishan telling him that he had claimed to be lost when he had wanted to slip away and visit him. He would probably make the same claim now.

"No." Dayyid gave him a look of sheer contempt. "He claims to have been lost, but he never is. His bones are the god's own. There is no place on this world unknown to them."

Because the world itself was the god's body, John quickly filled in the unspoken reasoning that Dayyid had to be following.

"Perhaps he's tired."

"Or injured," Dayyid countered.

The thought sent a sharp stab of worry through John. He'd left Ravishan in an ugly part of Amura'taye. Ravishan obviously hadn't returned to Rathal'pesha.

"He's never stayed away for an entire night before?" John asked.

"Never."

"Is there any way of tracing where he might have gone?" John asked.

"Certain men can feel the Gray Space." For the first time, Dayyid looked directly into his face. "I have the ushiri'im looking for him, but it never hurts to have another man."

"What do you need me to do?" John asked.

"I didn't mean you." Dayyid smirked. "Tell Hann'yu that I want to see him as soon as he is done here."

John scowled at Dayyid. But Dayyid had already turned away. He didn't spare John a glance as he strode out of the room. The door simply fell shut behind him. John hurled the clean sheet onto the mattress with unnecessary force.

"Ravishan really hasn't been up to see you today?" Hann'yu called from behind the panel.

"No." John frowned down at the sheet.

There was no further response from Hann'yu. John picked up the sheet but didn't move on. Finally, he said, "Do you think that I should go look for him?"

"Do you think you could find him?" Hann'yu asked back.

"I might."

"Then go," Hann'yu replied. "The beds will still be here when you get back."

John hardly heard the rest of Hann'yu's response. He was already heading for the door.

Chapter Thirty-Three

John closed his eyes, allowing himself to simply feel the scored lines that the ushiri'im often left when they tore into the Gray Space.

The walkways, walls, and the very air of Rathal'pesha were rough from the countless invisible abrasions. If he concentrated, John could feel them all. Lifting one hand into the air, he traced the finest imperfection, a sensation not unlike running his fingers across a pane of glass and having his skin catch on the razor-thin scratches marring the surface.

In the wastes, he had occasionally been able to feel Ravishan's passage by following the abrasion in space. But here in Rathal'pesha, the constant practices of all the ushiri'im made it impossible to distinguish one from another, much less track a single trail.

He supposed it wouldn't have mattered in any case. Ravishan hadn't returned to the monastery.

If he wanted to find Ravishan, he guessed that he would have to hike back down to Amura'taye. It would take the better part of the afternoon. He would arrive well after sunset. An ushiri could traverse the distance in an instant, so Dayyid probably already had several of them searching the town.

If Ravishan was there, they would eventually find him.

But then, there was no guarantee that Ravishan would be in Amura'taye. He was the strongest of the ushiri'im, able to cross mountain ranges in a moment. He could be anywhere in Basawar.

John leaned his head against the stone railing of the walkway. He shouldn't have left Ravishan the way he had. If anything happened to him, John knew he wouldn't forgive himself. He wished that he could just know if Ravishan was safe. Even if he couldn't find him, just knowing would make all the difference.

The entire walkway seemed to sway beneath him. John bolted upright, staring around him, but nothing moved. The stone walkway remained solidly where it had always been. There were no signs of a tremor in any of the surrounding towers or trees.

It hadn't seemed like an earthquake in any case. The movement had been silent and smooth. The land had seemed to simply slide beneath him as it so often did in his dreams. John remembered the same sensation coming to him the night before he had arrived in Amura'taye. Miles of land had whipped beneath him, leading him up from the flood plains, through the thickening forests, over the terraced farms of the mountain, and straight up to Rathal'pesha. It had taken him directly to Ravishan.

John lowered his head, again resting it on the railing. He closed his eyes, concentrating. Slowly, the walkway slid out from under him. He drifted over the monastery grounds, seeing gardens and stone paths pass beneath him. He recognized Samsango, lounging beneath a twisted pine with two other elderly ushvun'im. A moment later, John swept up over the walls and the watchtowers and then began to rise up the face of the mountain itself. The air was colder and thinner. The few trees that grew there were scrub, and as he ascended higher, even those disappeared. Soon, there was nothing but jutting stone and deep drifts of snow.

Ravishan was there, crouched beneath an outcropping of gray rock, staring down at the monastery below. His black hair blew across his face and he pushed it back. Absently, almost carelessly, he turned his black-bladed knife through his hands.

John opened his eyes.

He felt a slight shock as the surrounding stone walls and walkways of Rathal'pesha instantly rushed over him. Reflexively, he gripped the walkway railing, as if the world had truly shifted beneath him. For a few minutes, John simply stood where he was, wondering how he had just seen Ravishan.

His first instinct was to disregard the experience. For all he knew, it had just been an effect of a sleepless night, deep guilt, and wishful thinking.

It wasn't as if he'd opened the Gray Space or caused spontaneous combustion. He'd just imagined Ravishan, whose image came to him all too often and too readily.

Still, John decided that it was worth following. Seeing Ravishan turn the sharp knife through his hands so carelessly had disturbed him. Even if his vision had been completely wrong, John knew he had to go up the mountain.

He went quickly, only stopping to get a heavy coat and gloves.

☾ ☾ ☾

John followed the narrow animal tracks leading up between the outcroppings of rock and scrub pines. A few wild goats paused atop jagged stones to watch him pass beneath them. He climbed higher, and the air began to burn in his lungs. Despite the snow and wind, sweat beaded his body.

It was tiring work, and yet not as difficult as he had expected. He had anticipated more trouble keeping his footing, but that, at least, seemed to come easily. Even scaling the face of a steep incline, with his body pressed against the frigid rock, hand and footholds seemed to simply open where he needed them. It gave him an odd feeling of security, as if the mountain itself were cradling him, and it would not let him fall.

Just the kind of thought that would come to a man suffering from oxygen deprivation, John told himself. He shook his head and continued climbing. He was almost there. He could already see the outcropping where Ravishan knelt. John picked his way closer. Ravishan's black coat and hair stood out sharply against the white snow.

Ravishan's gaze was distant, almost unseeing. He raised his empty hands to his mouth and breathed over his fingers, presumably to warm them. A rush of relief washed over John as he saw that Ravishan had sheathed his black curse blade. Slowly, Ravishan shifted his gaze from the distant sky to the field of gray stone and white snow surrounding him. When he suddenly saw John, he looked as startled as if John had leapt out from nowhere.

John smiled and gave a tired wave.

Ravishan seemed expressionless. He straightened and stood. For a moment, John thought Ravishan might just slip away through the Gray Space. Instead, he remained where he was, watching as John closed the distance between them.

It was only when John stepped in close to Ravishan, sharing his shelter beneath the stone outcropping, that a red blush spread across Ravishan's cheeks. Then it seemed incredibly natural for John to wrap his arms around the other man and draw him close. Ravishan surged into the embrace, hugging John so hard that it was almost painful. When he pressed his face against John's neck, his skin felt icy. The fragrances of incense and pollen still clung to Ravishan from the night before. His body felt so good in John's arms.

"Are you all right?" John asked.

Ravishan nodded, not lifting his face from where it was pressed against John's neck.

"I shouldn't have left you the way I did," John spoke softly, his lips brushing Ravishan's cold hair. There was no one to overhear them, but secrecy had become a reflex to him. "I'm sorry."

"It's not your fault." Ravishan finally looked up at him. "I've been thinking about the things you said—"

"You shouldn't." John wished he could have taken the whole thing back somehow and been less of an arrogant bastard. "I don't know half of what I'm talking about."

"But you were right," Ravishan told him. "I hadn't thought about what could happen to us. When I did . . . when I thought of what Dayyid could do to you if he discovered us . . . " Ravishan bowed his head against John's chest.

"It's all right," John whispered. "We aren't going to do anything. So nothing will happen to us."

Ravishan lifted his face again. The afternoon light lit golden flecks in his dark eyes. Traces of a blush still colored his cheeks, but his mouth remained pale from the cold.

John bowed his head and gently kissed Ravishan's lips. He only meant it to be brief and sweet. But then Ravishan closed his eyes and opened his mouth to him. Desire surged through John's body. He pulled Ravishan against him hard, kissing him with a savage hunger.

Then John caught himself and drew back.

"Nothing's going to happen?" Ravishan asked. Slowly, he opened his eyes and offered John one of his dazzling, rare smiles.

John loved that smile—the joy in it, the honesty of it, and most of all the fact that it was meant just for him. Suddenly, John desperately wanted Ravishan. The wind, snow, and stone surrounding them didn't matter. All he wanted was to kneel with Ravishan beneath the shelter of this outcropping and make love to him. It took all of his will to stop himself from pulling Ravishan back into his arms.

"I told you, I didn't know what I was talking about," John answered.

John forced himself to let go of Ravishan and step back. Ravishan released him hesitantly.

John's entire body ached with an almost overpowering longing. It had been years since he'd touched another man and felt his arousal returned so fervently. And Ravishan wasn't just any other man. He was strong, smart, beautiful, and so very eager—everything John could have wanted.

But neither of them could afford to embark on this affair. Only this morning Hann'yu had warned him that at least one man had lost his life for such a thing. Homosexuality wouldn't be tolerated even in jest here.

John had to look away out over the frigid mountains for several moments before he could regain his composure.

"It's so cold," he said just to fill the silence. "You wouldn't even know it was spring."

"It always feels like winter up here," Ravishan replied.

John didn't trust himself to look at Ravishan, so he occupied himself by digging through his coat pockets for the pair of heavy gloves that he had brought.

"Here." John handed over the gloves. "Your hands looked cold."

"You could see them, behind your back?" Ravishan asked.

"Not just now. Earlier." John glanced to him and watched as Ravishan pulled the gloves on and flexed his fingers against the stiff leather.

"Thank you."

"It's the least I could do." John fell silent, unable to find anything safe to say. His mouth still burned from Ravishan's kiss. His body ached.

"So . . . " Ravishan said, but then didn't add anything else.

At last, John said, "I suppose we should get back to Rathal'pesha. Dayyid has the ushiri'im looking for you."

Ravishan sighed. As he gazed down at the monastery, that distant, hopeless expression returned to his face. From so far above, the stone walls and dark green trees seemed so small. John could blot the entire monastery out with one raised hand.

"I don't want to go back," Ravishan murmured. The words were so soft that John wasn't sure that he had been meant to hear them. "I hate it there."

John opened his mouth to tell Ravishan that he was sorry, that it was unavoidable, but then stopped himself.

When he had climbed up here he had only been thinking of Ravishan's safety. Obliquely, he'd imagined shepherding Ravishan back down to Rathal'pesha, as if he would be bringing Ravishan home. But now it struck him that the monastery offered Ravishan none of the security or protection of a home.

John knew that Ravishan's right arm, hidden beneath his coat sleeve, was swathed in bandages. John realized that at some point he had stopped thinking of the perpetual injuries those bandages masked. He had begun to accept the countless small scars and fresh cuts tracing Ravishan's body as if they were natural. Scars on the skin of an ushiri seemed as harmless as freckles. But they weren't natural, and they weren't harmless. They were years of pain carved into flesh.

Those injuries were all that Rathal'pesha offered Ravishan. Of course he hated the place. Of course he wanted to run away. Who wouldn't? He didn't cry like Fikiri, but John knew that Ravishan had endured far worse for much longer.

John frowned down at the monastery. In his own way, he needed Ravishan to be an ushiri and become Kahlil as much as the Payshmura priests did. The Kahlil offered him a chance to get back home. But if that meant that Ravishan had to endure injury and agony so routinely that pain became commonplace, then it wasn't worth it. Ravishan deserved better, and if there was nothing else John could do for him, he could at least give Ravishan his freedom.

"There must be somewhere you can go where Dayyid and the other ushman'im can't find you," John said softly. "Somewhere far from here. Nurjima, maybe."

From Hann'yu's descriptions, John knew it to be a vast city with a diverse and liberal population. It seemed like just the kind of place where a smart young man like Ravishan could remake himself and his life.

"You want us to run away to Nurjima?" Ravishan asked as if John had suggested something unimaginable and wondrous.

You want us to run away . . .

Yes, right now he wanted to go anywhere, so long as he could be with Ravishan. But John stopped himself from saying as much. He couldn't travel through the Gray Space, and it would be idiotic for Ravishan not to. If he was going to escape from Dayyid, then he needed to go very far as fast as possible.

Besides that, John knew he couldn't just abandon Laurie and Bill here.

"You should go," John told him. "You could probably be there in a few minutes. Dayyid would never be able to track you down."

Ravishan studied his face for several moments and John could see the realization dawning in his expression. Ravishan shook his head.

"I'm not going to leave you." He scowled down at the distant grounds of Rathal'pesha but then looked back to John. "I promised you that I would take you home and I will."

"You made that promise years ago—"

"I want to keep it. For you," Ravishan said firmly. He shoved his gloved hands into his pockets. "And in any case, you aren't the only one I made a promise to. There's Rousma as well."

"Rousma?" John thought he might have heard the name before but he couldn't remember when. Then he recalled the girl who Ravishan secretly spoke to through the Gray Space. John recalled her strange cadences and awkward sentences whispering through the air. The same tones often hunted him through his dreams of the holy bones.

"When we were children, they took her to Umbhra'ibaye," Ravishan said. "Now she's one of the Issusha'im Oracles."

"They're going to skin her?" A shudder of revulsion coiled through John's stomach.

"They did that years ago. At least she's still alive. By holy law, we both should've been executed along with our parents. But there was too much power in our blood and bones for them to let us go." Ravishan kicked at the snow beneath his feet. "If I run away, they'll take it out on Rousma."

It was so wrong, John thought. He wanted to curse the sheer injustice of Ravishan's entire life. But Ravishan's determined silence held him back.

"I swore to her that once I was Kahlil I would find a way to free her. So, you see, there's no running away for me," Ravishan said at last. He leaned into John's shoulder, and John instinctively wrapped an arm around him, offering his silent comfort.

"Don't look so grim, Jahn," Ravishan told him. "Before I met you, becoming Kahlil was something I had to do to keep myself and my sister alive. I endured my training. But after I met you, I began to truly want to become Kahlil. I want to cross into Nayeshi with you and . . . I want the life I can have there with you."

John met Ravishan's gaze, and Ravishan flushed and looked down at his boots.

"Things are very different for men like us in Nayeshi," John assured Ravishan. He didn't want to brood over the liberties he'd lost in Basawar, because it would only depress him, but in comparison Nayeshi was a welcoming haven.

"When we reach Nayeshi . . . " Ravishan began, but then faltered.

"Yes?" John asked.

"Will you live with me? Will you be my lover?" Ravishan asked in a rush.

Despite the surrounding snow, John felt a flush of warmth. He didn't know quite what to say. There were so many reasons that they shouldn't even be discussing such a thing.

"You don't have to say yes." Ravishan shied immediately, taking a step away, eyes downcast. "I'll take you back no matter what you say."

"Of course I'll be your lover," John said quickly. "I can hardly keep my hands off you now. Do you think anything would stop me once we're in Nayeshi?"

Ravishan looked up at him, as if he were startled, then slowly his expression melted into a radiant smile.

John realized that part of what made Ravishan's smiles so charming was the sense of surprised delight that they conveyed. He never seemed to expect happiness, and that made giving it to him so much more of a pleasure.

John leaned forward and stole one last quick kiss, then turned and started back down the steep trail.

Despite the fact that he could have stepped through the Gray Space and reached Rathal'pesha in an instant, Ravishan followed John on foot. When the path grew wide enough, they walked side by side, their arms brushing in an easy communion.

Chapter Thirty-Four

As the short months of northern spring passed quickly into summer, John managed little more than a furtive embrace and one desperate kiss with Ravishan. The rest of his time seemed dominated by Hann'yu's need for assistance in the infirmary.

It seemed that Dayyid pushed the ushiri'im harder every day, and steadily more and more of them suffered greater injuries. In early spring, John feared that bearing the brunt of the ushiri'im's wounds would kill him, but his body adjusted, and by the time the taye flowers were blooming on the mountainsides he found himself shrugging off even the deep punctures that seemed to plague Fikiri.

John took some consolation in the fact that he saw less of Ravishan because he was by far the least likely ushiri to be badly injured.

When Hann'yu didn't need John to bear the wounds of the ushiri'im, he kept busy with ushvun battle practice and studying holy texts for his formal initiation. Steadily, his knowledge of Payshmura history increased and his skill in dispatching an opponent became a reflex.

The only interruption of John's routine came one summer afternoon when Hann'yu attempted to teach him the spells that healed lesser injuries and eased pain. The result was disastrous.

Hann'yu had brought up two injured lambs for John to practice on. But the moment John had laid his hands on them, their skins had ripped open as their bones tore through their flesh. Shrieks of pain had choked as vertebrae had exploded into their throats. In an instant, they'd become nothing but blood, gristle, and fragments of bone.

John had staggered back in horror and vomited into an empty water basin.

"I don't think you were meant to be a physician," Hann'yu had remarked, his face pale.

John had nodded but hadn't been able to bring himself to look at what he'd done. After that, Hann'yu hadn't attempted to instruct John in any healing spells, much to John's relief. He continued to bear wounds, clean beds, bandage injuries, and prepare medicines, but did nothing beyond that.

Once he passed the trials of his initiation, winning the right to wear a single honor braid, he gained a little more free time.

Now as the summer neared an end, John took to visiting Samsango down in the kitchens. After long days in the heights of Rathal'pesha, bearing deep wounds, feeling the air tear asunder, and overhearing whispers of oracles and rumors of the destroyer god, he found Samsango's company relieving. They did simple work and often discussed the mundane news that the other ushvun'im brought up from Amura'taye.

"Another witch," Samsango said sadly. He settled his frail, aged body on a bench before one of the weathered cooking tables. "When I was a boy, there was only one witch that had to be burned. Now, it's nearly one a year."

John frowned at the pale flames flickering in the bread oven. Waves of heat rolled out over him. He shoved the tray of uncooked loaves inside and closed the oven door. Outside, predawn light had yet to soften the night sky. It would be hours before the majority of the ushvun'im woke.

John sat down at the table across from Samsango.

"It's the Fai'daum, you know," Samsango told him. He slowly measured out two more handfuls of ground taye into the mixing bowl. John cracked three weasel eggs into the bowl and began mixing as Samsango looked on. Slowly the red yolks of the weasel eggs colored the dough dull pink. John turned out the dough. Samsango scooped up the soft mass and began to expertly knead it.

"Their leader is in the thrall of the demoness, Ji Shir'korud," Samsango informed John.

John nodded. He recognized the name and remembered the large yellow dog he'd seen addressing the Fai'daum on the night he had been taken in by the Bousim. It felt like ages ago.

"The demoness teaches all the girls witchcraft and heresy. Then the poor, pretty things end up being burned. Such a waste."

John gazed at Samsango. A cold unease gnawed at him. The old ushvun went on working the bread dough as if the brutal murder of these girls was of no more consequence than wasted food. Samsango glanced up and gave John a gentle, warm smile.

"Up all day in the infirmary and now working all night with me in the kitchen," Samsango remarked. "You must be exhausted, Jahn."

"I'm fine," John said. He knew Samsango to be a caring man who had gone out of his way to help John settle in the monastery when he'd first arrived. Samsango took pains to see to the health of even the most ill-tempered goats and weasels. Yet, he could also easily conclude that a girl accused of witchcraft must be burned. He didn't seem able to even imagine any other course of action.

Intellectually, John knew that it was just a matter of culture. Samsango had no way of perceiving any morality apart from Payshmura holy law.

Within the Basawar culture, Samsango was perfectly consistent. He was kind and just. It was only from John's point of view that a contradiction emerged.

John wondered briefly if this was how vegetarians felt watching their companions eat meat. Or how pacifists felt watching popular war films.

He didn't want this sensation of revulsion. He liked Samsango. That was why he had come down to the kitchens in the first place. But he couldn't think of anything to say, any way to stop feeling alienated by the other man. He suddenly thought of Kyle, recalling the way his old roommate had, at times, just stood there staring at him. He, too, must have been shocked by the society around him. John wondered which of his own actions had sent waves of secret revulsion through Kyle.

"You look like you're about to fall asleep where you're sitting," Samsango said. The dull red glow of the kitchen fires softened the deep wrinkles of the old man's face. Samsango's expression was gentle, fatherly. John couldn't help but smile at him.

"I suppose I am. I'm probably slowing you down tonight," John said.

"No." Samsango patted a ball of dough down onto the cooking sheet. "This is the last. After it's baked, I'll be done. Though I have a little more room on the sheet . . . perhaps I should make a treat for our brothers who will be marching down the mountain."

He collected scraps of dough and worked them quickly into fat little buns. Once he was done, he laid a thin cloth over them and pushed the cooking sheet aside to allow the rolls to rise. Taye flour still caked his hands. He wiped them on a spare dishcloth, then looked up at John again.

John wanted to say something more, but he couldn't stop thinking of the girl who would be burned. Did she have friends or family? Was there anyone who would want to help her? Could they help her? What would he do if Laurie were ever discovered and condemned? The heat of the bread oven seemed suddenly more intense.

He didn't think he could imagine anything more painful, or terrible, than burning.

"I can see that you're troubled, Jahn," Samsango commented. "Would it help to tell me why?"

John didn't respond immediately; keeping his inner thoughts secret had become too much of a habit for him. But this was something he did want to share with Samsango, he realized.

"Did you know that before the first siege at Ganaa there were no witches?"

Samsango's bushy gray eyebrows shot up. "You have been listening to Ushman Hann'yu too much. He's from the south. They don't know anything there except what they read in books."

"But it's true. I looked it up."

Samsango cocked his head, seeming to contemplate something just past John.

"Long ago, they might not have been called witches," Samsango said at last, "but there have always been people who are tempted to misuse Parfir's blessings. They are not always bad people, but when they do wrong, they must be punished."

"But to burn a girl to death—"

Samsango held up a silencing hand. "I understand your turmoil, Jahn. If I'm honest, I will tell you that I share your sorrow for the poor child." He sighed heavily. "But remember, if the prior hears you repeating the things that Ushman Hann'yu tells you, you won't just be whipped. You might endanger Ushman Hann'yu as well. And you could lose that braid you fought so hard to earn or be barred from the presence of the ushiri'im!" Samsango looked truly distressed by the thought of this. He placed a callused, flour-caked hand over John's fingers. His touch felt surprisingly warm. "For the sake of the ushiri'im, if not yourself, you should keep your peace. They need your strength."

"The ushiri'im just need a body to bear their wounds. It doesn't matter if it's mine or not," John responded.

"You do them a great service," Samsango pronounced. He glanced at the raw scar that wound around John's wrist as he did so. The injury was recent and had been Fikiri's.

When the boy had been brought into the infirmary, his fingers had been gashed down to the bone. He had fixed John with a look that was half-shock and half-accusation, but he had said nothing. John had taken as much of Fikiri's wound as he could without losing his own fingers. Now both their palms and wrists were crossed with the same tender, red scars like some blood-brother pact gone terribly wrong.

"Modesty is good." Samsango's voice cut through John's wandering thoughts. "But you should take pride in your station, you know. Not many of the ushvun'im can serve the ushiri'im so well as you do. It's a great contribution."

John gave a lackluster nod. If it wasn't him, then it would have been someone else. But Samsango wouldn't see it that way.

"And to live up in the holy chambers." Samsango closed his eyes as if he were savoring a delicious sweet. "To be so near the holiest of the holy. I envy you a little."

"Only a little?" John teased.

Samsango opened his eyes. "Not so much that I'd want to be wrapped in bandages every day of my life."

"It's not the bandages that are so bad," John replied. "It's what's under them."

"Indeed."

The warm air hung thick with the smell of taye flour and faint dry spices. The moist scent of the loaves baking in the ovens began to spread through the kitchen. John took in a deep breath, knowing that the scent should have conjured images of his mother or grandmother, but neither of them had ever baked bread. His only association with the aroma was here in Rathal'pesha. When he returned to Nayeshi, he thought, the smell would remind him of sitting here in the flickering light of the cooking fires, watching Samsango.

"I imagine you're excited about the Harvest Fair," Samsango said.

Most of the men in the monastery were anticipating the annual fair with obvious excitement. Even Dayyid had mentioned it with a tone that struck John as almost enthusiastic.

"Now that you've earned your braid, you'll be allowed to attend. You won't believe everything you'll see there. I still remember the first time my father took me. The air was like perfume, with so many scents. Southern apples and honey sweets. Wine. And there were dancers and singers all the way from Vundomu. And the things there, glass lamps in every color you could imagine, embroidered bolts of silks, fat roasting dogs." He grinned wide, exposing the few teeth he had left. "I feel like a boy again just thinking about it."

John found himself smiling at the innocence of Samsango's nostalgia.

"You'd better watch for the game tables, though, and the wine sellers." Samsango's expression grew stern and John couldn't tell if he was joking or not. "They'll take advantage of even a poor old ushvun and then coldly turn him away when his few stones are gone."

"I'll be careful," John assured him.

"It's easily said, but harder to do. You get swept up in the music and colors and all the strange new people. And the dancing women. A young man like you has to watch out for them particularly. They're so lovely that it's easy to forget yourself. Then the prior will be shouting at you for months."

"Do you want me to keep an eye out for you?" John asked.

"At my age?" Samsango laughed. "The prior would proclaim it one of Parfir's miracles if I were to get up to trouble with a dancing girl. No, I'm just warning you. Some of these girls come all the way from Nurjima. They're clever and beautiful and some are a little wicked. A young man like you has to be careful."

"I will be."

"Should you keep an eye out for me?" Samsango shook his head as he repeated John's offer. "You can be so naive, Jahn. As if a lovely city girl is going to chase down an old prune like me."

"Some people like prunes," John replied.

"Not poor prunes," Samsango said. "Nobody likes a poor prune."

"I like you."

"I like you as well, Jahn. But you're not much of a substitute for a dancing girl." Samsango patted John's hand, as if he were indulging a child. "Now that bread needs to be turned, doesn't it?"

Taking the old man's implicit suggestion, John opened the oven door. Heat washed over him like a sudden afternoon sun. He wasn't very experienced at turning trays of bread, having spent far more time on the practice grounds than in the kitchens. He slid the large oven peel under the tray of bread and rotated it, careful not to upset the tray and send the rolls bouncing into the fire. The heat swallowed his arms and rushed over his face. Beads of sweat immediately rose across his brow and just as quickly evaporated.

Heat rolled over him in waves, growing steadily more encompassing. Flickers of discomfort built into an intensity. John could smell the fine hairs on his arms scorching. His fingers trembled as the sensation grew to searing pain.

When he finally finished and jerked the peel out of the oven, the warm air of the kitchen felt frigid against his hands.

"Oven too hot for you?" Samsango asked.

John only nodded.

"I used to be the same way," Samsango assured him. "But, you know, it's like anything. You get used to it."

"I don't know if I want to get used to it." John scowled at his red fingers.

"It can't be helped." Samsango shrugged. "You do something enough, and it becomes part of your nature."

John frowned at the inherent truth of Samsango's words. It was intrinsically human to adapt to his current surroundings. He had been living in Basawar for two years. Soon, it would be three. His body had grown used to hard labor. His skin was tanned and callused, his hair drawn back into an ushvun's braid. On the rare occasions that he caught his own reflection in a polished mirror, it looked strange to him. He could stare at himself and find nothing that marked him as foreign from the other men of Rathal'pesha.

Basawar vocabulary came to him easily. Even in his dreams, the words and images all arose from this world. When he thought of his home, he thought of Nayeshi, not Earth.

John suddenly realized why he had been so focused on his alienation from Samsango this evening. He hated it, but he also needed it. He needed that feeling to remind him of who he was. He needed its discomfort to keep him from becoming the man he played at being, because it would be easy and natural to adjust and settle into this life.

But he couldn't allow himself to overlook witch burnings just because they took place out of his sight. And he couldn't be proud of helping children like Fikiri learn to endure the pain of wounds that could kill or cripple them. No matter how much he wanted to feel at ease with Samsango or Hann'yu, no matter how desperately he wanted to lose himself in adoration of Ravishan, it couldn't come at the cost of his identity.

Once Samsango had settled back down at the kitchen table, he said, "You still look troubled."

"I'm just tired."

"Then you should sleep." Samsango smiled. "If man's hungry, then he should eat. If a man's tired, he should sleep. There are very simple solutions to most problems. It's only that men resist their natures."

John took in the pragmatic wisdom of this and nodded. "You're right. I'll go."

He started for the door and Samsango called out to him, "Thank you for coming down to see me. It's nice not to be lonely, even if you're not a dancing girl."

Chapter Thirty-Five

A day later, John was immersed in the exuberant atmosphere of the Harvest Fair. Grim, muddy Amura'taye had been transformed into something beautiful. Just as Samsango had predicted, the displays of color and noise did amaze him.

After living so long within the monastery, where the sacred quiet was broken only by solemn chanting, John had almost forgotten about the existence of music and dance. Now, the air seemed alive with it. As he walked through the rows of tents, makeshift wooden stalls, and painted carts, the sweet tones of flutes and stringed instruments whirled around him. Different melodies rose from different directions. They tangled with the scents of strange foods, strong perfumes, and living bodies pressed close in the afternoon heat.

In front of John, under the shade of a dull yellow tent, three women sang as they patted flatbread between their hands. Two of the women were older, their white hair partially hidden under red widows' veils. Doubtless, they had both lost the same husband. The third woman was younger, the daughter-in-law of the older two, John guessed. She, like most of the married women at the Harvest Festival, was obviously too poor to afford silver wedding rings. Instead, her fingers were banded with black tattoos.

Her voice rose in a pure clarity, striking notes as if she were ringing bells. Beneath her song came the constant, rhythmic slap of the flatbread cakes striking against palms. The three women worked in harmony, singing and pounding out the cakes, tossing them easily onto a thin sheet of heated metal and then flipping them up to the narrow counter where the vendor stood.

They sang of the Samsira River and the spring floods that fertilized the fields of Amura'milaun. John found the song beautiful despite its simplicity.

"Yellow honey cakes!" a man called out. "Fresh and sweet!"

His voice hardly carried over all the other vendors' cries. Countless tents, wagons, and stalls wound around each other, creating their own billowing bright streets. The Harvest Fair grew up like a second brighter, louder city outside the gates of Amura'taye. Crowds of people had come from all across the north to sell, buy, and gawk at the exotic goods of the farthest lands.

Hundreds of strangers moved around John like a living liquid, surging forward, rocking back, spilling into narrow spaces between wagons, then flowing back into the constant push and brush of bodies. Every human and animal odor washed over him and seeped through the scents of flowers, perfumes, fruits, and foods. The voices of hawkers cut through one another, only to be lost under the constant roar of the crowd. Children's squeals and screams split the air, as did the shrieks of caged birds and the bleats of agitated goats.

And yet, the music somehow carried through it all. It became a delicate stream of order flowing through the rolling chaos. As John walked further into the din of shouts and murmurs, he could still pick out the voices of the three women.

Only when John left the avenue of food and flower vendors did he lose the thread of their song.

He stood in a new maze of merchants that appeared to be dedicated to textiles and jewelry. Bolts of embroidered cloth and long swathes of delicate lace hung from racks. Strings of glass beads and beaten metal charms lay in heaps on tables. He wondered if he was getting any closer to where he should have been: Binders' Row.

None of the ushvun'im were supposed to travel outside the monastery alone, particularly not when they would be exposed to the delights and temptations of gambling tables and dancing girls. Before any of them had been excused to attend the Harvest Fair, they had been assigned partners. John had known better than to hope that Ravishan would be his. Ravishan's earlier transgression and his recent disappearance had inspired Dayyid to designate himself as Ravishan's partner for all three days that the priests were allowed to attend the Harvest Fair.

Hann'yu had requested John's company and Dayyid had agreed offhandedly. However, the moment they had reached Amura'taye, Hann'yu had simply wandered off, saying he would meet John in the Binders' Row after fifth bell. John hadn't minded at first. He could keep himself entertained easily enough. But soon he realized that without Hann'yu, he couldn't let Dayyid see him, and that meant that he couldn't see Ravishan either.

Twice already he'd been forced to duck into a tent to avoid Dayyid. And there were other ushiri'im, ushman'im, and ushvun'im at the fair as well. John didn't know any of them well enough to assume that they wouldn't report him to Dayyid. So John had spent the whole morning and most of the afternoon cagily scanning the gaudy crowds for dull gray Payshmura cassocks. Every time he glimpsed an approaching pair of his fellow priests, he was forced to plunge deeper into the crowds or hide in random tents. The situation had infused John's entire morning with a paranoid and furtive feeling of criminality.

Now, with fifth bell finally approaching, he could not find the rendezvous point. Sighing, he pushed his way forward through the throng of packed bodies. He watched enviously as two barefooted children darted between a bearded man and his wives. They dashed ahead and ducked through the flaps of a tent. His own progress had to be slower and more gentle. He was too big to easily slip between people unobtrusively. Though, he had noted that people tended to move aside the moment they noticed his gray cassock and holy braid.

Among the poorer population, the deference was most notable. The women bowed their heads and drew back beside their husbands or brothers. The men often averted their eyes or held up their hands in the Payshmura symbol of peace. John returned the gesture and passed on.

As a family of raggedly dressed herders pulled quickly aside for him, John caught a glimpse of a party of silk-clad women moving through the crowd. Their skirts were all made from the same shimmering swathes of green silk—the vivid color worn only by the Bousim family. John quickened his pace. He guessed that he looked particularly intimidating moving fast and with obvious intent. Young mothers jerked their children out of his way and men stepped aside. Only a few seconds later, he had caught up to Lady Bousim's entourage.

Pivan and his commander, Tashtu, both strode at the head of the large group. Their deep green uniforms looked crisp, and the silver emblems of their rank and honors gleamed from the straight collars of their jackets. Polished pistols hung from dark leather holsters at their hips. Their black riding boots shone with the luster of oil and snakeskin.

Behind them, Lady Bousim walked slowly, seeming hardly aware of the crowds of awed farmers and herders. Her black hair was strewn with silver, emeralds, and pieces of polished jade. Her long flowing dress shimmered like nothing worn by any of the surrounding throng. The silver rings on her fingers and the silver chains linking them swung and chimed like precious bells.

Even as tall and blond as he was, John realized that he was not as out of place as Lady Bousim. Among the poor herders and farmers of Amura'taye, Lady Bousim's wealth and noble rank placed her absolutely beyond their grasp. One glance at her smooth skin, her deeply curved breasts and hips, her luxurious clothing and lustrous hair informed any onlooker that she had never toiled in a field or gone hungry through a hard winter.

She was lovely and unobtainable. Even standing among common men and women, walking the same tight confines, she was distant. Her armed guards kept people away with just a glance. Her maids encircled her, smiling and talking, moving constantly, so that the lady herself could only be seen in brief glimpses.

Beside Lady Bousim, both Inholima and Ohbi wore their glossy black hair in long twisting masses of braids and tiny silver beads. Pale, translucent green veils floated over the long straight lines of their dresses. Laurie stood nearest to Lady Bousim, dressed just as Ohbi and Inholima were, but her platinum hair and pale skin lent her a radiance. The silver beads adorning her hair were nearly as long as Lady Bousim's. Strings of polished jade cascaded from her necklace down over her thin chest and shoulders.

Behind the women, John recognized Bati'kohl's round face and Rashan Mou'pin's startlingly vicious smile. Then there came another young rashan in a dark green uniform, and beside him, Bill.

Bill looked out of place with the other men. His pale skin appeared almost blue beside the tanned arms and faces of the rashan'im. His blue eyes looked like cut stones and his black hair spiked out from his face like strokes of ink. His slim body appeared delicate, almost girlish, in comparison to the thickly corded muscle of the rashan walking beside him.

At first, John thought that the rashan had slowed his pace to accommodate Bill, but then he noticed the limp in the man's step. The rashan laughed quietly at something Bill said and nodded.

Bill glanced up and immediately picked John out of the surrounding throng of onlookers and waved him over.

"Jahn," Bill said, "this is Alidas. Do you remember him?"

John regarded the rashan. He was younger than Bill but stood taller. His brown hair fell around his face, softening the sharpness of his jaw. He returned John's gaze with a knowing intensity.

"I don't think . . . " John said softly and then cut himself off as the man's features and his limp made a sudden connection. This was the rashan he had ridden behind that night on the Holy Road—the young man whose leg had been crushed beneath his fallen mount. He had looked so pale that night, like a corpse.

"You were to be Fikiri's attendant?" John asked, though he was sure of the answer.

The rashan smiled and nodded. "I didn't know if you would remember me. It was so dark when we met and so long ago."

"I saw you a few times after that, but you weren't well. I think you were sleeping most of the time," John said.

"I told you he'd remember," Bill said to Alidas. "Jahn doesn't forget much."

John didn't say anything to that. In truth, he had tried to forget as much about that night as he could. Before then, he had never seen men struggle, beat, and kill each other. He had never been responsible for a single life or death before that night. Involuntarily, he recalled the dirty face of the Fai'daum youth he had hidden. He had scrupulously avoided thinking of the entire matter, and yet he could still remember the boy's name: Saimura.

"I never had the chance to thank you," Alidas said. "Pivan says you saved my life."

"I don't know that I did that much—" John cut himself short, realizing that his words could seem insulting. It was Alidas' life, after all. "I'm glad that you were all right and that you've recovered," he added quickly.

"Recovered is a kind word for it," Alidas replied. "But near enough."

"We're going with the ladies to pick up some bolts of cloth for winter," Bill said. "Then we'll head back to the Bousim tents for a meal. I'm sure it would be fine if you joined us."

"I know Rashan Pivan would like to see you," Alidas added.

"And Fikiri should be meeting us there as well." Bill peered over his shoulder at the retreating backs of the rest of the Bousim entourage.

"I have to go to Binders' Row," John said. He didn't particularly want to see Fikiri. And he doubted that Fikiri wanted to see him. Still, it would be nice to talk with Bill and Laurie. "But after I'm done there, I should be free to come by. Seven bells?"

"That would be great." Bill took a half step back and bumped into a woman. She wheeled around about to hiss something at him and then went silent as her eyes fell on John. Immediately, she bowed her head and scurried deeper into the moving crowd.

Bill frowned after the woman and then eyed John. "Were you just declared scariest man at the fair, or did I miss something there?"

"It was probably just the Payshmura robes," Alidas remarked before John could explain. "You know what they say: the woman who crosses a priest steps straight into a fire."

"Sounds like something Rasho Tashtu would say." Bill gave a disgusted scowl and Alidas, too, displayed clear antipathy at the mention of his own commander. Then he glanced back through the clusters of people pushing past them. The Bousim entourage was nearly out of sight.

Alidas said, "We had better get going, or we'll never catch up."

Bill nodded. "But we'll see you later, Jahn?"

"Seven bells. I'll be there." John started to step away from them, but then paused. "You don't happen to know where Binders' Row is, do you?"

"Keep following this street south." Alidas pointed along the rows of cloth vendors. "You'll pass the leather tanners, then the binders."

"Thanks," John said.

"Tell me if you find any good books," Alidas commented. "I haven't had a chance to look yet."

"I will." John watched them go. It was strange to see Alidas, as tanned and muscular as he was, gripping Bill's slim shoulder for balance as they walked. An instant later, strangers closed in around them and John continued on his way.

He reached Binders' Row in a little under half an hour. Distantly, he could hear the city bells of Amura'taye ringing out the fifth hour. The sun was slipping from its blazing summer zenith. This far north it would still be a while before darkness, but at least the heat was beginning to relent.

The smell of leather hung over the two short corridors of wagons and wooden stalls that made up Binders' Row. Booksellers sat or leaned under the shade of their stalls, most of them quietly reading passages from their own merchandise. It wasn't a busy area. Only a few men and boys passed by John. None of them made eye contact with him or each other. John didn't see any women. It reminded him a little of his walk through Candle Alley.

"And a thousand bulls were tithed by the Lisam gaunsho to the Black Tower," an old man read slowly and solemnly as John walked past. "And the lands of the south were blessed a thousand times over by Parfir. In blossoms and fruit, in boundless fields of white taye and red, Parfir gave his holy blessings."

John leaned into the stall, peeking over the narrow shelves of books to search for Hann'yu. There was no one inside, so he walked on.

As he wandered farther along Binders' Row, the readings began to stray from purely religious works. He overheard passages that sounded more historical in nature, then those of technical works. John caught the partial descriptions of a miraculous steam engine, new printing presses, and the brilliant street lamps of Nurjima. Then he began to pick out hushed murmurs of "bare fingers, full breasts" and "red lips, sweet as nectar." Just once John caught a whisper of the word, "Fai'daum."

John paused, trying to locate the man who had said the name of the Fai'daum; even after a few minutes of listening, he didn't hear the name of the group again. Instead the air hummed with low murmurs of hushed longing and erotic desire. John continued his search.

At last, John caught sight of Hann'yu's gray cassock and black coat. The streaks of silver that twisted throughout Hann'yu's eight braids were hidden by the deep shadows of a covered stall. He stood, eyes half-closed between shelves of books, listening intently. His expression was gentle and appreciative, like a man hearing exquisite music.

The bookseller looked about thirty. He sat on a tall stool with the small leather book across one of his legs. He glanced up as John stepped into the stall but didn't stop reading.

"As she lifted the hem of her skirt to step across the stream, I caught sight of her dainty white ankle." The bookseller flipped the page. "I knew at once that she was no mere milkmaid as she claimed."

John supposed he should have predicted that he'd find Hann'yu in this section of Binders' Row.

"I've been looking all over for you," John whispered.

"What?" Hann'yu turned and swayed, then squinted at John. "Oh, Jahn. You should listen to this. Receive the wisdom of the more worldly . . . world." The thick, honey-like scent of mead poured off his breath.

John didn't find it unpleasant, but it struck him as too strong for so early in the day. He asked, "Are you drunk?"

Hann'yu frowned, as if he were concentrating on a difficult algorithm, and then slowly nodded. "It's really the only way that I get through the Purification Ceremony with Dayyid."

"Ceremony?" John couldn't recall any mention of a ceremony. "When?"

"Tonight." Hann'yu made a sour face and then turned his attention to the man reading. He made a quick gesture, and in response the man lifted his book to display the title embossed into the leather spine. *The Journey from Innocence.*

"You'd think, with such fine literature as this, that more boys would be interested in reading even in a cold, ugly wasteland like Amura'taye." Hann'yu paused, then added, "Especially in a cold, ugly wasteland like Amura'taye."

John waited for something more, but Hann'yu had fallen silent. He rocked back slightly and John realized that he was again listening to the reading.

"Her pink-tipped fingers worked apart the buttons of her wet blouse," the reader softly intoned.

"You say Dayyid is holding a ceremony tonight?" John prompted.

Hann'yu nodded, but offered no further explanation.

"What kind of ceremony?" John asked. "Is there something special we'll be expected to—"

"No," Hann'yu cut him off. "All we'll be expected to do is remain silent. Say nothing, do nothing. Just watch like corpses."

It wasn't a reassuring turn of phrase. John whispered, "But what exactly—"

"Hush." Hann'yu held his hand up in front of John's mouth. "This is a sweet story. We shouldn't ruin it. Just listen."

Hann'yu closed his eyes and John relented. He waited while the man on the stool read on to the end of the story.

The milkmaid turned out to be a noble girl fleeing an abductor. The hero was revealed to be her intended husband in disguise. Everything tied up at the end and finished with the passionate couple still in perfect moral standing. It wasn't much to John's taste, but Hann'yu seemed to enjoy it.

"Eloci Nass'ilem." Hann'yu smiled fondly. "She wasn't allowed to write nearly enough in her time."

"Yes, it sounded interesting," John said automatically. "But what is the Purification Ceremony for?"

Hann'yu gave John a weary look. "Don't look so concerned, Jahn. The ceremony won't begin until the last hour of the day at twelfth bell. There's nothing you'll be expected to do but chant and look holy. Nothing you need trouble yourself over."

"If it's nothing to worry about, then why are you getting so drunk?" John asked quietly.

"So drunk?" Hann'yu smirked. "You have no idea. You'll wish you had a whole vat of wine in you later tonight. It's the only good excuse a priest can claim for a weak stomach."

The man who had been reading watched them for a few moments, but then looked away as John caught his gaze. He flipped through the pages of the book on his lap but didn't begin reading again. John wondered how common it was for a pair of priests to be seen arguing in one of these bookstalls.

Hann'yu pulled a book out from the shelf and gave it to John. He chose another for himself. John looked down at the slim volume Hann'yu had given him. A circle enclosing a tree was embossed on the cover, but there was no title. John turned it over in his hands. The spine was bare.

"*Poems from Milaun*," Hann'yu supplied the title. "Even Dayyid couldn't complain. Well, I suppose he could, but not much."

Hann'yu took his book and approached the bookseller. John followed him to the front of the stall. Hann'yu passed the man two black-lacquered coins. One side was etched with the image of a tower, the other with gold sun.

"Thank you for coming so far from civilization and reading so well," Hann'yu said. "We will take these two."

The man smiled at Hann'yu and handed the coins back. "The compliment of Parfir's blessing would be a greater payment than any other."

"Of course." Hann'yu drew a small polished stone from the pocket of his cassock and placed it in the man's palm. "May Parfir protect you in the darkness of his sleep and lavish you with joy upon his waking."

The man lowered his head and remained bowed until after the two of them had left his stall.

As they worked their way through the rest of the Harvest Fair, John discovered that this was a routine interaction. Earlier in the day, he had been so focused on avoiding other priests that he hadn't watched them make any purchases. Now, with Hann'yu, he realized that they never really paid for anything. Hann'yu either gave out blessings and polished pebbles or lacquered wooden coins. Many of the vendors' wagons displayed large dishes of the polished stones. Others hung strings of the black coins above their entryways.

Hann'yu paused against the side of a seed-seller's wagon.

"We should find a wealthy merchant or one of the city judges to invite us into one of their tents," Hann'yu said.

"Not necessary. I've already been invited to the Bousim tent."

"That's right. You were Fikiri's attendant." Hann'yu grinned. "That's better than I could have hoped for. We'll drink ourselves sick and pass out."

"I really don't think that would be a good idea—"

"Don't be so serious, Jahn." Hann'yu rolled his eyes.

"I wouldn't be, but I'm not entirely sure you're joking."

Hann'yu sighed. "I would never embarrass myself or you in front of such esteemed company as Lady Amha'in'Bousim."

Knowing the kind of man Hann'yu was, John believed him. Hann'yu's warmth and reverence for noblewomen seemed innately ingrained in his nature. The presence of Lady Bousim would probably do more to encourage sobriety in him than anything John could do or say.

"All right. Let's go, then," John decided.

It didn't require much effort to locate the Bousim tents. They rose up in swooping emerald arcs behind the rows of flower sellers. Wealthy families of Amura'taye had erected tents for themselves as well, but none were as vast or as pleasantly placed. The natural perfume of cut blossoms and live flowers drifted over the heavier scent of tahldi hide and human sweat.

Rather than merely providing temporary relief from the sun, the main Bousim tent impressed John as a work of architecture. Massive carved timbers had been driven into the earth and secured with thick viridian-dyed ropes. The huge lengths of green cloth that stretched across the timbers were reinforced with worked leather displaying a pattern of the Bousim crossed arrows. Polished jade baubles hung from the timbers and lengths of silky green cloth, and silver bells were strung across the entry.

The four rashan'im who guarded the front of the great tent watched Hann'yu and John as they approached but didn't challenge them. As they entered, the faint sound of bells announced their presence. Inside, the air was cool. The tent's interior was suffused with an emerald glow from light passing through the cloth walls. Hann'yu's dark skin took on a pine tone. John imagined that his own pale hair had turned the color of a lime.

Aside from an open circle at the center of the tent, the rest of the floor was littered with low tables and embroidered cushions. Men wearing the badges of city judges, guild fathers, and scholars sat at the tables surrounded by their wives, unwed daughters, and favorite sons. Some glanced up as John and Hann'yu entered, but most seemed too engrossed in their conversations to take any note.

Every table was laden with dishes piled high with fragrant cut fruit or sliced meat. As he eyed these, John became suddenly aware of the absence of the flies and bees that had filled the open fairgrounds. He surmised that the veils of cloth and strings of bells over the entry weren't purely ornamental.

At the far end of the tent, Lady Bousim lounged with her maids and attendants. Two younger men were seated across from her. Their clothes, like those of the guild fathers, city judges, and scholars were well made and new. They wore clean, polished shoes instead of sewn goatskins or scuffed work boots. That alone marked them as better off than most of the people at the Harvest Fair. But compared to Lady Bousim and her entourage, they might as well have been peasants.

Lady Bousim looked up as John and Hann'yu approached. She gave John a gentle smile, but when she took in Hann'yu's face, her expression suddenly became radiantly happy. She stood.

"Please forgive me if I'm wrong, but you are the very image of Hann'yu Shim'arun of the Lisam House," Lady Bousim said.

"I never did the name service enough while it was mine." Hann'yu bowed smoothly and then straightened. "Now I am only Ushman Hann'yu."

Both Hann'yu and Lady Bousim turned expectantly to John. His grasp of Basawar etiquette was poor when it came to women, but he knew that it was rarely desirable for them to introduce themselves to unrelated men, particularly if the men were of a rank close to or higher than their own. Hann'yu cleared his throat quietly. Suddenly, John realized that they were waiting for him to introduce Hann'yu to Lady Bousim.

"Ushman Hann'yu, please allow me to present the benevolent Lady Amha'in'Bousim to you."

Hann'yu bowed a second time and Lady Bousim invited them both to sit and dine.

Once the formality of the introduction had been dispensed with, Hann'yu installed himself at the table across from Lady Bousim and the two of them immediately began discussing their native city of Nurjima. The two handsome young men who had been attempting to entertain Lady Bousim were all but forgotten. Hann'yu opened the book he had purchased and read a brief passage. Lady Bousim recited the passage that followed from memory. A classic of Basawar literature, John supposed.

He worked his way back to where Bill sat, just behind Laurie. He wasn't surprised to see that Alidas was seated there too. His right leg jutted straight out over a pillow in an awkward fashion. The maids and rashan'im all around Lady Bousim were talking to each other but with their voices lowered. The sound created a soft, almost insectile hum.

"You just missed Fikiri," Bill remarked.

"He brought me flowers." Laurie held up a small bouquet of red blossoms. "It was so cute. He ran off like a little kid right after handing them to me."

"I'm seething with jealousy," Bill said.

"I'm quite attracted to the bouquet myself," Alidas told Bill. "I would try to steal it, but I'm sure your wife would break my good leg."

Laurie snickered and lifted one tiny, white fist. "Yeah, watch out, Alidas. I'll take you out."

"If you keep bullying me like that, Behr is going to take pity on me, and you know where that could lead," Alidas murmured.

"Brutal fists of fury for you both." Laurie held up her balled fists and made a tiny jabbing motion.

"Is there anything you'd like to eat or drink?" Bill asked.

"Anything, really," John said. "But no wine. I'll just pass out."

Bill waved one of the Bousim serving girls to him. He ordered white taye cakes and roast lamb and blossom water.

"And spring cheese," Laurie added. "Be sure to bring a big block of spring cheese."

The servant girl nodded and slipped away.

"Did you find something in Binders' Row?" Alidas leaned forward slightly, as if to read the title of John's book.

"*Poems from Milaun*." John offered the slim volume to Alidas.

Alidas took the book and held it with reverence. He didn't flip through the pages as John had; rather, he treated them with care and read with interest.

"These are the old plains songs. You hear field women singing them in rounds when you ride through the southern countryside. They sing them in the kitchens as well." Alidas turned the page that he had been reading. "You can tell that some of them come from the apple orchards near Umbhra'ibaye because of the mentions of the bones. The Issusha'im Oracles are there, you know."

"Yes, of course," John replied. He was only half listening to Alidas.

He hadn't realized how tired he was until he sat down and relaxed. He'd been up since dawn, and the walk down from Rathal'pesha was always tiring. He noticed that a number of people had stretched out on the ground with their cushions propped under their elbows or beneath their heads. He lay back.

The green tent above him glowed like the underside of an immense leaf. John closed his eyes.

"Would you like me to read some aloud for you?" Alidas offered.

"Certainly," John replied. Laurie laughed.

"I think Alidas was asking the ladies, Jahn," Laurie whispered. John shrugged in reply.

Alidas' voice was soft as he read, and the cadence of the poem reminded John of a lullaby:

"Fine men may court you with silver and stone.
Spring blossoms will promise an autumn delight.
But bless us, our sisters of holy white bone,
Lest day break too swiftly and turn into night . . . "

Alidas continued reading, but John's thoughts lingered on the words of the first poem: *sisters of holy white bone.*

The existence of the Issusha'im Oracles seemed too strange to be believed. Living bones. They frightened him and fascinated him at the same time. Eyeless skulls somehow watching, searching, looking into the unknowable future. Yet Ravishan's sister was one of them.

John didn't know exactly when he drifted into sleep. But his thoughts began wandering from the oracles to the great stone gateways that they commanded. With the Nayeshi'hala, they could tear apart the fabric of existence. John's dreaming mind created images of black holes ripping through the skies, tearing away color and light from the land the way a rupture in the hull of an airplane could whip away all life within. He shuddered in revulsion—as if those two lambs were once again dying in his hands and he couldn't stop it from happening.

John bolted upright.

The tent was darker, lit now by hanging oil lamps. More people had gathered inside. Many of them were in the open space at the center of the tent, dancing. John straightened his cassock. He could only catch glimpses of the people around him as they moved between the luminous oil lamps and the deep shadows of the night. Their bodies melted into one another, forming one swirling silhouette.

Music rose up from the far left side of the tent where a dozen musicians were gathered on a raised dais. John was a little surprised to see Bill among them, strumming an instrument that looked like an overgrown mandolin. Alidas leaned at the edge of the musicians' dais, watching Bill play. He held a small bone flute in his hands. John guessed that he, too, would be playing along with the musicians.

For a few minutes, John simply watched Bill play. In Nayeshi, he had never shown any aptitude for music. Or perhaps, he just hadn't shown any interest in it. He hadn't shown any interest in anything, really. He was the friend who everyone thought was smart enough to be outstanding in any field he chose, but who never made a choice. He had seemed content to do nothing but rent odd videos, memorize obscure, useless trivia, and wander through dance parties dispensing misinformation.

Now it was strange to see him so deeply focused and eager. John noted the way Bill's fingers slid and jumped along the strings. He could pick out the distinct tones of Bill's music as it floated through the surrounding pipes and drums. The purity and skill of it was obvious.

John searched the wide space of the tent for Laurie. He caught sight of her at the entry, nearly opposite him. She stood beside Ohbi, watching Bill. A moment later, she glanced to the pile of cushions where John had been sleeping. Seeing him awake, she waved and held up a small hunk of what looked like bread and began working her way around the edge of the crowded tent toward him.

John caught glimpses of her between the raised arms and turning bodies of the dancers. For a second, she dropped into a deep shadow and then emerged again, her pale hair gleaming in the lamplight. She wasn't far from him when, suddenly, a dark form seemed to melt out of the silhouettes of the dancers and jerk her back into the darkness. At first, John mistook it for a play of the flickering light.

But Laurie didn't reappear.

A sudden fear seized John. He rushed forward, brushing dancers and onlookers aside, hardly taking note of them as he raced along the edge of the tent.

He could feel some strange power radiating from within the curtain-like folds of the tent wall. It shimmered through the darkness like heat waves dancing across a desert horizon. It drew him.

John tore back one of the deep folds of the tent to discover Rasho Tashtu holding Laurie from behind in a tight grip. One of his thick arms crushed across her throat, while his other hand groped at her breast.

"If you don't let me go," Laurie hissed, "I swear I'll make you wish you were dead."

John knew she could and would. He could feel the fury and power emanating from her in waves.

"You need a little training." Tashtu's words were slurred. "A real man—"

John didn't let him get any further. He caught hold of Tashtu's hands and ripped them off of Laurie. She immediately bolted free.

"Who the hell do you think you are?" Tashtu roared. The alcoholic flush in his face looked almost black in the shadows of the tent. "Release me, peasant!" Tashtu snarled. "I'll have your head for this."

He attempted to jerk free but John held him, grinding his thumbs into the soft flesh of Tashtu's wrists. He wanted to snap the man's hands off. He wanted to feel the bones crack and the tendons tear. But Tashtu was too high-ranking in the Bousim house. Harming him would only end up endangering Laurie and Bill. John knew that, and yet it was incredibly hard not to keep twisting the man's arms, grinding into his bones.

John released him and Tashtu stumbled sideways.

John glanced back to Laurie. Her jaw was clenched, her lips pressed tightly closed as if she were fighting to remain silent. Her pale eyes looked unnaturally bright. Her entire body trembled, but John didn't know if it was with fear or rage.

"Are you all right?" John asked.

Laurie managed a tight nod.

John caught a movement from the corner of his eye and turned in time to see Tashtu straighten. His hands were clenched into fists.

"Fucking priest!" Tashtu swung for him.

John blocked Tashtu's punch and then caught the man's throat in one hand. John's fingers felt hot as they closed around the supple muscles and delicate column of cartilage that encased Tashtu's trachea. John flexed his hand and Tashtu choked.

"I could kill you." John's words came out evenly, as if he was not seething with anger, as if it was a simple statement of ability and not a driving desire. He was so enraged that he could hardly think of anything else. His attention locked on the kick of Tashtu's desperate pulse against his palm.

Only slowly did he become aware of how quiet the tent had become. Distantly, he registered the circle of startled and fascinated men and women surrounding him.

Tashtu swayed in John's grip, his mouth wide open, his face dark purple. John instantly released him. Tashtu collapsed to the ground. This time, he didn't struggle back up. He lay, sprawled out and gasping.

John turned back to find Laurie, but she had disappeared into the crowd. John thought he saw her far back with the other members of the Bousim household, her face buried against Bill's chest.

"Interesting choice of entertainment, Ushvun."

John turned to meet Dayyid's unamused face. John opened his mouth to offer his explanation but then realized that Dayyid appeared to be in no mood to hear anything he had to say.

Chapter Thirty-Six

John hung back between Ravishan and Hann'yu as they trailed Dayyid back across the fairgrounds. In the depths of the night, John expected the stalls to have been locked up and the vendors to have bedded down. Instead, torches had been ignited, and oil lamps lit and hung. Fairgoers still packed the narrow avenues between the stalls, tents, and wagons. There were fewer children but far more men.

The smell of burning oils and strong wine wafted through every other scent on the air. The music that John picked out through the roar of fast bargaining and loud drunken voices was oddly slow. Smoky, sensual melodies curled out from the closed flaps of the tents they passed.

Dayyid glanced back over his shoulder at Hann'yu.

"I would have thought that you'd have remained sober enough to keep Ushvun Jahn from embarrassing himself in a common brawl."

Hann'yu grinned. A red, alcoholic flush spilled across his nose and cheeks. The strong smell of wine and mead clung to his breath. There was no denying that he had been drinking. But compared to Tashtu, Hann'yu only seemed slightly tipsy.

"It was hardly a *common* brawl." Hann'yu gave John a slightly lopsided grin. "That was a rasho that our Jahn took down. And the man had been mistreating ladies all evening. Jahn may very well have been acting as Parfir's wrath for the offenses. It was magnificent."

John glanced to his right to see Ravishan's reaction. So far he had been silent, keeping his eyes focused on Dayyid's back. Ravishan looked over to him at the same moment and gave him a brief, approving smile.

John imagined that an entire day spent with Dayyid had to be miserable and exhausting. He wished he could offer Ravishan some consolation.

"You would have been proud to see him move, Dayyid," Hann'yu continued. "It was like lightning. Something to put the fear of god back into the masses."

"Ushvun Jahn's prowess does nothing to excuse you," Dayyid responded coldly. "I shouldn't have to come and fetch you for the Purification Ceremony every year. If you had minded the hour and kept your eyes on Jahn, none of this would have happened."

"But as it was, Jahn saved a very pretty girl," Hann'yu countered.

"For all you know, she was one of the whores who follow the fair," Dayyid said.

"She was Jahn's sister." The playful tone dropped from Hann'yu's voice.

Dayyid glanced back, this time to John. John met his gaze. Dayyid's scowl seemed to soften. He turned his attention back to their path.

"Was she . . . is she unharmed?" Dayyid asked after several minutes of silence.

"I think so," John said.

Dayyid nodded and said nothing more.

They continued threading their way south through the fairgrounds until they reached the last wall that enclosed the terraced steps of Amura'taye. City guards, armed with archaic-looking bows and spears, stood on duty at the heavy gates. They bowed as Dayyid approached and remained bent down until John, Ravishan, and Hann'yu had all passed through the open gates.

Outside, John expected to only see the flat expanse of the Holy Road, the small shrine to Parfir, and the surrounding forest. Instead, he found that they had stepped out into a second fairground. But a single whiff of the air told John why this one was kept so far from the city.

The air was choked with the smells of blood, meat, excrement, urine, and fires. Makeshift pens held fattened goats, young sheep, and old gaunt tahldi. Dogs crouched together in cages. Coops of weasels hung from the eaves of wagons. Smoked and salted carcasses dangled from walls and over entryways.

Tahldi bellowed and dogs whimpered as they were dragged from their pens. Teams of sweating, muscular men wrestled the animals down. Butchers slashed open the animals' throats with fast, practiced strokes of their gleaming knives. Blood splashed and sprayed. Almost immediately, women and girls took over the work of skinning, gutting, and butchering the slaughtered creatures.

In the flickering red torchlight, the bodies of butchered animals seemed to melt into the blood-stained sweating forms of the men and women moving between them. Crowds of buyers shoved their way to the pens. They pointed and shouted out which animals they wanted, many demanding the same dog, goat, or sheep. Arguments seemed to break out constantly.

"You haven't been here before, have you?" asked Hann'yu.

John shook his head. He had tried to hide his revulsion at the vast, open-air abattoir, but Hann'yu must have noticed it.

"I was astounded the first time I came as well. I couldn't believe how many people were up and about this late. They don't even have proper lights." Hann'yu shook his head. "But the blood market is always busiest at night, when the air is cooler and there aren't so many flies."

John simply nodded. The fact that it was so busy at night hadn't really made an impression on him. His deep familiarity with the twenty-four-hour conveniences of Nayeshi made the idea of nighttime shopping unremarkable.

It was the way the blood and butchery seemed so routine, the straightforward brutal slaughter that shocked him.

"The night brings out its own kind of vermin." Dayyid threw a pointed look to the shadowy alcove between two wagons where a group of men seemed to be lounging. John wasn't sure what Dayyid was referring to. The men looked bored, but hardly like vermin. In fact, some of them seemed very well dressed. Then John saw a woman farther back in the shadows. The thick body of the man thrusting between her sprawled legs hid most of her nudity. Her thin arms absently clung to his back as she stared up at the dark sky.

Noticing John's stare, one of men waiting his turn lowered his gaze. Others shifted so that that John wouldn't see their faces.

"It wouldn't be half so bad if the girls were allowed to ply their trade indoors," Hann'yu said. "In Nurjima, the laws have been changed and the diseases—"

"This isn't Nurjima," Dayyid cut him off.

Hann'yu sighed and didn't make a reply. His amused energy seemed to be evaporating. His steps had grown steadily slower and clumsier as he continued walking.

John looked to see how Ravishan was responding to all of this. His expression was distant, his eyes still fixed on Dayyid's back. He didn't even seem to be listening to the conversation.

As they pressed through a crowd gathered around a bull calf, John very briefly allowed his hand to brush against Ravishan's. Ravishan's expression didn't change at all, but he grasped John's hand in a tight, almost desperate grip. John held his hand for an instant and then broke away before anyone could notice the exchange.

They continued working their way through the crowds until they reached the middle of the blood market.

There, two small braziers stood about four yards in front of the aged building housing Parfir's shrine. Other ushvun'im and ushiri'im had gathered outside the weathered wooden walls. John recognized Samsango and Fikiri among them. Samsango gave him a brief wave.

Dayyid stopped just short before the open doorway of the building and turned, scowling at Hann'yu. "You're sober enough to inspect her, I hope?"

Hann'yu nodded.

"Go on, then." Dayyid waved a hand at the shrine. "We don't have much time, so try to be quick."

Again, Hann'yu only nodded. His lips were pressed closed in a hard line. His face looked pale even in the warm red firelight. John wondered if he was going to be sick. Hann'yu took a deep breath and then walked into the shrine.

"My brothers." Dayyid raised his voice, addressing the rest of the ushvun'im and ushiri'im. "It is time to begin our prayers."

Immediately, the gathered men knelt in rows along either side of the doorway. They filled the entire space between the shrine and the two lit braziers, only leaving a narrow path between the two. John wasn't sure where he was supposed to sit. The ushiri'im seemed to have taken the spaces closest to the braziers. John guessed that he should be back farther with Samsango and the other ushvun'im. He began to go but Dayyid caught him by the arm.

"Harvest wines affect Hann'yu more than they ought to," Dayyid whispered. "When he's done in the shrine, make sure he doesn't come back out and embarrass himself in front of the ushvun'im. Wait for him by the door."

John strode quickly to the doorway and crouched down, leaning his back against the wooden frame. He had a terrible feeling about all of this.

The small flames in the braziers snapped and flashed behind Dayyid.

Dayyid remained standing, making sure that all of the men were properly spaced and solemn. Behind him, Ravishan also stood, waiting. When Dayyid turned and strode to the closest fires, Ravishan followed him.

Dayyid raised his hand, signaling the prayer with a quick motion of his fingers. Instinctively, the words came to John, as they did to the priests surrounding him. The low, deep invocations rolled from them like a sudden flood. Their voices washed through the air, engulfing the cries of animals and drowning the noise of commerce.

Behind him in the darkness of the shrine, John thought he could hear a faint sound, a whimper. He turned his head just slightly to look back into the dark chamber. Inside, five city guards stood circled around Hann'yu and the naked girl he knelt over. One of the guards absently toyed with the head of a sledgehammer. Another held a small lamp out over Hann'yu. Its light cast Hann'yu's face in shadow but burned into the girl's features.

She was young, probably still in her teens. Her head had been carelessly shaved. Dirt and scabs mottled her bare skin. She tossed her head and cried out, but a tight leather gag muffled her voice. Her scraped, bruised arms were bound back behind her. The guards held her legs apart as she struggled to pull them closed.

"Well?" The guard's voice hardly carried over the waves of chanting that enveloped John. "Has she got a whelp in her, or not?"

Hann'yu glanced up at the man. His skin looked deathly pale as it caught the light. He lowered his face again before he spoke. "No, she isn't carrying a child."

"Then it's the fire for this bitch." The guard holding the lamp grinned. "Ring the bell."

Hann'yu didn't look at any of the guards, but simply walked away from them as if he were half-asleep. He reached the doorway of the shrine but didn't come out. Instead, he slumped down to the floor and pressed his forehead against the wall. His eyes were clenched shut, but tears still dribbled down his cheeks. He clamped his hands over his mouth to cover the sound.

John looked away as a brassy bell clanged overhead.

Ahead of him, men and women from both fairgrounds were gathering. More city guards arrived, leading tahldi hitched to wagons bearing wood, kindling rags, and oil.

He could hear the girl whimpering and moaning behind him as he watched the unlit pyre steadily growing in front of him. He tried to imagine what he could do to free the girl. But there were too many guards. Even if he could overpower all five of them, then what would he do? There was nothing.

Women from the city threw bundles of dried herbs and flowers into the heap of kindling. Many of them knelt and added their voices to the prayers of the priests. The men seemed less solemn. Several youths passed drinks among themselves and exchanged jokes with the guards building the pyre.

John closed his eyes and chanted along with the priests around him. He all but shouted the words out, drowning out the pathetic noises of the girl behind him and the laughter of the gathering crowds of men.

"Let the flames shine," he called out, "and this darkness will be consumed. It will not share your breath, holy Parfir. It will not touch your flesh. It will not taste your sacred blood. It will burn away from you and never have shape again."

The prayers went on. John had recited them before. He had practiced them with Pivan and Bati'kohl here in the shrine. He had recited them almost daily in the monastery. He had known them for years, but he had not understood them.

A sacred fire, parting shadows from forms—it had seemed so abstract. But it wasn't. A genuine pyre was being built in front of him and it was a real girl who they would strip of her living form.

John glanced back to Hann'yu. He lay on his side now, his face buried in his arms. John guessed that he had passed out and envied him.

Dayyid stood, overseeing the construction of the pyre. There was a focused intensity to his expression. The light from the two braziers gleamed over his long black braids and glowed in his eyes. He chanted, his low strong voice carrying over all the rest. He held an unlit torch in one hand.

Ravishan knelt beside Dayyid with his head bowed, his loose black hair hiding his face. Fikiri sat a little further back among the rest of the ushiri'im. He stared out past the pyre into the gathered crowd of townspeople, tradesmen, and city guards. His mouth barely moved with the words of the prayers.

John heard the squeal of a hinge from behind him, and then the five city guards marched out of the doorway, dragging the girl between them. She sobbed and made pleading noises around her gag. The fingers of her bound hands were swollen, black, and horribly bent back. Her legs scraped the ground like broken branches as the guards dragged her past the line of priests.

Dayyid held up his hand to end the prayers. All of the gathered ushvun'im and ushiri'im went quiet. The city guards stopped in front of Dayyid, lowering the girl to the dirt at his feet.

"Unholy creature." Dayyid glanced down at her for only an instant. "You have been found barren of even Parfir's smallest blessing. Once, he fed you with his own flesh, quenched your thirst with his very blood. He brought you the abundance of summer and gave you shelter in winter. You knew only his kindness and yet made yourself like a poison to him. You gave yourself to his enemies as a whore gives herself to greed.

"You have so defiled the blessings that he placed upon your flesh that even your woman's womb is a place of desolation."

The girl's mouth worked around the gag, making the motions of denials and pleas, but only choked animal sounds came out. Dayyid scowled down at her, then glanced to Ravishan. At first, Ravishan simply remained where he was, head bowed, arms hanging limply. Then he stood. He didn't look at the girl. Instead, he stared at the small clay pot in his hand. There were markings on it, little gold suns and silver moons.

"Unholy creature," Dayyid began again, "you have fouled yourself beyond repentance or redemption. You have refused his love and now you can only know his wrath."

Dayyid stepped to the side as Ravishan spilled the glistening contents of the jar over the girl. It was lamp oil, John realized. The city guards heaved her back up off the ground and dragged her to the pyre. With a swing, they hurled her onto the low mass of oil-soaked wood, sticks, and flowers. In a panic, she tried to get to her feet. Her broken legs collapsed under her. She flailed and jerked, trying to push herself off of the kindling. Her motions only seemed to tangle her further in the broken wood and slick oil.

"Do not pity her!" Dayyid shouted over the girl's howls. "Evil feeds on honest men with teeth carved from pity!" Dayyid turned and handed his unlit torch to Ravishan. "Look upon her and do not flinch. Her despair is Parfir's triumph. Make yourself worthy of him."

Ravishan took the torch. His face was nearly expressionless. John could see the muscles of his throat working, swallowing back sickness. He lowered the torch into the brazier on his right and then into the one to his left. Flames immediately rushed up the torch. Ravishan stepped up to the pyre. The girl screamed at the sight of him, the sound coming out like the raw shriek of a crow. Ravishan lifted the torch. His arm trembled but then he steadied it.

John clenched his mouth shut. His hands curled into tight fists. He didn't want to see this and yet he couldn't make himself look away.

Ravishan leaned forward slightly and touched the flame of his torch to the pyre. It was a graceful motion, almost a bow. Flames gushed up over the oil-soaked wood. The girl screamed again. This time it was a purely animal sound of agony. Ravishan stepped around the pyre and lit it again and again, until it was engulfed in flames. Black billows of smoke churned up against the much paler night sky. Then the air began to fill with the smell of burning hair and flesh.

Cheers rose up through the gathered crowd. Somewhere farther back, someone was playing a happy melody on a flute. People were laughing.

Ravishan stood in front of the pyre as the flames gushed and hissed outward. His face was like a corpse's. His dark eyes were wide, staring into the writhing fire. John could see droplets of oil spattering down from the torch in Ravishan's hand. He didn't flinch from them.

Revulsion and sorrow welled through John. He wanted to be sick, to cry or rage. Anything to exorcise the horror in him. Anything to get it out. But none of those courses were open to him. He closed his eyes and simply dug his fingers into the hard-packed earth beneath him.

Above them, the sky split with a massive crack of thunder. Then a heavy, hard rain began to pour down on them all.

Chapter Thirty-Seven

Most of the ushiri'im and ushvun'im took shelter from the pounding rain in the shrine. Others fled with the crowds of men and women. All around, people scattered, rushing back to the cover of their wagons and stalls or running farther to their homes in the city. Lamps and small fires died out. But the burning pyre only snapped and hissed in the face of the rain. Flames floated on thin slicks of oil and dribbled down the heaps of wood. The heat of the pyre seared the rain to white steam.

John felt the earth slowly softening beneath him. His fingers curled through the mud. Slivers of lightning splintered through the smoke-blackened sky. Thunder crashed. The music and laughter of a few minutes ago had changed to shouts and curses as lamps guttered and people tripped. Farther back in the blood market, John thought he could hear an old woman shouting. Someone had crashed into a pen and knocked the gate loose. John glimpsed escaping goats bounding between clusters of human bodies.

In the midst of it all, Ravishan stood, still staring into the flames of the pyre. Rain beat down on him, plastering his black hair to his face and drenching his clothes. The flame of his torch crackled, spit sparks, and then went out with a hiss. He remained, the firelight of the pyre illuminating his dark form.

John got up. He expected to slip in the mud, but the ground felt oddly firm beneath his feet. He walked, hunching against the pounding rain, to where Ravishan stood shuddering from the cold. His eyes were like black chasms against the bloodless white of his face. His jaw was clenched so tightly that John could see the muscles bulge and tremble.

"You need to get out of the rain." John gently took the dead torch from Ravishan's stiff hands and let it fall to the ground. "We can't just stand here all night," John said firmly. He grabbed Ravishan's hand and started for the city gate. Ravishan didn't resist him, but he didn't throw himself into action either. He followed John in clumsy, stumbling steps. The normal grace of his motions seemed utterly lost.

John led Ravishan past floundering drunks, through the city gates and up along the now nearly deserted avenues of the Harvest Fair. John tried to think of a place to shelter. He certainly wasn't going to turn back and join Dayyid and the other priests in the shrine. The church hostel in the middle of Amura'taye, where they would have slept, was too far. And in any case, John didn't know if he could stomach any more sanctimonious exchanges with the other men who would be staying there.

Briefly, John considered taking Ravishan to the Bousim tents, but he hadn't left there under the best circumstances. The last thing he wanted was to get into another fight with Tashtu or the rashan'im who served under him.

The surrounding tents and stalls were crowded with people taking shelter from the rain. Men bumped and pushed each other, trying to get further under the cover of eaves. Women huddled close, keeping the few children still awake protected between them.

John headed for the city proper, but once they arrived he found that he had no more idea where to go than he'd had when they'd left the shrine. Dozens of streets shot out between countless hunched buildings. He looked to Ravishan for guidance.

"You know this city better than I do. Where should we go?"

Ravishan stared at him blankly, not seeming to understand his words.

"I'm getting soaked here, Ravishan," John prompted.

"The hostel in the Carvers' District." Ravishan pointed to the road to their left.

John nodded and started down the muddy street. He doubted that he needed to lead Ravishan by the hand any longer, but he didn't want to let go of him, either.

The hostel was a small wooden building with a reed-thatched roof and an outdoor toilet. Because it was the Harvest Fair, few rooms were available. The man at the door seemed relieved when John told him that he and Ravishan could share a room. John gave the man three wooden coins and a polished blessing stone. While the man didn't look too pleased with the payment, he didn't argue about it either. He accepted John's quick blessing and handed him a cut-tin key.

The room was hardly more than a closet with several blankets and a straw-stuffed mattress on the floor. It was dark with a pungent scent reminiscent of a stable. There were no lamps or even candles. After John closed the door, he had to wait for his eyesight to adjust.

Once inside, Ravishan just leaned against the door, wet and miserable and seemingly unaware of how violently his own body shivered.

"You should get out of those clothes," John said. He winced at the words as he said them. It sounded like some kind of cheap come-on. John supposed that if Ravishan hadn't looked so pathetic and if the evening hadn't been so utterly ugly, it might have been.

As it was, John simply turned his back and quickly stripped off his own soaking clothes. He took one of the blankets and wrapped it around himself.

When he turned back to hand the other blanket to Ravishan, he found that Ravishan still wore his wet cassock. Some color had come back into his face and a blush was spreading across his cheeks. His expression was a weird mix of arousal and misery.

John sighed.

"I don't think your clothes are going to drip dry anytime soon, do you?"

Ravishan flushed and then began pulling at his heavy cassock. His hands were still numb and clumsy from the cold. The sodden fabric slipped out of his grip.

John stepped closer and took hold of the dripping wool, saying, "Here, raise your arms."

Ravishan quickly lifted his arms over his head. John pulled the cassock up and off him. He tossed it into the pile with his own clothes. He'd worry about getting them dry later. For now, he concentrated on Ravishan.

The thin white material of the undershirt and pants was plastered to Ravishan's body. The wet fabric did nothing to hide the deeply tanned expanses of Ravishan's lean chest and muscular legs. Even in the dimness of the room, John could see the dark hair of Ravishan's chest and the way it tapered into a fine line leading down to his groin.

An instinctive flush of desire surged through John. His skin felt suddenly much hotter. John forced his thoughts past it. The night had already been too desperate and repugnant. Ravishan was a stunned, shivering mess. The last thing he needed was a seduction. John doubted he was up to it himself.

He quickly untied the knotted laces of Ravishan's pants. Then he straightened and stepped back. Ravishan could handle the rest for himself. Once Ravishan had undressed, John handed him a blanket, which he wrapped around himself. His black hair was beginning to dry and curl just slightly.

He looked like he could have been some young, biblical prophet draped in shadows and flowing cloth.

"Are you tired?" John asked.

"I don't know. I think I am but I don't feel—" Ravishan cut himself off. "I don't want to go to sleep."

"I don't either," John said. His own mind was in too much turmoil to sleep. Still, his body ached with exhaustion and hunger. There was nothing to eat, but at least he could get off his feet. John sat down on the mattress. Ravishan joined him. Despite the dousing of rain, the smell of smoke and roasting meat still clung to both of them.

John didn't want to think about it. And yet each time he tried to think of something to say, his mind was overwhelmed with the image of that girl, struggling, shrieking as she burned. He didn't know if merely witnessing an atrocity could harm a man, but it seemed that way.

Somewhere in him there had been a self-image of a man who was brave enough to suffer for his convictions. A man who would not stand by as a girl was murdered in front of him. Now revulsion and recrimination were eating that ideal away.

He glanced to Ravishan. He knew it was a double standard of the deepest affection that kept him from applying the same expectation to Ravishan. He wouldn't have wanted Ravishan to fight to save the girl. He wouldn't have wanted Ravishan to die for her.

"I can't think of anything to say," Ravishan whispered. "I can't stop seeing the fire."

"You did what you had to."

"I know," Ravishan replied far more easily than John expected. "She murdered her husband's first wife. She misused the power that Parfir had entrusted to her. But . . . "

John frowned. The revelation that the girl was a murderer herself shouldn't have mattered. It didn't justify her brutal treatment. But it seemed to make it easier for Ravishan to accept.

"I don't know why, but this entire day I've felt like I was eight again. I felt like I did when my mother burned, like a stupid little child who couldn't do anything." Ravishan's voice choked. He lowered his head so that his loose hair hid his face. "I haven't thought about her or my father in years. I don't know why now . . . " Ravishan wiped the back of his hand across his face. He kept his head lowered. "I think I always knew they were criminals, but they weren't bad. They never hurt anyone. There was even a big, golden dog. Nobody tried to kill her or cook her. They were people who never hurt anyone . . . Damn it, I'm babbling like a baby." Again Ravishan wiped his face. He drew in a deep breath. "How am I going to be Kahlil when I can't even burn a witch?"

"You did burn her." The words came out with a flatness that John wasn't used to hearing in his own voice. Ravishan didn't seem to notice it.

"But I didn't want to," Ravishan said quietly as if it were the worst confession. "It made me feel sick, like they were making me burn my mother again."

"They made you burn your own mother?" It seemed too horrible to be true. Even as he asked, John knew it had to be. It would have been the only act that could have proven Ravishan's loyalty to the Payshmura. It would have been the only way he could have saved himself and his sister.

"She was a traitor, a holy sister who turned to witchcraft. She aided the Fai'daum. The punishment had to be burning."

"And your father?"

"They shot him. I didn't see it, but Rousma did. She still has nightmares about it."

"I'm sorry," John said. He wished he could say something else, something that would make it all less terrible.

"It could have been worse." Ravishan shrugged and leaned back against the wall. It was an act of boyish bravado, an attempt to regain his composure. John could see that Ravishan's face was streaked with tears but he didn't say anything. Anyone else sitting in the darkness with him wouldn't have known.

"They were going to shoot me as well." Ravishan gazed up at the ceiling. "They had me on the ground with a gun right up to my head. But I moved."

"Through the Gray Space?" John asked.

Ravishan nodded. "Then Dayyid wanted to keep me alive to train me."

John leaned back beside Ravishan. "You've had a crappy life."

Ravishan looked startled for a moment and then laughed.

"Yeah, I have." He leaned his head against John's shoulder. John slid his arm around Ravishan and held him. "But it doesn't seem so bad right now." Ravishan closed his eyes.

John held him until he fell asleep.

Chapter Thirty-Eight

John awoke early. Thin predawn light seeped in through cracks between the planks of the walls. Ravishan's warm skin pressed against his own. Their legs and arms had curled around each other as they slept. John pressed his lips lightly against Ravishan's.

Slowly, Ravishan responded. He opened his eyes and smiled, still half-asleep. Lazily, he brushed a hand across John's chest. John leaned in to kiss Ravishan a second time, but then John's stomach let out a growl of hunger. John felt a small flush of embarrassment spread over his cheeks. "I haven't eaten since yesterday afternoon."

"And I smelled too delicious?"

"You are delicious," John replied.

"Am I?"

"Yes." He kissed Ravishan again, much more deeply this time. Ravishan leaned into him. John slid his hand over the edge of blanket that lay across Ravishan's waist. His fingers curled around it and he forced himself to uncurl them. Anyone could be outside that door. Listening. Maybe it was just paranoia, but he had a strange sense of being watched.

John drew back from Ravishan and forced himself to sit up. "We have to get to the church hostel before Dayyid notices that we're missing."

Ravishan groaned but sat up as well. "What will we tell him if he's already noticed?"

"The truth, I suppose," John said. "We picked the closest hostel we could find and got out of the rain."

John picked up his pants. They were cold and still damp from the night before. His undershirt and cassock lay crumpled together on top of his sodden wool socks and filthy boots. Ravishan's wet clothes flopped beside his own in a second, unappealing mound. Not for the first time, John wished he had access to a washing machine and dryer.

He sighed and pulled the pants on. A clammy chill slid up his legs.

"Dayyid probably spent all last night sharpening his razors for what little hair I've managed to grow out," Ravishan muttered.

"Maybe not? He wasn't paying much attention to you when we left."

"He always notices when I'm gone, and he's going to be in a foul mood. He hates to get wet." Ravishan scowled at his soaking clothes. "Right now, I'm not relishing the idea myself."

"I'd tell you that it's not so bad, but I'd be lying," John replied.

Ravishan took his own clothes and dressed quickly. John did the same. It did no good to draw out the unpleasant sensation of the damp cloth folding over dry, warm skin. And after a few minutes, John found that the heat of his body had at least warmed the wet clothes.

They left the hostel without even a nod from the man who had rented them the room. Now the man lounged in a chair beside the door, sleeping. John imagined he'd been up most of the night allowing drenched strangers in. John left the room key in his lap.

Outside, the sky was still dull and the streets were muddy. Little white seabirds clustered together under eaves of many of the buildings. No one else seemed to be up yet.

"If we cut through the Smiths' Rows—" Ravishan began then stopped and scowled at the countless rows of stone buildings before them.

"We cut through and . . . " John prompted.

"We'll run straight into one of the inner city walls." Ravishan shook his head. "I'm not used to traveling with someone who can't cross the Gray Space."

"Would it be better if you arrived alone?"

"No. If I was out with an ushvun, Dayyid might suspect I was up to some mischief, but if he thought I was alone, then he'd be sure," Ravishan said. "We'll just have to take the main road."

"He doesn't trust you much, does he?" John asked as they walked.

"Dayyid? Not even as far as he can throw me. But I'm his best chance for a Kahlil, so he can't afford to be rid of me." Ravishan glanced up at John and smiled. "Your braid is a mess."

"You're on the scruffy side yourself."

They walked up the slow incline of the main road. As they traveled, the gold edge of the sun began to rise. People awoke and began the first activities of the morning. The scents of cook fires drifted through the air. Wisps of smoke curled up from chimneys. The strong aromas of cooking meat floated out from the buildings.

It was normally a smell that John would have welcomed—the promise of a warm meal wafting on the cold air. But this morning the fresh memory of the girl burning on the pyre choked his appetite.

"Rousma says that the Issusha'im Oracles have almost found the Rifter," Ravishan said casually.

"Here?" John's thoughts jumped immediately to Laurie.

"Of course not. In Nayeshi. You think I'd be this calm if the Rifter were here?" Ravishan shot him a disbelieving look. "They could find him in a year or so. Then they'll have to send out the Kahlil."

"That's not too long," John said absently. A sweet, fruity scent rolled over him. Someone was baking apples.

Ravishan dropped his voice to a whisper. "It means we could be leaving for Nayeshi in a year."

"We might miss the next Harvest Fair."

"I wouldn't mind that a bit," Ravishan replied and he looked suddenly hurt and haunted. Ravishan needed the escape Nayeshi offered. Perhaps he needed it as much as John did.

As they walked on, the buildings they passed appeared better kept. John picked out shop signs hanging over freshly painted doors. A few blocks away, a street vendor called out that daru'sira and taye cakes were for sale. If they hadn't needed to reach the church hostel as soon as possible, John thought he might have hunted the vendor down. A taye cake would have settled his stomach. As was, they kept walking. John caught the voices of other street vendors offering more dishes and passed them by.

John could see the gilded silver dome and golden filigree of the church hostel a few blocks ahead of them. It was the only building in Amura'taye adorned with such extravagance. While the last few decades of crops and grazing lands had been stunted and sickly, the tithes the Payshmura church demanded remained high. With their massive holdings and wealth, the gaun'im could afford it, but most common men and women barely managed subsistence. With such blatant inequity, it was no wonder that the Fai'daum had come into being.

He wondered what Ravishan made of the Fai'daum. Before John could ask, Ravishan suddenly waved to someone ahead of them. Hann'yu rushed down the block toward them. As he came closer John saw that he was carrying a bundle of blue leaf cakes. The smell reminded John of sage.

"I've been looking for you," Hann'yu said. He smiled with obvious relief.

"Dayyid isn't already sending people out to find me, is he?" Ravishan glanced up and down the street with a hunted expression.

"I don't think so," Hann'yu said. "Are either of you hungry?"

"Starving," John admitted.

"Have some. They're best when they're still hot. A very kind woman made them for me, though I think she over-estimated my appetite." Hann'yu offered them the bundle of blue leaf cakes.

Both John and Ravishan helped themselves to the steaming, fragrant loaves. John ate his with a famished intensity. Once he had something in his stomach, he seemed to realize how hungry he really was. Ravishan smiled at him as he eyed the last cake in Hann'yu's bundle. Hann'yu, too, noticed John's attention.

"Have it," Hann'yu told him. "I've already stuffed myself on them."

"Thank you." John picked up the warm cake but years of Nayeshi etiquette stopped him from just devouring it. "Would you like half?" he asked Ravishan.

"Yes, thank you," Ravishan replied.

John handed him half the cake and they both ate quickly.

"I've found myself in something of a bind," Hann'yu said while John and Ravishan chewed. "I was thinking that the two of you might be able to help me out."

John simply nodded and took a last bite. Ravishan made an affirmative noise around his food.

"Last night, the rain woke me up and I saw the two of you leaving so I followed. I had thought we three could share accommodations but I lost my bearings before I even got out of the fairgrounds. I wasn't in the best state." Hann'yu gave John a slightly embarrassed smile. "In any case, a widow took pity on me and allowed me the shelter of her home since it was close."

"That was nice of her," Ravishan said. He took the last bite of his cake.

"She's a kind woman," Hann'yu replied. "But you can see my predicament. It looks bad if I return saying I spent the night alone with a woman. Dayyid might make a fuss over it. It would be a terrible way to repay the woman for her goodness."

Knowing so little of women, Ravishan seemed to accept Hann'yu's story with no apparent suspicion. But John suspected that Hann'yu might actually have something to hide. It wasn't just any woman who invited a strange man into her house and then who got up and baked him breakfast. Especially not in Basawar, where most women wouldn't have gone near a Payshmura priest for fear of offending him in some manner. Hann'yu plainly needed a cover story even more badly than Ravishan and he did. Their mutual corroboration could shield all three of them.

"Why don't we tell Dayyid that all three of us spent the night at the same hostel?" John suggested.

"That would be an excellent idea," Hann'yu replied.

"It's nothing." Ravishan shrugged. "If the weather hadn't been so bad, you probably would have been with us."

"Yes, absolutely," Hann'yu agreed. "The rain certainly came on suddenly."

John didn't know why, but a slightly guilty feeling crept through him at the comment, as if he were somehow responsible. Perhaps it was just that he had been so relieved that the storm had broken. If only it had come earlier.

They reached the hostel and found Dayyid. He seemed angry until he heard that Ravishan had not been alone. After that, he sent the three of them down to breakfast with a warning not to wander away before prayers. It went much more easily than John had expected.

He supposed that was because he wasn't used to having alliances. He was accustomed to thinking of himself as a lone foreign man set against the world around him. But he had friends now, and soon he discovered that he'd also gained a kind of respect.

He noticed it throughout the next two days at the fair when his fellow ushvun'im as well as several of the ushiri'im paid him passing compliments on his battle prowess. Samsango pronounced him Parfir's protector of all men's sisters. Ravishan grilled him about which holds he'd used to defeat a rasho so quickly. John noticed two other ushiri'im listening intently to his response, though Hann'yu looked immensely bored by the entire exchange.

After they returned to Rathal'pesha, the ushiri'im's interest in him only seemed to grow. Most of them already recognized him from the times that he treated them in the infirmary. But after the Harvest Fair, they seemed overtly friendly toward him. In the halls of Rathal'pesha, they greeted him casually and struck up conversations with him as they would never have conversed with the other ushvun'im.

Soon it became obvious that they wanted to test their own battle prowess with him. John agreed to it, so long as they fought without blades. It was a good excuse to see more of Ravishan. Dayyid couldn't criticize them for practicing battle forms together.

Familiarity with the ushiri'im gave John another advantage. They often allowed him into forbidden chambers, if he was walking with them. Slowly, over the course of several months, he gained access to room after room of Rathal'pesha's greatest heights.

Soon he was familiar with the barrack-like chambers where the ushiri'im slept as well as the small treasuries where relics from Nayeshi were housed. Locked cabinets held tattered white T-shirts, work pants, a baseball, and a wide variety of postage stamps. One glass case contained bills and coins from a scattering of years. The earliest John could find seemed to be 1935, but he didn't look too long or too intently. He wasn't supposed to be capable of reading any of it.

An ushiri named Ashan'ahma even pointed out that John's ignorance rendered his presence in the sacred rooms harmless. "It isn't as though he could carry our secrets to the Fai'daum. He can't read a word of the holy script."

Ravishan had added his agreement to Ashan'amha's and the matter had been settled among the ushiri'im. None of them mentioned it to Dayyid. They simply allowed John to go where he pleased.

The highest chamber both drew and repulsed him. It was like a scabbed injury that he wanted to forget about but always found himself scratching. When he stepped onto the stairs leading up he felt a change, as if the stones themselves had become infused with something terrible.

As he ascended, John heard voices. They were not the clear human sounds of the ushiri'im speaking through the Gray Space. These were quiet and strangely distorted, almost indiscernible. They piled over each other. They bumped and muttered through each other, building hundreds of tones, thousands of words. As John came closer, the voices grew louder but not more distinct. He only became more aware of the chaos of them. Their disjointed sentences crashed and jarred, hissed and murmured, like the ramblings of a hundred paranoid schizophrenics.

At the top of the stairs, the gray stones of the floor and walls seemed to have been infected with the same disorder. They were pitted and yellowed, like diseased teeth. The grain of the stones jutted in one direction and then abruptly broke into a different formation. Wisps of bluish smoke curled out from the edges of the single iron door in front of him. The smell of seared ozone mixed with an odor of taxidermy.

John stepped closer and placed his hand against the cold iron. A feeling of utter revulsion swept over him. He pulled his hand back. The same feeling had come to him from the yasi'halaun and from the broken stones of the Great Gate.

"The men in red ride south. We holds them back. Then men in red ride north. We cannot sees them. We cannot sees . . . "

John picked out one murmuring voice only to lose it in the hisses of another. "We sees the tower. Falling. The tower is falling. The tower falls. The tower burns . . . "

"It is near water. The water knows it, loves its flesh . . . "

"Blue eyes. We sees it. Yellow hair. Running. Dirty feet . . . "

"The convent burns. We smells our bones blackening. We smells us . . . "

"Traitors in the palaces. Gold and guns to the men in red. Traitors . . . "

Then a shriek suddenly broke through all of the soft whispers. "NO! IT HURTS! I HATES YOU! It hurts! It hurts, it hurts, it hurts . . . " Slowly the cry died to a whimper and then was lost in the depths of countless other murmuring voices.

"Quiet her, can't you?" This time the voice was distinct and familiar. It was Ushman Nuritam.

"Forgive us, Ushman." The response came from a strong, female voice.

"Rousma is young and still not broken into the collective of the Issusha'im. But her potential is great. She has given us our first glimpses of the Rifter."

Rousma. Ravishan's sister. She had sounded like a little child. It was wrenching to hear her in such obvious pain and yet John knew there was nothing he could do. She was one of the Issusha'im now, pared down to a skeleton, strung together with copper wires and carved with Payshmura incantations.

The Issusha'im were kept in the southern convent of Umbhra'ibaye, and yet it had seemed like they were just behind that door. There had to be some kind of gateway between the two places, here in the highest chamber of Rathal'pesha. He remembered Ushman Dayyid and Hann'yu both mentioning conversations with the ushman'im in the Black Tower of Nurjima. Perhaps there was more than one gate.

"I dislike her outbursts." Ushman Nuritam's harsh voice cut through John's thoughts.

"She will be reprimanded," the woman assured him.

"Very well. What of the Rifter?"

"Rousma has caught glimpses. We hope to bind him to the Kahlil within two years. That is, if a Kahlil has been ordained by then."

"He will be." Ushman Nuritam sounded slightly annoyed at the question. "The Issusha'im have seen as much, have they not?"

"What they have seen changes, Ushman," the woman replied. "You have heard them yourself. Since Fikiri'ro'Bousim survived his passage over the Holy Road, their visions have broken and altered. They have become divided even among themselves."

"And there is nothing to be done about it?" Ushman Nuritam asked, but his tone was more accusatory than questioning.

"The problem does not originate from the Issusha'im Oracles, Ushman." The woman's voice remained supremely calm. "They can only look into the future. They cannot alter it. That is the work of the Kahlil. Perhaps your question should be put to him."

"Yes, I'm sure it will be," Ushman Nuritam responded coldly. "But, for now, you can tell me nothing?"

"We can tell you many things, but none are certain and many are lies."

"Spoken like a true sister of the bones, Ushvran Polima," Ushman Nuritam said.

"I could hope for no greater compliment."

John heard Ushman Nuritam's derisive snort, but if the woman did, she made no response. The voices of the Issusha'im continued to mutter and mumble. John caught whispers of ruin and fires, the lost key, the demoness, the Rifter, and Jath'ibaye.

"If there is nothing more for you to tell me, then I will be going," Ushman Nuritam said after a moment. "I have no wish to further exhaust the bones."

"Of course," the woman responded. "Peace to you, Ushman."

"And to you, Ushvran."

Outside the door, John felt a sudden shudder of cold pass through him. He knew the feeling from witnessing the ushiri'im move through the Gray Space. The gateway inside the room had closed. The place went instantly silent. Then John heard Ushman Nuritam's footsteps slowly approaching.

"The greatest compliment, indeed," Ushman Nuritam muttered to himself.

John rushed back down the staircase. The ushiri'im might allow him into forbidden chambers, but Ushman Nuritam wouldn't so easily overlook his trespass.

He reached the hall a floor below and hurried back to the scroll room. He was supposed to meet Ravishan there after the next bell. It was a relief to escape the staircase and those voices.

Hundreds of small, deep nooks had been carved into the walls of the scroll room. Delicate silver grates hung from hinges over each one. Inside were dozens of cloth and leather scrolls enclosed in wooden cases. The writings here were older than the books in the library. The Basawar words were archaic and difficult for John to read.

But oddly, no matter how old a scroll was, the Nayeshi words it contained were always modern English. Ages passed between writings, but the Nayeshi that they described was always within the same few decades. It made John suspect that the Great Gates could only allow travel between a very limited area and age of Nayeshi. That was good, in that it meant he, Bill, and Laurie would be sent back to the same region. But it also brought up a far more troubling thought, one that John had never considered before: It was time as well as space that they would be crossing.

At first, John had hoped that each of the Kahlil'im's crossings into Nayeshi had progressed chronologically in Nayeshi history as they had in Basawar history—the first crossing into the forties, the second into the fifties, and so on. That would have ensured that he, Laurie, and Bill would return a few years after they'd left. But reading the scrolls, he had discovered that this was not the case.

The Issusha'im hunted the limited window of access that they had to Nayeshi. They searched back and forth, past and future. They accepted the first Rifter they could find. Then they cast a spell that bound the Rifter and the Kahlil together. That bond drew the Kahlil to the correct time and place.

That meant that whatever decade this new Rifter was living in, it would be the decade that Ravishan would be taking them into.

John drew out one of the scrolls. A perfume that almost smelled like cinnamon drifted off of it. The supple leather was familiar in his hands. He had looked over this scroll several times already, slowly deciphering the ancient script. Faded sepia images of flowers ran along the top of the scroll while skeletons knelt in prayer on the bottom. He read the first lines easily.

The holy bones, the Issusha'im Oracles, saw far and spoke the words of ruin. They spoke of the end of kingdoms, of the fall of those who had crafted them.

And so we called the blood of the seas and the breath of the air, the rage of fire and the strength of stone. We called Parfir to us and would have given him form, but it would not hold. For he was all life, land, water, fire, and sky. No body of this world could contain all his vastness. Only cut away, only wounded and severed, could he be captured in flesh.

And that flesh was of Nayeshi, near as the night, distant as the day.

And the world of Nayeshi held him, for it did not know him as god. And he did not know himself.

John felt the chill and heard the hiss of the Gray Space. He turned, expecting to see Ravishan. Instead, Dayyid stood frowning at him. John rolled the scroll closed.

"Already reading the divine history." Dayyid glanced at the scroll in John's hands. "Hann'yu said that you learned your letters quickly. I see that he was right."

"He's an excellent teacher," John replied offhandedly. He had no idea how Dayyid could find fault in any of this but he suspected that the ushman would try.

"Indeed." Dayyid gave John a piercing look. "I've heard the same said of you."

"What do you mean?" John asked.

"My ushiri'im seem to have taken to practicing battle forms with you." Dayyid watched John like a cat preparing to pounce on an unsuspecting robin.

"I think they just enjoy beating me." John returned the scroll to its case, then slid it back into its nook and closed the silver grate over it.

"I've been told that they rarely have that pleasure." Dayyid stepped up next to John. "In fact, none of them have bested you. Isn't that so?"

"I'm sure some of them have. They're probably just being modest." John wondered who had passed all this information on to Dayyid. It wasn't like one of the ushiri'im to brag about being beaten.

"Who's bested you?" Dayyid asked.

"I don't know," John replied as casually as he could with Dayyid staring so intently at him. "We've been practicing so much that I don't recall all the matches."

"When I asked, each of them told me that you had won every bout." Dayyid remained standing just a little too close. "Why do you think they would wish to lie to me?"

"I'm sure that none of them would have lied to you," John said quickly. Lying to Dayyid could get an ushiri whipped mercilessly. "We just practiced holds and defenses, so it's hard to say who's won."

"You seem to be the only one who is uncertain of the outcomes," Dayyid replied.

John sighed. A year ago he would have just bowed his head and apologized until Dayyid sent him away in disgust. But John didn't think he could stomach any more of that. It wasn't that his fear of Dayyid had lessened, but rather that his anger toward the man had grown.

There had been the beatings during his first days in Rathal'pesha. There had been the slights and only half-veiled insults; he'd constantly reminded John of his lowly rank. But none of that infuriated John as much as the memory of how easily Dayyid had condemned that girl to burn while knowing that Ravishan would be the one to take her life.

"I beat them." John straightened so that Dayyid had to look up to meet his gaze. "So what?"

Dayyid stepped back just slightly. His dark eyes narrowed, as if taking John in for the first time. Distantly, John heard the bells ringing out the new hour.

"Hann'yu is expecting me in the infirmary," John said. It was a lie that meant that he would miss Ravishan, but he couldn't stay in this room with Dayyid. He was too likely to lose control of his temper and lash out at the man. That wasn't something he could afford to do.

John walked out before Dayyid could make a response. It was one of the only times he had gotten in the last word. Not much of a victory, but John supposed it would be enough to enrage Dayyid.

At the moment he didn't care.

Chapter Thirty-Nine

Autumn passed quickly in Rathal'pesha, and deep winter soon settled over the monastery. John searched out work that would keep him clear of Dayyid. He had spent most of this day chopping wood for the fires and hauling casks of oil up from the storerooms. It had been dirty, tiring work, but at the end of the day he felt good, knowing he'd accomplished so much.

Now John gazed down from one of the raised walkways. Snow swirled past him. The empty grounds below appeared deceptively still and peaceful. Thick white drifts smoothed the stone paths and raised garden beds into a single flowing plane. The perfect white was broken occasionally by stone walls or the exposed branches of a dark pine. Just below him, smoke billowed from the kitchen chimneys like clouds.

"You're going to freeze out there," Hann'yu commented loudly from the shelter of the kitchen doorway two stories below. The two ushiri'im standing next to Hann'yu studied John. The shorter of them waved John over. He crossed the walkway and then took a staircase down to meet them.

All three men wore heavy wool coats and scarves. Their thick wool caps were pulled so low that their eyes were barely visible. It took John a moment to recognize Ashan'ahma. He could have been any of the ushiri'im in those clothes. Only the loose strands of his light brown hair and the sharp crescent scar that bit into his right cheek identified him.

Ravishan, however, John knew instantly. He had hit his last burst of growth this winter and now stood only a hand shorter than John himself. Of the rest of the ushiri'im and ushman'im, only Dayyid came close to Ravishan's height. Ravishan's summer tan had faded and the dark stubble along his jaw stood out clearly. Deep shadows showed beneath his eyes as well, a sign of the intensity of his training.

Now that the Rifter was so close to being found, Dayyid was working the ushiri'im relentlessly. At the center of Dayyid's attention was Ravishan, his best hope for a Kahlil.

Ravishan leaned against the doorframe, letting the building take his weight. His hands were loosely tucked into the pockets of his coat while his arms hung slack. No twenty-year-old should have looked so at ease with exhaustion.

Behind Ravishan John could see the oven fires flickering. He thought he smelled bread. Samsango must have started baking already. Normally he waited for John to join him.

John regarded Ashan'ahma, Hann'yu, and Ravishan curiously. The kitchens were one of the last places he expected to see any of the ushiri'im, much less two of them and an ushman. Hann'yu's mouth kept curling up at the edges as he tried to suppress one of his huge grins.

"Dayyid gave all three of you scullery duty?" John asked.

"He can be so cruel," Hann'yu said.

"If he had me cook, it would be more than cruel," Ashan'ahma said. "It could kill us all."

Ravishan simply yawned.

"So?" John asked. "What are you doing down here?"

"You'll never guess." Hann'yu was beaming.

"All right," John said. He waited a moment. "You're not going to tell me?"

"No, you have to try," Hann'yu insisted.

"You've baked Dayyid into a giant cookie which we will offer to the unsuspecting leaders of the Fai'daum?" John responded glibly. Both Ravishan and Ashan'ahma exchanged a brief smile.

"No. Where do you get these ideas?" Hann'yu shook his head. "I can't believe you can't guess. It's so obvious."

John frowned. What could be so obvious and yet elude him? Snow continued falling. The tops of John's boots were slowly being hidden under a layer of white.

"I have no idea," John admitted at last.

Hann'yu looked at him in disbelief. "You have no idea what might be special about today?"

"It's snowing?" John guessed. Hann'yu's exasperated look told him that he had given the wrong response. Then Samsango stepped out through the doorway. He wore only his undershirt and pants and his cheeks were still red from the heat of the cooking fires.

"With all respect, Ushman," Samsango lowered his head slightly to Hann'yu, "Ushvun Jahn is going to freeze to death if we keep him out here guessing all night."

Hann'yu sighed. "All right. But I can't believe you, Jahn. Such a sharp mind and then to miss something like this."

"I told you he wouldn't remember," Ravishan said. "We common people don't celebrate our births the way you gaun'im do."

A celebration of his birth, John thought, and then he suddenly remembered.

Today was the tenth day of the Snow Month, the day John had supplied to Samsango as his birthday. That had been years ago. It hadn't come up again and John had almost forgotten about it. The tenth day of the

Snow Month was nowhere near his real birthday. At the time, John hadn't been sure of the names of the summer months so he had simply chosen a date that he knew how to say.

"None of us are gaun'im any longer," Ashan'ahma said.

"A tree can never forget its roots," Ravishan replied. Then he glanced to Hann'yu. "We should get inside."

They hurried into the warmth of the kitchen. John pulled the door shut. When he turned back, he saw that the worktable had been covered with a cloth. Two bundled gifts were placed on it, as well as a pot of daru'sira and a platter of stuffed rolls.

"Goat cheese," Samsango said to John. "I'm afraid this late in the winter there wasn't much else to make them with."

"You shouldn't apologize," John said. "They smell delicious."

They all seated themselves. Ravishan dropped down next to John on the long bench. Ashan'ahma and Hann'yu sat across from them. Samsango remained on his feet, obviously unsure of where he belonged at the table. Normally, he would never have been allowed to seat himself next to an ushiri or ushman. He eyed the edge of the bench next to John, but it was too short for him to fit. John started to move, but then Hann'yu invited Samsango to sit with him.

"Jahn has spoken so highly of you," Hann'yu said.

"Has he?" Samsango looked almost bashful.

"He certainly has." For his part, Hann'yu seemed amused by Samsango's obvious awe. John could see why. Of the two of them, Samsango was certainly the more pious. "Jahn said you were originally from the Hishii Monastery."

"Yes."

"You must have come here before the fire."

"No," Samsango replied, "I was there when the Fai'daum burned it down. After that, the few of us who escaped fled to Rathal'pesha."

"The winter march," Hann'yu said. "I've read about it. I can't imagine how you lived through it."

Samsango looked a little embarrassed. But the attention had to be expected. Even John had heard of the winter march from Hishii. Over three hundred ushvun'im and ushman'im had started out, and fewer than twenty had survived. The mountain winter had been harsh and the Fai'daum relentless.

"Parfir was watching over me." He glanced to the steaming stuffed rolls as Hann'yu started to reach for one of them. "Perhaps we should have a blessing so we can eat." Samsango bowed his head.

"Yes, of course." Hann'yu drew his hand back from the rolls. John caught Ashan'ahma's grin at the exchange. John had only seen Hann'yu say a blessing on the most formal of occasions, when Dayyid or Nuritam was present. Otherwise, he was known for being lax.

"Jahn," Hann'yu said, "why don't you speak for us?"

"You should wake Ravishan up first," Ashan'ahma said.

"I am awake," Ravishan answered. His eyes remained closed and his head was bowed to his chest. Under the table one of his hands rested against John's thigh. Even through his cassock John could feel the heat of Ravishan's skin.

"I'll make it fast in case you nod off," John said quietly.

Ravishan frowned slightly but didn't open his eyes.

John bowed his head. "Holy Parfir, we thank you for your blessings and your bounty. From your sacred body you have fed us and given us shelter. You are with us always and we are forever thankful—"

"Well spoken," Hann'yu cut in. "Let's eat." He snatched up one of the rolls.

Samsango seemed surprised by this new abbreviated blessing, but he said nothing. Ashan'ahma helped himself to a roll, and then John took one for himself and handed a second to Ravishan. Samsango took one of the rolls as well but just held it, obviously watching for the others' reactions.

Hann'yu let out a groan of delight as he took his first bite. "This is delicious. These aren't the rolls we normally have, are they?"

"No, they're something I like to make for special occasions."

"I haven't tasted anything like this since I lived in Nurjima." Hann'yu sighed. "You could have been a private cook to a gaunsho."

"Delicious. Truly delicious," Ashan'ahma added. He took another.

Bald, weathered, and nearly toothless, Samsango still managed to take on the air of a starstruck girl as he beamed and blushed at Hann'yu's and Ashan'ahma's compliments.

John smiled and ate his roll. The bread was soft and simple, while the hot cheese inside burst with a subtle sweetness of toasted spices.

Ashan'ahma helped himself to a third with a look of slight guilt. Hann'yu had his second. Ravishan gazed at the roll in front of him, his eyes only half open. John imagined that he was assessing whether the sustenance was worth the effort of eating it. After a moment, Ravishan picked up the roll and ate.

"It's good," Ravishan said.

"I think that you've outdone us all in our gifts, Samsango." Despite their difference in rank, Hann'yu's manner was effortlessly gracious. He addressed Samsango not as a lowly ushvun but with the warmth and familiarity of a respected elder. Both Ashan'ahma and Ravishan followed his example.

Briefly, John wondered what Rathal'pesha would have been like if men like Hann'yu were in charge of it instead of Ushman Nuritam and Ushman Dayyid. He didn't get far with the thought before Hann'yu pushed a bundle of cloth in front of him.

"Here, open it up and see what you think," Hann'yu instructed him.

"Thank you." John took the bundle. It was light and soft. He unwrapped the scrap of cloth and lifted out a pair of supple leather gloves. Fur lined the insides. John carefully pulled them on and flexed his hands. The leather stretched and gave without binding.

"You're a hard man to fit," Hann'yu remarked.

"I know." John gazed at the tiny stitching that decorated the backs of the gloves. It was a simple pattern of two leaves curling out from a single vine.

"Thank you," John said again. Hann'yu smiled.

Ashan'ahma handed a second bundle to John. "Just remember that we aren't all able to appropriate funds from the treasury as easily as Ushman Hann'yu."

Like Hann'yu's gift, Ashan'ahma's was wrapped in rough scrap cloth that would later be used as rag for making paper. John unwrapped it and found an ivory and silver pen inside. It had obviously been used. Most likely it was one of the few things that Ashan'ahma had been allowed to bring with him when he had been tithed to the Payshmura. The arching Basawar letters of John's name had been freshly carved into its body.

"It's not so bad, is it?" Ashan'ahma asked.

"No, not at all. It's beautiful." John held the pen. It looked incredibly white against the dark leather of his new gloves. "It was yours?"

"Yes." Ashan'ahma nodded. "Before my ushiri talents were discovered, I fancied the life of a writer for myself. Everyone gave me pens, of course. So, now I'm passing one on to you."

"Thank you," John said.

Ashan'ahma smiled and then looked oddly embarrassed. He squinted at Ravishan's still form. "He's asleep, isn't he?"

"No." Ravishan's voice sounded rough, but the response came quickly.

"So what have you got for Jahn?" Ashan'ahma asked.

"I've got some laundry." Ravishan yawned.

"You're not fooling anyone," Ashan'ahma said.

Ravishan frowned at him but then straightened. "All right, but it's not much to look at." He dug into the deep pockets of his coat and then brought out three small red apples. The flesh of each of them bore a number of sharp gashes, the kind of injuries that came from the Gray Space.

"Fresh apples," Samsango gasped. Hann'yu and Ashan'ahma looked amazed as well. It was the dead of winter. The last fresh fruit or vegetables any of them had eaten had been bitter greens a month ago. It would be another three months before they had anything better than leathery pieces of dried berries.

John could smell the sweet tang of the apples rising from their sliced skins.

"How did you get them?" Samsango asked.

"I picked them this afternoon from an orchard in Umbhra'ibaye." Ravishan smiled slightly.

"No wonder you were so torn up in the infirmary," Ashan'ahma said. "Umbhra'ibaye is too far to go."

"I'll go farther when I'm Kahlil." Ravishan shrugged. "Anyway, it was only a few scratches."

John glanced questioningly to Hann'yu. Hann'yu only gave a small shake of his head. John glanced down at the apples again. Their red skins and pale white flesh were split and torn. One of them was sliced all the way to the core. It was no wonder Ravishan was so exhausted.

"Well?" Ravishan asked. "Are they too ugly to eat?"

"Not at all," John replied. It embarrassed him to feel so touched while staring at three small apples. "We should cut them up and share them," John decided.

All five of them carried knives. But only Samsango's short paring knife wasn't infused with curses or carved from sacred bone. John stood and found clay cups for all of them. He poured out servings of the strong daru'sira.

The sweetness of the apples balanced the bitter edge of the daru'sira. John closed his eyes, savoring the taste. In Nayeshi, this would have been nothing to him. He could have gotten all the varieties of apples he liked at a grocery store. The gloves and the pen, even the stuffed rolls were things that he would have taken for granted.

But here, he knew the kind of rarity and effort that they represented. Because life was harder here, because resources were more scarce and convenience virtually unknown, each offering meant much more. Hann'yu couldn't just pick up a pair of gloves at a department store. Ashan'ahma wouldn't ever be able to replace his pen with another. Samsango couldn't just order a meal in. And Ravishan had bled to bring him these three sweet apples in the dead of winter.

If he had never lived here, he never would have been able to understand how precious each of these gifts was. For a brief moment, John was so moved that he felt tears begin to wet the corners of his closed eyes. He quickly drew in a breath and stopped himself from going any further with these thoughts.

"So," John said, "do you think that the sisters in Umbhra'ibaye would like to trade residences with us?"

Hann'yu laughed.

"Wouldn't that be a treat?" Ashan'ahma asked.

Samsango nodded. "I suppose it's warm there, even now in the Snow Month."

"It's like a nice day at harvest," Ravishan said. "You can smell the ripe fruit and the leaves are just beginning to turn gold. I don't think it ever snows there."

"It doesn't," Hann'yu said. "I lived in Amura Milso when I was young. I never saw snow until I went north to Nurjima for my schooling."

"In cold months like these, I imagine you miss it." Samsango refilled his cup of daru'sira.

"I miss Nurjima more," Hann'yu said. "But there's no point in brooding over it. And Rathal'pesha has its good qualities."

"Does it?" Ravishan asked.

"Certainly it does." Samsango smiled. "It is the most sacred honor to be so near the holy ushiri'im."

John could see how that wouldn't be much of a consolation to Ravishan, or to Ashan'ahma, for that matter. But for Samsango it truly was a kind of blessing. The ushiri'im were living testaments to Parfir's power. They were men who carried the god's own bones.

"There is something very sacred about the presence of the ushiri'im," Hann'yu agreed. "At times, the very air feels different in the rooms where they have been housed for so many generations."

"And there are all those fine lines left behind from where they've passed through the Gray Space," John added. He poured more daru'sira into his cup.

Hann'yu regarded him questioningly. "Fine lines?"

"Well, not obvious lines but, you know, scratches. You can follow them . . . " John trailed off as he became aware that none of the other men at the table were showing any sign of recognition of what he was describing.

"You can follow where we've gone?" Ashan'ahma asked.

"Yes, but . . . " John tried to think of a way to retract what he had said. "It's just what Hann'yu was describing, the texture of the air is different. It's scratched. You can feel it like a scrape in the grain of wood."

"You can, perhaps," Hann'yu said. "But I certainly can't."

"I've never noticed it either," Ashan'ahma said, "and I am an ushiri. You, Ravishan?"

Ravishan shook his head.

"I'm probably not describing it correctly," John said.

"No, I think you're describing it perfectly," Hann'yu said. "I've never seen it, but I've read about it. The Kahlil Vash'illoun wrote about a current running through all of Parfir's creations. When an ushiri opens the Gray Space, he cuts into that current and either moves with it or against it. Most ushiri'im can't sense it, and so their movements are at odds with Parfir's currents. The paths they leave were described as the marks a sharp blade leaves on ice."

"Exactly," John said.

"And you've seen this?" Samsango stared at John.

"Just once or twice," John lied.

"That's how you can always find Ravishan for me. You can see the path he's left." Hann'yu shook his head. "Dayyid really should have accepted you as an ushiri."

"It wouldn't have made a difference if he had," John said. "Ravishan is going to be the Kahlil."

"But having you with the others might have allowed you to share your sense of the currents sooner," Hann'yu said. "From what I've read, it's moving against those currents that causes injuries to the ushiri'im when they are within the Gray Space."

"What do they look like?" Ashan'ahma asked.

Ravishan also looked intently at John, waiting for his answer.

"The currents or the paths?"

"The currents," Ashan'ahma said.

"They don't look like anything. They just feel right. I don't know how to describe it except . . . you know when you're swimming, and you can feel the water flowing around you? It's like that."

"Just like that," Ashan'ahma said ruefully.

"If you can feel these currents," Ravishan said quietly, "you ought to be able to open the Gray Space."

"I can't," John said. The idea of touching, much less creating, an opening to the Gray Space repulsed him utterly. He had no idea how Ravishan or any of the ushiri'im managed to overcome the feeling of revulsion that the Gray Space generated.

"But you can feel Parfir's living current?" Ravishan asked. "Right now in this room, can you feel it?"

"Yes," John admitted after a moment.

"So," Ravishan held up his hand over the table, "if I were to open a space, you could tell me which way the current was running?"

John gazed at Ravishan's hand. His long fingers were nicked and scraped. Faint red lines streaked across his palm where earlier cuts had only half healed.

"I think so," John said.

"All right then." Ravishan's tone was almost challenging. This was an area that Ravishan was used to dominating. Perhaps a hint of combativeness couldn't be helped. John didn't bother to linger on it. Ravishan had a right to his pride.

John concentrated on the empty air surrounding all of them. He felt the weightless atmosphere that washed over him, caressed his skin, and rolled into his lungs. Each breath he released sent tiny breezes rolling through the room. Invisible currents slipped out cracks in the walls to rejoin the cold night sky. Outside, it was snowing and the winds chased each other like children intent on a game of tag.

John reached out and gently turned Ravishan's hand through the sweeping play of the elements.

"There," John said. He drew his own hands back.

Ravishan snapped his fingers apart, cracking open a thin slice of the Gray Space. The hiss was hardly audible but John still felt the chill. Ravishan closed the space immediately. He dropped his hand back to the tabletop.

Only the faintest trace of the opening remained hanging in the air. It was almost invisible compared to the others John had seen. No one else seemed to notice it.

"It opened so smoothly," Ravishan said. "I hardly felt any resistance." He lifted his right hand again. "Show me again."

"But—" John began.

"Not tonight, Ravishan," Hann'yu said. "You've already exhausted yourself, and Jahn should be allowed to relax on this one day."

Ravishan gave Hann'yu a harsh frown that was distinctly reminiscent of one of Dayyid's scowls. "This is important."

"So is Jahn's day of birth," Hann'yu replied.

Ravishan glanced to John and then sighed. "All right. But you have to show me tomorrow."

John just nodded his agreement. He would have shown Ravishan now, but he thought the others would have been bored. And Ravishan had to rest sometime.

"You're never going to be free of him now," Ashan'ahma told John.

"But this is wonderful, isn't it?" Samsango smiled. "What a perfect thing to discover. A great talent hidden in a lowly ushvun."

Hann'yu smiled warmly at that and nodded. "I suppose it's to be expected that Parfir's gift to Jahn would be so much greater than all of our material offerings." He poured himself another cup of daru'sira and filled Samsango's cup as well, then glanced to John. "So how does it feel?"

"What?" John asked.

"To be twenty-five," Hann'yu said. "It's been so long I can hardly remember what it was like."

John shrugged. The last birthday he had celebrated had been his twenty-second. It seemed as if it had been decades ago, ages ago. He couldn't even remember what he had been given or done then.

"It feels older than I expected," John said.

"Just wait for forty-six," Hann'yu replied.

"Forty-six?" Samsango waved his hand as if brushing the comment aside. "You wait until you've turned sixty. Sixty. That's nearly the ages of all four of you put together."

Hann'yu smiled. Ashan'ahma was well into his thirties, John was twenty-five, and Ravishan was twenty. Their four combined ages put them well over a hundred. But they all let Samsango's bad math pass without comment.

"You're older than the bell tower, aren't you?" Ashan'ahma asked Samsango.

Samsango nodded. "I was here when they pulled the old one down. That's when you know you're old. When you've outlived the architecture."

"So, you'd remember Gaunsho Par'taum?" Ashan'ahma asked.

"Of course." Samsango smiled broadly at the mention of the man's name. "He had such a voice! Women came from miles to hear him sing at the Harvest Fair. He was born the first son of the Du'yura Gaunsho, the heir to the entire family. But he must have felt a great calling because he disguised himself as a common pilgrim and came to the monastery. Of course they admitted him, but only as a lowly ushvun. He was the worst worker I had ever seen." Samsango shook his head. "He didn't know how to light a fire, couldn't sew a stitch, and he was scared of the goats. He complained and wouldn't eat the food. Ah, and he refused to clean out the privies. No matter what, he wouldn't do it. But when you heard him in prayer . . . such a beautiful, sacred voice would rise out of him. It was as if warm sunshine filled the chamber. Eventually the ushman'im noticed and sent him to the Black Tower to sing for the Usho. Then, of course, his brothers recognized him and he was returned to the Du'yura family."

"He was my grandfather," Ashan'ahma said.

"Really?" Samsango looked Ashan'ahma up and down, searching for traces of the man he remembered. "How is your singing?"

"Not as good as his, I'm afraid. But not bad."

"It's quite good," Ravishan said.

"It is," Hann'yu agreed.

John hadn't noticed it, but then he was rarely among the ushiri'im when they sang their prayers. More often he was working with his fellow ushvun'im or running errands for Hann'yu.

"You must let me hear you," Samsango said.

"You'll be disappointed," Ashan'ahma warned.

"I know that I won't," Samsango replied. "You must sing something."

"Come on," Hann'yu said. "You always want to sing."

Ashan'ahma relented easily. His voice was deep and rich. John leaned onto his elbows and simply listened. Ravishan leaned beside him, half-asleep but smiling. Both Hann'yu and Samsango seemed lost in remembrances. Doubtless Hann'yu's recollections were of the operas of Nurjima, the costumes, lights, and late night conversations. Samsango seemed to simply be recalling his youth and the sacred voice he had known.

John closed his eyes and let his own thoughts wander with the song. Despite the cold and his aching muscles, the night seemed perfect.

Chapter Forty

Ravishan woke John before daybreak, demanding instruction. He bounded up the stairs to the infirmary and John followed in a groggy daze. They worked together while the sun slowly crept up over the mountain peaks.

Outside the infirmary window, the sky was a pale white expanse. The rising sun only burned a faint white circle through the walls of falling snow. John yawned and frowned at the smell of ozone and smoke that hung in the air. He turned back to Ravishan. He had expected that Ravishan would want to train with him. But he hadn't thought that Ravishan would wake him up before the break of day for it.

"Show me again." Ravishan stood, tensed as though he were preparing for an attack. His right hand was slightly extended, his left drawn back, closer to his chest. A fine sheen of sweat already covered his bare chest and arms. Wisps of his shaggy black hair hung around his face.

"Try to feel it for yourself," John said.

Ravishan closed his eyes and frowned intently. He shifted his hand slightly, but then scowled. "I can't . . . I thought I did, but it was just the wind."

"The wind is part of it," John assured him. The living current, as Ravishan called it, suffused the wind and rolled with it.

"Here?" Ravishan moved just a little more.

"Close," John said. "You're really close."

Ravishan shifted the angle of his right arm, turning it by slow degrees. John felt him move into and then out of the delicate current that surrounded them. Ravishan suddenly punched his hand forward, rending the Gray Space open. Flames arced through the air. The sound of tearing metal cut through the morning silence.

"Damn it!" Ravishan jerked his arm back to his chest. The Gray Space snapped closed. Ravishan squeezed his left hand over the bleeding cut in his right forearm.

"How can I be getting worse the more I practice?" Ravishan glared at his arm.

"You're trying too hard," John said. "I don't think it's something you can force. More finesse, less force. Less Dayyid, more Hann'yu."

"So I should be drunk?" Ravishan asked with a smile.

"Maybe not that much like Hann'yu." John went to the drawers and dug out a roll of bandage. "Let me see your arm."

Ravishan held it out. The cut was deep and narrow. John bandaged it. Not for the first time, he wished that he possessed a little of Hann'yu's skill at healing. He tied Ravishan's bandage. There were other, much smaller scratches across Ravishan's arm and even one thin red welt across his cheek.

"Maybe you should try this with something that's easier to feel," John said.

"What do you mean?" Ravishan asked. He was still scowling at his arm as if it had betrayed him.

"It's hard to feel the atmosphere. It's too prevalent and we're too accustomed to it. But maybe something else. Maybe water."

"You want me to go swimming in the dead of winter?"

"No, just . . . " John looked around the room and at last caught sight of one of Hann'yu's porcelain bowls. "Here, let's try it with this." John got up and filled the bowl with clean water.

"If you put your hand in, you can feel the pressure of the water." John slipped his own hand into the bowl. The water was icy. He closed his eyes, concentrating on the texture of the water surrounding his fingers. A moment later he felt Ravishan's hand slide into the water next to his own.

"What do you feel?" John asked.

"Wet," Ravishan replied.

"Other than that."

"I don't know."

"There are strong and weak forces," John said. "Elements like oxygen and hydrogen bond together firmly. They're the hard grain of the water. The force pulling clusters of molecules together is different. . . . Can you feel it?" John asked.

"I don't know what you mean by oxygen," Ravishan said.

"It's a molecule. Something that you'll feel in both the air and the water."

"I don't—"

"It doesn't matter," John assured him. "It's just a name. What's important is to feel the difference between the strong and the weak forces. You want to open the Gray Space by cutting through the weak forces, not the strong ones."

John knew that what he was describing was not the whole experience of the currents he felt. But he had no words to describe the living force that seemed to saturate not just the chill water but the bowl containing it. The air, the stones, everything around them overflowed with that deep energy. When he concentrated on it, John felt as if it was surging up to meet him, churning and pressing against his skin. He could feel it twisting on the cold drafts that slipped through the window. He imagined that he could turn it through his hands or snap it apart. It was a strange sensation.

Ravishan's eyes were pressed closed in concentration. His dark brows compressed, nearly forming a single line. Ravishan turned his hand through the water, slowly. Then suddenly he stopped. His fingers straightened.

John quickly withdrew his own hand from the water. He didn't want to get hit by the Gray Space that Ravishan would open.

Ravishan flicked his fingers apart. A burst of water splashed out of the thin air a foot behind John. Ravishan looked up and grinned. "I think I got it that time."

John nodded. He'd hardly felt the chill of the space opening.

"There's a texture," Ravishan marveled. "A grain. Like you said, it's weak in one direction, strong in another." He stared at John for several moments. "How did you know?"

"That's just how it felt to me," John said. Hann'yu wasn't going to be pleased about the spill of water. John glanced to the shelf to see if there were any towels.

"John," Ravishan said his Nayeshi name in a low whisper, "you would tell me if you were . . . if there was something more, wouldn't you?"

John focused on the towels. There was so much he didn't say. He didn't even know why, exactly, except that he knew their lives here were fragile. He didn't want to discover something that would change the way they were, right now, together.

"I would. I—" John started to turn back towards Ravishan but something caught his attention—a distortion in the air. A faint blur hovered just a foot from him. Someone was in the room with them, spying from the Gray Space.

A shot of anger rushed through John. Without thinking, he bolted forward and grabbed the scrawny ushiri by the arm. A wave of nausea rolled through him as his hands drove into the Gray Space. John jerked the ushiri out as if he were hauling a fish out of the water. The air screamed, and a frigid blast whipped across John's face. Fikiri howled in shock as John hurled him onto one of the infirmary beds.

"What do you think you're doing?" John demanded.

Fikiri scrambled upright. His face and arms were crisscrossed with scratches. His lips looked blue.

"I didn't do anything," Fikiri said quickly.

"You were spying on us?" Ravishan stepped forward.

"It was Dayyid's order," Fikiri snapped. He glared at Ravishan. "He doesn't trust you."

"He didn't trust you either. Now I can see why he's changed his mind. You've turned yourself into his little bootlicker. You're pathetic," Ravishan replied.

"And you're a pervert—" Fikiri hardly got the last word out. Ravishan lunged onto him, gripping his throat.

"I'll kill you in the Gray Space, and no one will ever find your body. Not Dayyid. Not even your precious mommy," Ravishan hissed.

"Ravishan." John pulled him back from Fikiri. "No one is going to kill anyone. Just calm down."

"He—" Ravishan just clenched his mouth shut and looked away from Fikiri. "Fine. Let him go crying back to Dayyid."

John addressed Fikiri, "How long has Dayyid had you watching Ravishan?"

"Long enough," Fikiri responded.

John took one step closer. "How long?"

"Since that night he disappeared." Fikiri narrowed his eyes at John. "There are things I could tell him that I haven't . . . not yet."

"Such as?" John asked. A cold revulsion that had nothing to do with the Gray Space churned through John's stomach.

"I heard you two talk about going to Nayeshi together," Fikiri said.

"And?" John asked. Dread gripped him as he remembered that Fikiri had called Ravishan a pervert. They had been careful, but there had still been moments when Ravishan had pressed a hand against his. There had been small gestures, brief overtures. How much had Fikiri seen and how much had he understood?

"And I want to go too," Fikiri demanded.

"What? No!" Ravishan snapped.

"If you don't take me and my mother with you, I'll tell Dayyid everything." Fikiri looked at John. "I'll tell him about the night you two spent in the hostel. I'll tell him what you did in the morning."

"You'll die before you can say a word!" Ravishan started forward again but John caught him by the shoulders.

"Calm down," John said softly.

"I'm not going to let this piece of snot blackmail me," Ravishan growled.

"You're not going to kill him," John said flatly.

"I can beat him till his tongue falls out," Ravishan countered.

"Just calm down," John told him. "Beating up Fikiri certainly won't make Dayyid less suspicious."

Ravishan stepped back again and turned away from Fikiri.

"All right," Ravishan said. John could see the muscles in his jaw working.

John turned back to Fikiri. "So you and Lady Bousim want to go to Nayeshi?"

"We're going to live there with Loshai," Fikiri said firmly.

"With my sister?" John asked. "Why do you think she'd be going?"

"Because I've watched her." Fikiri's pale face flushed slightly. "I've listened to her and Behr when they thought they were alone."

"Now who's the pervert?" Ravishan demanded.

"At least I didn't have my head shaved for whoring with a goat herder," Fikiri spat back.

Ravishan glared at Fikiri. "If Jahn wasn't here, you would have my blade through your throat, Fikiri."

"Well, he is here," Fikiri answered. "So just shut up."

John caught Fikiri's jaw in his hand and turned his face so that they were staring directly at each other. He leaned a little closer to Fikiri.

"Don't push your luck," John said slowly. "And don't insult Ravishan."

Fikiri blanched. John continued, "What are you going to do if we don't agree to take you with us?"

"Then I'll tell Dayyid everything." Fikiri lifted his chin slightly.

"Tell him," Ravishan said suddenly. "He can't afford to kill me now. I'm his Kahlil and he knows it."

"Maybe, but we all know he's dying to beat the life out of Ushvun Jahn," Fikiri replied.

A look of horror washed over Ravishan. Then his eyes narrowed and he shifted his weight into a battle stance. His right hand flexed and John could almost feel him summoning the force to create a Silence Knife. John thought he might really kill Fikiri.

"So you'll be coming with us," John said quickly. "You and your mother."

There was no point in arguing. He had to tell Fikiri what he wanted to hear, even if it might not turn out to be true.

"I want your word," Fikiri said.

"What?" John asked.

"I want your word that you'll take us," Fikiri repeated.

"All right." John agreed. "I promise that we will take you and your mother to Nayeshi when we go."

"Ravishan has to promise as well," Fikiri added.

"You have my word." Ravishan's voice sounded flat but his expression was filled with contempt.

"It's your own fault," Fikiri snapped at Ravishan. "If you weren't a disgusting pervert, there wouldn't be anything for me to tell Dayyid. But you—"

"Fikiri," John cut him off. "You've gotten what you want, so don't keep goading Ravishan into murdering you."

Fikiri bowed his head and glowered down at his scraped hands.

"You should go," John told him. "Now."

Fikiri stood and started for the door. Ravishan watched him with narrowed eyes. John could see his hands shaking with suppressed fury.

John almost swore when Fikiri stopped at the door. Why couldn't he just stop baiting Ravishan and get out? But this time he focused his attention on John.

"How did you pull me out of the Gray Space?" Fikiri demanded.

"I don't think knowing how is as important as remembering that I can," John replied. "Don't spy on us again."

A look of genuine fear crossed over Fikiri's face. He left quickly then.

John sat down on the corner of the bed. He rubbed his hand across his forehead, massaging the beginning of a headache away.

"You should have let me kill him in the Gray Space," Ravishan said.

"Would you really have done it?"

"What he said about Dayyid beating you to death is true. I think I'd kill anyone before I'd let that happen."

"Well, it's not going to happen," John assured him. "So let's just put the murder plans aside for the moment."

Ravishan nodded. He glanced down at the floor, looking almost lost. "I should probably clean this water up before Hann'yu gets here."

"I was about to do that," John said.

Ravishan had already reached the shelves. He found one of the rags and tossed it down over the small spill. John watched the water soak into the cloth. He felt tired and a little sick.

"How did you pull him out, Jahn?" Ravishan whispered.

"I don't know. I just did it."

"You have witch's blood, don't you?" Ravishan asked.

"Maybe, I don't know. No one does things like this in Nayeshi. No one walks into thin air or has witch's blood or god's bones. We're just people."

"You're not a Kahlil?" Ravishan asked.

"No." John almost laughed at the thought of it. "No. We don't have Kahlil'im in Nayeshi. You know that."

"I just wanted to be sure."

"Well, be sure. I'm not a Kahlil or a witch or an ushiri. I'm just a person."

"You're something." Ravishan smiled and stepped closer. John caught the flirtatious curve of his smile. It hardly began before Ravishan stopped himself. He stepped back from John and turned to stare out the window.

John understood. Who knew if Fikiri was the only spy that Dayyid would send out? They couldn't afford even the slightest overture of affection now.

"I should go," Ravishan said.

John simply nodded.

"Be careful," John told him as he opened the red door.

"You as well." Ravishan gave him a smile and then left.

By the time Hann'yu arrived, John had thrown out the water, put away the bowl, and begun the tedious work of grinding down the dried herbs that would be needed for poultices. The smell of earthy roots hung in the air, but it couldn't mask the odor of burnt ozone.

Hann'yu sniffed and pulled a sour face. "Fikiri?" he guessed.

"Ravishan," John said.

"He normally doesn't leave such a strong smell." Hann'yu contemplated the snow falling outside the window, then opened the window anyway. Icy, fresh air rushed in.

"We were practicing with the currents," John said. "I think he got a little frustrated."

"Did he make any progress?"

"He did, actually."

"Good," Hann'yu said. Then he looked John over. "But you look dead on your feet."

"I didn't sleep well." In fact, his nights had been restless for months. More and more the image of the Issusha'im's bones infiltrated his rest. The hollow, black chasms of their eyes stared, unblinking, into his sleep. Even in his most mundane dreams he thought he heard them whispering after him. Lately, it seemed to be growing worse.

"I suppose Ravishan woke you before the first bell?"

"He's dedicated," John replied.

Hann'yu studied the dried roots as John ground them in the mortar.

"If so much didn't depend on him, I would say that he was too dedicated." Hann'yu went to one of his shelves and opened a jar of desiccated leaves. He dropped two of the leaves into the mortar and then put the jar away.

"Yellowpetal leaves," Hann'yu explained. "They dull pain somewhat."

John ground them in with the knotted pine root. Hann'yu would use it as an antiseptic later.

"Did you get anything to eat?" Hann'yu asked. He walked back to the window and closed it.

"Cold taye and goat milk," John said.

"Sounds awful."

John didn't think it was any worse than some servings of oatmeal he'd eaten. Hann'yu wouldn't have understood that response. "It could have been worse."

"Yes, most things could be," Hann'yu said. "But it's a sad consolation to have to take, you know."

"I know." John smiled.

"Would you like a nap?" Hann'yu offered.

"I'd love one, but—"

"Go on." Hann'yu waved him toward one of the beds. "You're no use as you are now."

"No use?" John couldn't help the tone of protest in his voice. He'd been working all morning.

"Oh, you can work well enough," Hann'yu replied, "but you're a terrible conversation partner when you're tired."

"I see." John set the mortar aside. "Are you sure?"

"Positive," Hann'yu told him. "Take a nap. I need someone who can appreciate my gossip like a second wife."

"You don't have a first wife," John said.

"We can all dream," Hann'yu responded. "Especially you. Go to bed and dream me up a wife. A pretty wife."

"I make no guarantees." John wasn't sure how well he would sleep, but his body hungered for rest. He lay down and closed his eyes. Hann'yu spread a blanket over him.

"Give her red hair and big breasts. Maybe a full, pouting mouth like the women from the Anyyid lands," Hann'yu said.

"I think you're going to have to come up with her for yourself," John mumbled. He heard Hann'yu drawing the canvas curtains closed around the bed but didn't bother to open his eyes.

"I have," Hann'yu replied softly, "many times over. I've just gotten lazy. I'm hoping you'll do the work for me."

"You don't want me to. I'll get her all wrong." John yawned. "You'll end up married to a sheep. Something with a giant udder."

"A giant udder. Really?" Hann'yu asked. "Perhaps you shouldn't tell me any more about your dreams."

"My dreams." John's words came out in a groggy murmur. "Hardly." Moments later, he was asleep.

Dark insentience coiled around him, and yet at the edges of his senses he felt as though he was still awake, watching as Hann'yu separated leaves and dried flowers for teas. He heard the hard snap of boot heels outside the door and knew immediately that Dayyid stood there.

Dayyid knocked and Hann'yu called him in.

"Is he here with Ushvun Jahn again?" Dayyid asked.

"Who?" Hann'yu didn't look up from his herb table.

"Ravishan." Dayyid scanned the infirmary, seeming disappointed with its emptiness. For a moment, a small pile of dull green leaves and white flowers bore the brunt of his disapproving expression. Then he looked to Hann'yu.

"No, they've finished their practices. Ravishan has gone to the golden chamber, I imagine, and Jahn is sleeping." Hann'yu glanced to the curtained bed. It gave John an odd feeling of vertigo to take in the space where he knew his own body lay in a deep sleep.

"In the middle of the day?" Dayyid frowned at the canvas panels.

"He was up early training with Ravishan." Hann'yu looked up at Dayyid. "Did you know that he goes down to the kitchen after the eighth bell and helps the ushvun'im bake for the next day? He hardly sleeps at all."

"How could he, when he's so busy doing every job that isn't his to do?" Dayyid responded.

Hann'yu sighed. "You sound jealous, Dayyid. I can see why you would be. The ushiri'im practice with him and Ravishan follows him around like a milk-pup. It leaves you out. But it's unbecoming to succumb to such a petty feeling."

"I'm not jealous," Dayyid replied coolly. "If he improves the ushiri'im, then I'm glad for it."

"You don't seem glad for it," Hann'yu replied. He stood and picked out another jar. A dark golden fluid swirled in it. "But perhaps I'm misinterpreting your glares, scowls, and threats."

"I don't trust him."

"Is there anyone you do trust?" Hann'yu searched his shelves. At last he found two small clay cups. He set them down on the herb table.

John would have liked to have heard the answer to Hann'yu's question but Dayyid offered none. He stood in silence and watched as Hann'yu filled the two cups with golden liquid. It poured like honey. Hann'yu pushed one of the cups to Dayyid and took the other for himself.

"Fathi?" Dayyid raised a dark brow.

"The drink of divine truth and joy," Hann'yu confirmed. "It suits our conversation, don't you think?"

Dayyid eyed the small cup as if it were a trap of some kind.

"He hides things," Dayyid suddenly stated. "When I placed the curse blade before him he felt its power, and yet he didn't choose it."

"He has a right not to choose it," Hann'yu replied. "Anyway, you were the one who said that you didn't want him as an ushiri."

"I didn't and I don't." Dayyid picked up his cup. He held it between his hands as if it offered him some kind of warmth, but he did not drink. "He's hiding something."

"What?" Hann'yu laughed. "His dread of being cut to ribbons by the Gray Space? It's not all that desirable of a test to pass, really."

"You know that's not what I mean," Dayyid grumbled.

"I don't, actually." Hann'yu met Dayyid's intense expression with an easy smile. "So tell me what you're really bothered by."

"He holds back," Dayyid said. "When he first arrived, I took it for pure cowardice. He took his beatings like a dog. But when he came to the golden chamber, I felt something stir in him and he restrained it. He tried to hide it from me."

Hann'yu frowned. "Hide what, exactly?"

"Power. Immense power," Dayyid said after a long pause. "When he collapsed the God's Razor, I felt it for just a moment. A raw, dark power. It struck me, but then he pulled it back. During the test he suppressed it and lied. I assume you've noticed it as well?"

"There is a force to him," Hann'yu admitted. "But it's, as you say, raw and strong. That makes it no use in the infirmary. As far as I'm concerned it's best if he does hold it back."

"Then you have sensed him hiding it." Dayyid's voice rang with vindication.

"Certainly," Hann'yu agreed, but he only appeared amused by Dayyid's serious expression and tone. "But don't you think that would be natural for a man who obviously comes from Eastern blood? He has 'witch's child' all but written across him. He's probably had to hide his power all his life just to keep clear of harvest fires."

Hann'yu frowned down at his small cup. Dayyid said nothing. John wondered if the conversation would end there. It seemed unlike Dayyid to allow anyone else to have the last word. Hann'yu drank from his cup while Dayyid simply held his.

"If he had done nothing wrong," Dayyid spoke as if the long silence in their conversation had never occurred, "then he would have no reason to hide. In itself, his power could be Parfir's blessing. Only if Jahn misused it could he have been accused of witchcraft."

Hann'yu gave a dry laugh at that. "Well, that's the letter of the law," Hann'yu replied, "but we both know that misuse is a matter of interpretation. There are jealous, petty people willing to cry foul against anyone they can. And Jahn doesn't just have himself to think of. He has a sister as well."

"Yes, I recall that he made a spectacle of himself for her sake." Dayyid took a small sip from his cup. He closed his eyes, savoring the taste.

"Don't pretend that you weren't proud to see one of ours knock a rasho flat." Hann'yu grinned. To John's surprise, a slight smile tugged the corners of Dayyid's mouth upward.

"Perhaps," Dayyid admitted. "But his prowess isn't a matter of contention."

"Of course it is," Hann'yu replied. "You just won't admit it."

"No," Dayyid replied.

John wasn't sure if Dayyid meant that he wouldn't admit his jealousy or if he was refuting Hann'yu completely. Hann'yu seemed not to need to pursue the matter further.

"How's the fathi?" Hann'yu glanced to the small cup in Dayyid's hands.

"Still too sweet," Dayyid replied.

"Better than last year's, though." Hann'yu poured himself another serving.

"Much," Dayyid agreed.

"Another five or six years, and it may be quite smooth," Hann'yu pronounced after another sip.

"If there's any left," Dayyid replied.

This time Hann'yu's laugh sounded genuine and warm. "The pursuit of perfection has its costs," he declared.

Dayyid sipped a little more of the golden drink.

"Go on," Hann'yu said to him at last. "Sit down, before it knocks you down."

"I have no intention of drinking it all," Dayyid replied. He set the small cup aside on Hann'yu's table. It was still nearly full.

"You need to relax sometime, Dayyid," Hann'yu said. "Go ahead. Have the rest."

"No." Dayyid shook his head. "I should find Ravishan and make sure he's at his practices."

"He's at his practices," Hann'yu said. "He's always at his practices. He wakes Jahn up before sunrise to practice. He stays in the golden chamber until sunset. He does nothing but practice."

"You disapprove?" Dayyid asked.

"I just wonder what he's going to do when he crosses to Nayeshi."

"Find the Rifter," Dayyid replied as if there could be no other response.

"Yes, obviously, but I mean besides that. It takes years, doesn't it? Then he has to wait for word from the Black Tower. He hardly knows how to relax or talk about anything but becoming Kahlil. What will they make of him in Nayeshi?"

Remembering Kyle, John had a good idea of what people would make of Ravishan—a weird, knife-wielding, scarred milkman. But it would be different for Ravishan. John planned on being there with him, helping him.

"My only concern is that he becomes Kahlil," Dayyid replied.

"He will." Hann'yu gestured as if waving any doubt aside. "The Issusha'im Oracles have seen the Prayerscars over his eyes. They have seen him cross through the Great Gate."

"They also saw Fikiri's blood spilled on the Holy Road." Dayyid reached out to the cup he'd set aside and ran a finger over the rim before drawing his hand back. "We can't depend upon their scrying."

"Then perhaps we should have faith in Parfir," Hann'yu said.

"You'll say anything not to have to drink alone, won't you?" Dayyid picked his cup up again and took a quick drink from it. He closed his eyes. "Even now, drinking fathi," Dayyid said softly, "he doesn't stop picking at my thoughts."

"Ravishan?"

"Ushvun Jahn." Dayyid opened his eyes and gazed back to the curtained bed. "He's like a splinter in my mind." Dayyid stepped closer to the bed and caught hold of one of the canvas panels. "He learns too quickly, fights too well. . . . What will we do if he's one of theirs?"

"Fai'daum?" Hann'yu asked. He looked amused by the idea.

Dayyid drew one of the panels back and scowled at John. Seeing his own body stretched out in the bed utterly exposed as Dayyid leaned over him sent a shudder of fear through John. He wanted to wake up but couldn't quite rouse himself.

Dayyid released the panel and it fell back closed.

"He isn't Fai'daum," Hann'yu stated with certainty.

"You can't know that." Dayyid turned back to Hann'yu.

"I can." Hann'yu's smile was a little crooked. His small cup of fathi sat nearly empty.

"You think you know him," Dayyid said. "You think he's trustworthy, but to me he reeks of lies."

Hann'yu rolled his eyes. "Even if I didn't like him, I would still know he isn't Fai'daum." Hann'yu leaned back in his chair. A soft pink glow had spread across his nose and cheeks. "The Fai'daum brand their men so that one can never desert the cause."

"I've heard the same thing, but it could just as easily be a rumor, like almost everything else you hear about the Fai'daum."

"No, I met members when I lived in Nurjima." Hann'yu smiled at Dayyid's horrified expression. "In the south, it's not like it is here. It's not an all-out war. There are public speeches and debates. . . . Well, there used to be. It's all changed by now, I suppose."

"Southern intellectuals making speeches and giving themselves burn scars hardly speak for the true Fai'daum. They're children compared to the real insurgents we battle here in the north."

"Yes, so I've been told many, many times," Hann'yu said. "But even if I know nothing of the northern Fai'daum, Jahn is the last person you should suspect of being one of their spies. What would he be doing? If he was going to kill the Kahlil, he's had more than ample opportunities to end both Ravishan's and Fikiri's lives. Instead, he's improving the ushiri'im by training with them. He's born wounds for all of the ushiri'im. He could have refused and let several of them die. What kind of Fai'daum member does that?"

"I don't know," Dayyid admitted.

"You do know," Hann'yu stated firmly. "He's not a member of the Fai'daum. He's a man who Parfir has blessed with strength and power, and that threatens you. Jahn has the potential to become a powerful ush-man, perhaps even more powerful than you. The ushiri'im sense as much and so do you. That's why you mistrust him. That's why he nags at your thoughts."

"If you weren't drunk on fathi," Dayyid glowered at Hann'yu, "I would call you out onto the fighting grounds for saying such a thing."

"But I am drunk."

Dayyid leaned across Hann'yu's table and glared down at him. "Someday you will have worn that excuse too thin," Dayyid growled.

"Today?" Hann'yu's smile faded but his tone remained teasing as he met Dayyid's glower.

"Not today." Dayyid straightened. He turned and started for the door. "When he wakes, send him to the golden chamber."

"Ushvun Jahn?" Hann'yu asked.

"Of course." Dayyid stopped at the door and glanced back to Hann'yu. "Don't make me wait too long." Then he left.

Hann'yu took Dayyid's abandoned cup of fathi and raised it toward the curtained bed. "Well, Jahn, let's pray that wasn't the wife you dreamed up for me." He tossed back the last of Dayyid's fathi. "Sheep are sounding better already."

☾ ☾ ☾

John no longer found the chill and harsh odor of burnt ozone remarkable when he entered the golden chamber. Even those faint bloodstains that marred the perfect white practice mats no longer perturbed him. He'd fought and seen blood spilled—both his own and that of the ushiri'im—in combat practice.

But the emptiness of the space bothered him. He was used to entering the chamber to find many ushiri'im practicing their battle skills. Some afternoons, the number of men and the intensity of their exertions managed to warm the chamber, despite the cold that emanated from countless rifts in the Gray Space.

This afternoon, only Dayyid occupied the room; John recognized him despite the fact that he wore neither his black coat nor his cassock. Dozens of long white scars marred the dark skin of his bare arms. He knelt before the large iron statue of Parfir, dressed in simple pants and an undershirt. His long dark braids were tied back, and he gripped a black curse blade in his right hand.

Powerfully built and handsome, he reminded John more than a little of Ravishan, and yet as John studied him, he felt nothing but loathing for the man.

"You sent for me, Ushman Dayyid?" John called from the doorway.

"I did." Dayyid remained where he was. John waited for him to complete his prayers. At last Dayyid stood and turned to face John directly. He didn't sheath his curse blade.

"I will not pretend to like you, Ushvun Jahn," Dayyid announced.

"I don't think you ever have," John replied before Dayyid could go on.

Dayyid narrowed his dark gaze, and John knew he should have remained silent. But ever since the Harvest Festival, when he'd realized just how cruelly Dayyid used Ravishan to enforce his own brutal ideals, John had found himself overwhelmed by his outrage at the man.

"Perhaps I have not. Such deceit is not in my nature, after all. Just as honesty is not in your nature." Dayyid gave him a hard smile and made a small sweep with his curse blade, almost absently.

John ground his teeth but kept his mouth shut. He wasn't going to be baited into attacking Dayyid and being run through with that poisonous blade.

"Hann'yu seems to think differently of you," Dayyid stated. "And it seems that many of my ushiri'im have found a use for you as well."

John nodded, not trusting himself to speak just yet. He hoped this wasn't going to be a repeat of the interrogation that Dayyid had already put him through in the library.

"I won't have my ushiri'im training against an inferior opponent. After all, one cannot sharpen a blade with a soft stone." Dayyid watched John like a cat watching a fallen crow. "From this point on, I will personally see to your battle training . . . unless, of course, you wish to withdraw from practices with my ushiri'im."

John stared at Dayyid for a moment, almost unable to believe that the man could be so petty. At the same time, he knew Dayyid was serious and would take the greatest satisfaction in beating him to a pulp while claiming that it served a higher good. The smartest, fastest way to diffuse the entire situation would be to withdraw from practicing with the ushiri'im as Dayyid wished.

But even knowing as much, John couldn't bring himself to do so. Training was the only excuse he could claim for time alone with Ravishan, and it offered John a reason to be in the upper reaches of the monastery. More than that, he refused to give up his friendships with the ushiri'im and the freedoms they had won him just to mollify Dayyid's jealousy.

"When do we begin training?" John asked.

"I believe your first lesson will start right now," Dayyid replied. He sheathed his black curse blade, and then with a flick of his hands, wrenched the Gray Space open and punched it toward John's chest.

John lunged back. Dayyid pursued him with fast, sure strides and an expression of pleasure on his face. John's heel hit the wall behind him. No further retreat in that direction.

Dayyid obviously saw as much as well and pressed his assault with a quick jab for John's face.

John dropped to a crouch, feeling the sick cold of the Gray Space slash the air just above his head. He immediately pounced up, driving both fists into Dayyid's exposed torso. Dayyid stumbled back and John bounded after him. He landed another powerful body blow to Dayyid's chest and saw the look of pain and fury as he knocked the breath out of Dayyid. But in an instant Dayyid struck back with a hard kick into John's right knee. Pain shot through John's leg and he staggered.

Dayyid pressed his advantage, tearing open the Gray Space to create a Silence Knife. The air screamed and flames followed the arc of Dayyid's fist as he plunged the Silence Knife down.

Two years ago, John would have been too overwhelmed, too hurt and off balance to do anything but fall beneath the killing edge of Dayyid's Silence Knife. But since then, John had trained hard and constantly, not only against his fellow ushvun'im, but also against Dayyid's ushiri'im.

They fought just as Dayyid fought, because he had trained them. Their speed and relentless attacks were Dayyid's, but so too were their weaknesses. They never expected anyone to challenge their divine weapons; they could not seem to even imagine an attack across the line of their Silence Knives and Unseen Edges.

With a roar of sheer rage, John punched directly into Dayyid's Silence Knife. Agonizing pain tore across the back of his hand, but John threw himself into the blow. Blood gushed from his hand and then the frigid cold of the Gray Space snapped closed and John's bloody fist smashed into Dayyid's jaw. Dayyid's eyes went wide with shock.

John hooked Dayyid's ankle with a fast kick and pulled him off his feet.

As Dayyid hit the practice mat flat on his back, John dropped to one knee, aiming a blow straight down into Dayyid's exposed throat. A killing strike.

Then, reflexively, John pulled back. He wasn't about to kill another human being, not even someone as cruel as Dayyid.

For a stunned instant he stared at Dayyid, horrified by what he had almost done. It had come so easily that John felt almost sick with himself. Dayyid stared back up at him, his dark eyes wide and his breath coming in gasps.

"I'm sorry. I didn't mean—"

"Idiot!" Before John could react, Dayyid brought up his leg and landed a solid kick into John's stomach. John tumbled back and Dayyid rolled up to his feet. In an instant, he stood over John with one foot placed on John's neck.

"The win is mine," Dayyid declared with a smirk.

"Yes," John conceded before Dayyid placed any further weight on his throat. "The win is yours."

Dayyid stepped back, allowing John to regain his feet.

The wound across the back of John's hand hurt like hell, but it didn't seem too deep, despite the volume of blood spattered across the training mats.

John noted the numerous welts and scratches that stood out across both of Dayyid's hands and forearms.

"Do you understand why I defeated you, Jahn?" Dayyid asked the question over his shoulder as he strode to the dressing table where his cassock and coat lay. He dressed quickly, hiding his injuries.

Because you're a dick, John thought, but he said nothing. The last thing he wanted was to start a real fight.

"It is because I am a true servant of Parfir. My entire being is dedicated to him. I never have to question myself or fear that I am on the wrong path, because Parfir is with me in everything." Dayyid looked up to the towering statue with an expression of reverence. Then he cast John a disdainful glance. "You have not taken Parfir into your heart, and so you question your actions. You hesitate in battle because you do not know if you are just or not. I never hesitate. That is why I beat you and why I will always beat you."

John cradled his bleeding hand and glared at Dayyid's back. Very briefly he imagined himself drawing his own knife and plunging it between Dayyid's self-satisfied shoulder blades.

But John quickly stopped that line of thought.

He wasn't here to fight the injustices of the Payshmura religion or to teach Dayyid some humility. He had come to Rathal'pesha to find a way for himself, Bill, and Laurie to escape this entire world. He'd promised to show Ravishan a kinder, better life in Nayeshi. No matter what, he couldn't lose sight of those things. He just needed to endure all of this. After all, Ravishan had assured him that the Issusha'im were closing in on the Rifter. It could be any day now. They would escape Basawar and he would never see Dayyid again.

John drew in a deep, calming breath and slowly released it.

"You're right," John told Dayyid.

"Of course I am." Dayyid turned back to John with a smug expression. "These lessons will ensure that you never forget that."

John lowered his gaze but couldn't help noticing how gingerly Dayyid held his left hand. John suddenly realized that he must have hurt Dayyid badly when he'd punched through his Silence Knife. And then he recalled that brief expression of shock that had flickered across Dayyid's face.

John bowed his head to hide his smile. Dayyid could talk all he liked about being Parfir's holy servant, but for that instant at least, he had to have known that Parfir hadn't been with him. Though it was petty, John took more than a little consolation in the thought.

That became more true, especially as the weeks passed and his training with Dayyid intensified. He always conceded the win to Dayyid, but more and more often he exalted in those brief moments when he broke through Dayyid's divine weapons and forced Dayyid to feel defeat.

Chapter Forty-One

As the months passed, spring grew into summer, and even in the heights of the mountains, beds of berries ripened and the scents of fruit and flowers carried on the warm winds.

Despite the balmy weather, John woke, shaking and clammy. He'd dreamed of the bones again. Their strange voices hissed and murmured through his groggy memory. He tried to recall the dream, but it, like others, faded to fleeting impressions of black hollow eyes and thousands of skeletal hands searching for him. He'd been terrified, but now he couldn't recall exactly why. It was something he was happy to forget.

He stared at the dim white expanses of the canvas panels that surrounded his bed. The first bright rays of morning light played across the cloth. The strong scents of other men's bodies hung in the warm air of the dormitory. He thought suddenly of the one morning he'd woken with Ravishan in his arms. If only they could have lingered. . . . Then his reverie drifted to the few minutes he and Ravishan had stolen alone in the pine garden last evening.

Compared to the nights of easy, anonymous sex he'd known in Nayeshi, the simple act of holding Ravishan in his arms should have felt dull, almost chaste. And yet the warmth and strength of Ravishan's embrace had electrified John's entire body. The smell of his skin, the feel of his fingers curling along the nape of John's neck, even the soft rhythm of his breathing had suffused John with arousal.

This morning, he allowed himself to remember and ease his desire.

At last he sat up and tossed his sticky blankets aside. His body ached a little as he stretched and washed at his water basin. Just looking over his chest and thighs, John could see where Dayyid liked to strike and where his own defenses were too slow. But he was improving. Most of his bruises were old and fading.

Somewhere nearby, birds called out. John listened to their tiny, shrill voices as he dressed. He recognized the songs. Brownish birds with black heads made them. Doubtless the two singing were males challenging one another for territories. By late summer, they would be settled and much more quiet.

"If only Dayyid would have been satisfied with a song," John mumbled to himself.

"He's not a man like you and I," Hann'yu had told John a month ago. "Dayyid doesn't compromise. He doesn't relent for the sake of human comfort or mercy. But he's the most genuinely pious man I have ever known. It can make him hard on the people around him, but his only true concern is how best he can serve Parfir."

John had simply nodded at the time, but he had known that Hann'yu was wrong. Piety was not the cause of Dayyid's brutality, but a tool with which he justified his abuse of those around him. John knew as much because he'd seen the best ideals of the Payshmura religion embodied by Samsango. Parfir's edicts of generosity, humility, and compassion moved Samsango to do what Dayyid never would: to celebrate the prowess of those who surpassed him while offering aid and sympathy to those beneath him. His serene piety at times made John wish he could believe in Parfir as Samsango did. Dayyid's piety only made John want to get as far from him and his church as he could.

Today, at least, his wish would be granted. Hann'yu needed him to go down to Amura'taye and fetch supplies for the infirmary. One day down the mountain and one day back up. That meant two days free of Dayyid.

John finished cleaning his face and teeth and poured the used water into the rain gutter outside the window. The morning bells began to ring, and John heard his fellow ushvun'im groaning and mumbling as they too arose from slumber. He made his way out of the dormitories and back to the kitchens. The morning meals wouldn't be ready for an hour. Fortunately, Samsango always left out bread and cold cheese for the ushvun'im who would be leaving for Amura'taye. John helped himself and then went out to join the other ushvun'im at the iron gate.

The sky was pale blue and cloudless. Woody herbs displayed yellow and violet blooms from where they nestled along the path. John brushed his hand against the bare stone of the mountain wall as he strode down the Thousand Steps.

The rock beneath his fingers was cold and hard, and yet it struck John as fragile at the same time. There was brittleness in its nature, like the bones of an old woman; it felt aged and depleted.

John supposed he was projecting the decay he saw in Rathal'pesha and now below him in Amura'taye. The clear sky allowed him a sweeping view of the city. It stretched out beneath him like a map. He easily picked out the white curves of the inner city walls. They arched out and enclosed each other, reflecting the city's growth and decline. He recognized a cluster of small structures that would have been the first refuge of a few dozen farmers and herders. Larger walls and buildings spilled out from there.

Clearly, Amura'taye had flourished once. Its walls swept and curled out over the entire side of the mountain.

It was still a lively city, but now wide stretches of the periphery stood abandoned and crumbling, like the collapsed walls in Candle Alley where he had first kissed Ravishan. Most of the buildings there had been deserted and derelict. Now, John picked out other districts that resembled abandoned ruins more than an inhabited urban area.

It was a backwater. More than one person had told him so. And seated so close to the Payshmura stronghold of Rathal'pesha, the tithes were strictly enforced. It was no wonder that the city, like Rathal'pesha itself, was being abandoned.

What young herder would choose to struggle for a living in a desolate, repressive land when there was the promise of an easier living to be made in a developing city like Nurjima? Stories of city lights, railroads, and loom factories all attested to the rise of industry there.

At the same time, John couldn't help but wonder how many of those same herders might instead choose to join the Fai'daum and fight to destroy the theocracy that so relentlessly drained them of resources and drove them from their homes.

"It looks so peaceful from up here, doesn't it?" an older ushvun commented to John.

"Yes, it does." John turned his attention back to the men traveling with him.

"Just past the city wall there," the man said as he pointed to a tiny cluster of huts, "you can see what remains of my uncle's farm."

"He raised taye?" John guessed the obvious and the ushvun nodded.

"But the crops aren't what they used to be. He moved to Gisa and left the land to me." The ushvun gave a dry laugh. "As if I could afford to pay the tithe for a property. . . . Still, it's pretty, isn't it, with the wild flowers all blooming across the old fields."

"It is," John agreed.

And soon other ushvun pointed out the farmlands or hill pastures that had once been their homes. John shared what he could of his own history as they descended.

His strides were naturally longer than those of the other ushvun'im, but he slowed to their pace, and when a gray-haired ushvun seemed to flag, John took the pack of oil jars that he'd been hauling to ease his burden. All of them then paused to share a flask of daru'sira.

When they reached Amura'taye, his fellow ushvun'im wished him luck in finding all of the herbs Hann'yu had requested, and one handed him a blessed stone to give to his sister. They had all heard that she had been unwell of late.

John accepted the stone and thanked them, though he knew Laurie would have no use for it. Then he marched off to find the medicinal supplies Hann'yu needed. He purchased boughs of pungent southern herbs, jars of arcane brown syrup, and glistening, succulent green blossoms. Samsango's knuckles had been bothering him recently, and so John added a jar of camphor-scented analgesic. The thick, musty smells of the apothecaries clung to him. It reminded him of days he had spent wandering between the cramped shelves of used bookstores.

They needed needles in the infirmary as well. John walked across town to the open streets of the Smiths' Rows. Most of the goods were crude. Rough knife blades, ax heads, bicycle chains, and scythes were common. It was only among the cases of delicate gold and silver jewelry that John at last found medical instruments. He chose twenty of the finest silver needles. Then, out of curiosity, he looked over the other devices in the medical cases.

John picked up an instrument that resembled a pair of surgical scissors. There was an odd wire loop up by the blades. He frowned at it.

"Gelding shears," a familiar voice supplied from behind John.

He turned to see Bill grinning at him. A faint tan colored his skin, and his thin frame showed traces of muscle. John couldn't remember him looking so well since they had left Nayeshi. Laurie's spells were making obvious improvements in his health.

"We just heard that the ushvun'im had come down for supplies. I figured I should see if I could hunt you down." Bill eyed the shears in John's hand. "Looking for just the right gift for that special someone?"

"Something like that." John set the shears aside.

"Do you think you have time for a lunch break?" Bill asked.

"Sure. I'm done here." John shrugged. When neither the prior nor an ushman accompanied them, the ushvun'im tended to be lax. They rarely paired off or bothered to supervise each other's activities. So long as he got back to the church hostel before dark, no one would care what he did with the remaining free hours of the afternoon.

"Good. Loshai is dying to talk to you."

"How's she doing?" John stowed the needles in his pack and then swung it up onto his back. "Is her stomach still bothering her?'

"Oh, yeah." Bill looked almost pleased. "Apparently, it comes with the territory."

"What?" John frowned at the reply.

"I think she wants to tell you herself," Bill said quietly.

John decided not to ask anything more, not out here on the open street where they could be overheard.

He suspected that Laurie's recent bouts of sickness were linked to the spells she poured over Bill. John didn't know much about working a healing spell, but he had been watching Hann'yu for more than a year now. Hann'yu always chose another priest—generally John—to bear the brunt of the wounds he treated; Laurie only had her own strength to call on. It had to wear her down.

"We've heard that things are moving along in Rathal'pesha," Bill commented as they crossed the street.

"So I'm told," John said. He guessed that Fikiri had been keeping them informed.

The walk to the Bousim house went quickly. They only had to pause once, halfway up a steep hill, for Bill to catch his breath.

"Oh, yeah, feeling the burn," Bill whispered between deep breaths. "I have no idea how other people walk around all day long."

"It's not nearly as easy as it looks."

"Tell me about it." Bill straightened. "Okay, let's not keep the ladies waiting."

John followed Bill to the Bousim house and up to one of the more elegant chambers of the second floor where Lady Bousim preferred to receive her guests.

Breads, fruit, and cuts of lamb had been laid out on the long wooden table. Thinner tapestries embroidered with images of summer flowers and fruit-laden trees hung in the place of the heavier tapestries that had insulated the room the last time John had visited.

Lady Bousim greeted John with a smile as he followed Bill in. Laurie beamed at him from the seat to Lady Bousim's right. A healthy blush colored her skin, and she'd at last put on enough weight to make her slim figure truly feminine. Her eyes were bright.

John grinned at her, feeling overwhelmed with relief to see her looking more than well—radiant, in fact.

The other two attendants, Ohbi and Inholima, sat to Lady Bousim's left. They bowed their heads when John entered the room. Ohbi's glossy black hair had grown even longer than John remembered. Clusters of sliver beads and ribbons hardly held back all of her twisting braids.

Of the four women, only Inholima appeared ill. A sallow tone pervaded her once-golden skin, and dark purple bags hung beneath her eyes. She smiled faintly, showing the small gap between her front two teeth. Most disconcertingly, the tinge of oxygen-starved blue that had once colored Bill's mouth now saturated Inholima's lips.

John suddenly had a terrible idea of who had been chosen to bear the brunt of Bill's illness.

He knew Inholima was a spy, placed in Lady Bousim's entourage by Lord Bousim. If she were to ever discover the witchcraft that Lady Bousim, Laurie, and Ohbi practiced, she could get them all killed. So John could see why they wouldn't hesitate to make her weak and ill.

Still, just sitting there at the table, she seemed young and pathetic. It made John feel sorry for her in spite of himself.

"Ushvun Jahn." Lady Bousim waved him to a seat at the table. "Is it possible that you have grown even more handsome? It is such a delight to see you again."

"Thank you, Lady Bousim." John bowed to her.

"Tell me, how is Ushman Hann'yu?"

He had almost forgotten that the two of them knew each other. His memories of last year's Harvest Fair had been so dominated by the witch burning and his fight with Rasho Tashtu that he hadn't remembered introducing the two of them.

"He's well," John told her. "A little overworked, but well."

"You must inform him that I am anxiously looking forward to this Harvest Fair so that we can talk again."

"I will."

Inholima cupped her hand over her mouth and coughed. It was a sticky, gasping sound. She looked embarrassed at the ugliness of it.

"My dear," Lady Bousim said to Inholima, "are you sure you're well enough to be out of bed?"

"You look terrible," Ohbi said softly.

"Maybe you should rest," Laurie added.

"I don't think I could stand much more bed rest. Lying on my back all day, I feel like I'm withering away." Inholima smiled weakly. "I want to stay up at least long enough to hear Behr play."

Bill glanced to Inholima. "That's flattering. I had no idea you liked it so much."

"It's soothing," Inholima said.

"Well, if Lady Bousim doesn't object, I'd be happy to play for you," Bill said.

"Of course you should play, Behr," Lady Bousim said. She turned easily to John. "You must try the white rolls. The flour was brought all the way from Milaun. They're so soft, nothing like the tough bread you find around here."

"Thank you." John took a roll. It wouldn't taste like anything to him. He added a slab of pale yellow cheese to his plate as well as several slices of lamb cutlet.

Bill walked across the room to where a polished wooden case lay on top of a small table. He opened the case and gently lifted out a mandolin-like instrument. John ate while Bill tuned it. A few moments later, Bill began playing. The music was simple and soothing. The melody struck John as familiar. He wondered if Bill had adapted it from some popular song from Nayeshi.

Inholima closed her eyes. Laurie quietly rose from her seat and stepped back behind Inholima. She gently set her hands on either side of the girl's temples. Inholima glanced up, and Laurie smiled down at her. Inholima closed her eyes again as Laurie massaged the sides of her head.

"Just relax and rest," Laurie said quietly. "Sleep."

John's head snapped up as the last word escaped Laurie's mouth. The air had seemed to shudder around her. He'd felt it. Inholima slumped forward. Laurie caught her, stopping her from falling flat onto the tabletop. Slowly, Laurie and Ohbi lowered Inholima down to the table and let her head rest there.

"Sleep, deaf, dumb, blind." Laurie's words seemed to distort the air like waves of heat. They poured from her mouth and wrapped around Inholima's head. "Sleep, free of thought and mind."

Inholima's breathing suddenly slowed. Her head lolled to the side.

"I hadn't even finished the first song." Bill placed his hand against the strings of his instrument, silencing the notes.

"Jahn doesn't have all day to wait for her to nod off on her own," Laurie replied.

"Is she going to be all right?" John asked. Inholima looked like a corpse collapsed across the table.

"She'll be fine," Laurie assured him. "A little sleep isn't going to hurt her."

"Which is a pity, if you ask me." Ohbi scowled at Inholima's unconscious face.

"There's no need to be cruel," Lady Bousim said. "If it wasn't Inholima, then it would just be another girl sent to spy on us." She turned her attention back to John. "How is the bread?"

"Very soft," John replied.

"I thought you would like it." Lady Bousim smiled.

Laurie returned to her chair. She took several cuts of lamb and a sliced apple. Bill began playing again. John was almost positive that this time it was some variation on a Led Zeppelin song. They all seemed to take Inholima's collapsed, unconscious form in stride. He wondered how often this happened.

"So, how much longer until the Great Gate will be opened?" Laurie asked.

"Soon," John said quietly.

"She's not going to wake up," Ohbi said. "You don't have to whisper."

Suddenly John wondered just how many people Fikiri had told about their plan to leave.

"Soon as in a week, or soon as in this year?" Laurie asked.

"I don't think the Issusha'im are good with exact dates," John responded. "Soon is all they've pinned down as far as anyone seems to know. I would guess within the year."

"Is there any way to hurry it along?" Laurie finished off the last of her lamb and frowned. She laid one hand against her belly.

"Your stomach's still bothering you?" John asked.

Lady Bousim gave a silent shudder of laughter at this. John had no idea why. Both Ohbi and Laurie smiled at him. When he glanced to Bill, John saw that even he seemed amused.

"It's still bothering me, but it should clear up in about nine months," Laurie said.

"Nine . . . " Suddenly John realized why they were all looking so pleased. "You're . . . " John began but then couldn't go on. He hadn't thought of this, and didn't know what he should think of it. He stared at Laurie, stunned.

"Pregnant," Laurie supplied.

"You're going to be an uncle." Bill clapped him on the shoulder. John simply stared at Laurie.

"So, you can see why I would want to know when we're going to be crossing through the Great Gate," Laurie told him. "That last trip through wasn't exactly a roll in the hay."

"Maybe if the hay was mixed into a stack of needles," Bill suggested. He strummed the strings of his instrument softly.

"I don't . . . " John began, but then trailed off. He glanced to Ohbi and then back to Laurie. He'd been so stunned by the news that he hadn't wondered why they would be discussing Nayeshi in front of Ohbi and Lady Bousim. Both Bill and Laurie had just offhandedly mentioned their previous passage through the Great Gate.

The reason was obvious, John realized. They had informed Lady Bousim and Ohbi that they had come from Nayeshi. This meant Fikiri probably knew . . .

Laurie and Bill had to be planning to bring them all along. Fikiri must have told them that John had already agreed to it. John ran his hand across the back of his neck, massaging uselessly at the tense muscles there. Fikiri, Lady Bousim, Ohbi. Doubtless they would be planning to bring Ohbi's brother, Bati'kohl, as well. John had no idea how Ravishan would manage to sneak three of them through the Great Gate unnoticed. Adding in Fikiri, his mother, Ohbi, and her brother was simply impossible.

He knew he couldn't say so, not in front of Lady Bousim and Ohbi. He had to find a time when he could talk to Laurie and Bill alone.

"I don't know when," John said. "It depends on the Issusha'im. But from what we've heard, it sounds like the Kahlil will be leaving by the end of the year. Early in the next year at the latest."

"Earlier would be better," Laurie said. "I think I can protect our little girl as long as she's inside me, but after that I don't know."

"How far along . . . " John wasn't sure why he was having such difficulty even talking. It just seemed like so much to take in. He'd known Laurie since they were children themselves. He couldn't imagine her as someone's mother.

"Six weeks." Laurie grinned at John's awkwardness.

"That's really early, isn't it?" John asked. A distant memory of his developmental biology class floated up to him. The first month. At this point the fetus would be a clump of red pulsing cells clinging, fragile and microscopic. If it had been a root ball or mineral deposit, he would have been utterly at ease. Even in the animal realm, contemplating gestation periods, rates of miscarriage and stillbirth, he was comfortable. But this was his friends' child. The closeness of it made him feel nervous and uncertain.

"It's early, but I can feel her perfectly. She's very strong," Laurie assured him. "Still, I'd like it if we could leave in the fall."

John stole a glance back to Bill and caught him gazing at Laurie with a wide, almost goofy smile.

"Maybe after the Harvest Fair. I think that would be the best," Laurie said.

"Before would be nice." Ohbi closed her eyes for a moment. "I would be so happy not to see another of those fires ever again in my life."

"This year it isn't a witch," Lady Bousim said. "They're going to burn one of the Fai'daum, the man that killed a garrison commander at Gisa."

"I still don't want to see it," Ohbi whispered.

"I don't think any of us do," John agreed. Ravishan would be the one forced to light the fire. John closed his eyes as if it could shut out his memory of the last fire.

"You should try one of these pears," Laurie told him.

John opened his eyes to see that Laurie was already spooning several slices of poached pear onto his plate.

"Thank you," John said.

"Don't look so glum," Laurie told him. "It'll all work out. We'll make it work out."

John could have told her that he very much doubted that they had the power to do that; instead he took a bite of soft pear. It tasted like wine and honey.

"Any suggestions for names?" Laurie asked.

"It's hard to think of good names for girls," John said. It struck him as the least of their problems.

"Don't name her Ohbi," said Ohbi. "It's such a desolate name for a little girl to have to live with."

Lady Bousim nodded. "Wounin'an is sweet. It was my mother's name."

"I like Billy-Joe," Bill remarked dryly.

Laurie laughed. Both Lady Bousim and Ohbi frowned in confusion.

"Bayal'go?" Ohbi worked hard to pronounce the foreign name.

"No, Behr is joking." Laurie quickly explained. "It's a man's name in Nayeshi."

"What does it mean?" Ohbi asked.

"I don't really know," Laurie said but her tone was pondering. "Billy is a type of goat . . . "

"A male goat," John supplied automatically.

"Joe's another word for coffee." Bill gave John an impish grin as he spoke. "That's a drink like daru'sira."

Ohbi nodded seriously, as if committing this all to memory. Lady Bousim picked up one of the soft rolls and nibbled on it thoughtfully.

"It's a strange name," Lady Bousim pronounced at last. "A name suitable for a wily young man, but not a pretty girl."

John tried not to picture the absolute disaster of the two of them attempting to integrate with people back home. That was assuming that any of them even made it home. His head was beginning to throb. He poured himself a cup of the pale green daru'sira.

While Laurie, Ohbi, Bill, and Lady Bousim discussed possible names for the baby, John drank his daru'sira. At last, he heard bells beginning to ring in the new hour. It would be getting dark soon.

John stood. "I should go."

"But you just got here," Laurie protested.

"I have to be back at the hostel before dark or the other ushvun'im will miss me."

"I wish you could stay here with us," Laurie said.

"Sorry." John turned to Lady Bousim. "Thank you for everything."

Lady Bousim inclined her head graciously. "It is always a pleasure to see you, Jahn. Thank you for looking after my son."

John simply nodded. He doubted that Fikiri would have shared her sentiment.

"Stay out of trouble," Bill told him.

Ohbi held her hand up in a sign of peace. John returned her gesture and departed.

When he reached the hostel, he stored away Hann'yu's supplies and then went to the room he was to share with the other ushvun'im. None of them had returned yet. Most would stay out as late as they could, drinking hard taye liquor and gambling on goat races. John sat down on a bed. The fires hadn't been stoked for the evening and the sheets felt cold. He stared at the plain wall and tried to think.

How would seven people slip unnoticed through the Great Gate? One of them heavily pregnant, or worse yet, carrying a newborn baby. It would never happen. The Issusha'im were watching everything now. The full force and attention of the Payshmura Church would be focused on the Great Gate and the Kahlil.

John fell back against the bed and stared up at the ceiling as if it would offer him some new insight. For an instant, he thought he glimpsed white skulls staring back at him. And for the first time they didn't seem like a dream, but a premonition.

People were going to have to be left behind or they would all be killed.

To Be Continued in Rifter Volume Three: The Holy Road

Characters from Kahlil's Story

Alidas—Captain for the Bousim in Nurjima; partly crippled
Desh'oun—The house steward in the Lisam Palace
Saimura—Jath'ibaye's house steward in Nurjima
Esh'illan Anyyd—A young gaunan allied with Ourath
Fensal— A Lisam runner
Fikiri Bousim—An ushiri from the fallen Payshmura Faith
Ji Shir'korud—Dog demon; called Jath'ibaye's bitch by some gaun'im
Jath'ibaye—Leader of the new Fai'daum kingdom
Joulen Bousim—Bousim heir after Nanvess. Currently serving military duty in the northmost Bousim holdings
Kahlil— Kyle'insira, also called Kyle
Mosh'sira'in'Bousim—Gaunsho Bousim; aged and weak ruler
Nanvess Bousim—A gaunan; named the Bousim heir for political reasons
Nivoun Bousim—Nanvess' father; highly ambitious for his son
Ourath Lisam—Gaunsho Lisam
Parfir—God of the banned Payshmura Church; his worship is now forbidden
Yu'mir—A servant woman in Lisam Palace

Characters from John's Story

Ashan'ahma—An ushiri studying at Rathal'pesha
Alidas—A rider for the Bousim family; partly crippled
Amha'in'Bousim—Lady Bousim, third wife, exiled to the north
Bati'kohl—A servant of Lady Bousim; brother of Ohbi
Bill—Called Behr in Basawar
Dayyid—Second ushman at Rathal'pesha
Fikiri Bousim—An ushiri candidate; son of Lady Bousim
Hann'yu—An ushman exiled to the north; specializes in healing
Inholima—Spy in Lady Bousim's household
Issusha'im—The Payshmura oracles
Ji Shir'korud—Dog demon; one of the Fai'daum
John—Called Jahn in Basawar
Laurie—Called Loshai in Basawar
Mosh'sira'in'Bousim—Gaunsho Bousim
Mou'pin—A rider under Pivan
Nuritam—The ushman at Rathal'pesha
Ohbi—A loyal servant to Lady Bousim
Parfir—The earth god
Pivan—The second in command of the Bousim rashan'im
Rifter—The destroyer incarnation of Parfir
Ravishan—The most promising of the ushiri at Rathal'pesha
Rousma—Ravishan's sister
Sabir—The leader of the Fai'daum
Saimura—A member of the Fai'daum
Samsango—An elderly priest at Rathal'pesha
Serahn—Powerful ushman in the Black Tower of Nurjima
Tashtu—Pivan's commander
Wah'roa—Leader of the kahlirash'im at Vundomu

Titles and Ranks

Usho—Leader of the Payshmura Church.
Kahlil—Holy Traveler and Companion to Parfir.
Ushman—High Ranking Clergy in a position of responsibility.
Ushiri—Talented Priest studying to become Kahlil'im.
Ushvun—Priest.
Ushvran—Nun.
Kahlirash—Military sect devoted to Parfir's destroyer incarnation.
Gaunsho—Lord of one of the seven noble houses.
Gaunan—Nobleman.
Gauniri—Noblechild.
Gaunvur—Noblewoman.
Gaun'im—Nobles (as a group).
Laman—Scholar, Doctor or anyone learned.
Lamiri—Student.
Rasho—Military leader, particularly cavalry.
Rashan—Soldier.
Vunan—Common man.
Vuran—Common woman.
Shir—Animal; derogatory when used to address a human being.

Basawar Dictionary

Ahab•how/because
Alidas•hawk
Amha•joy
Amura•place
Ashan•brothers
Ayal•time/year
Bahab•why
Bai•idiot
Bamura•where
Ban•who
Bati•what
Bayal•when
Behr•bee (honey)
Bish•strike
Daru•fire
Daru'sira•tea
Daum•red
Domu•good/pretty
Du•yes
Fai•river
Fathi•sacred drink
Faud•fuck
Fik•goat
Ganal•weasel
Gasm'ah•lost (object or thing)
Gasmva•to be lost
Gaun•noble
Hala•key
Halun•knife
Hel•but/however
Holima•blue
Ibaye•green
Iff•and
Illin•none
In•from/of
Iri•little/diminutive
Isma•fruit tree
Iss•no
Issusha•the holy bones
Ista•tree
Istana•tree bark
Itam•quiet
Jahn•blond hide
Jath•solitary
Ji•yellow/gold color
Jid•shit
Jima•gold metal
Jiusha•money
Kin•same
Kohl•dog (domestic)
Korud•unholy/unclean
Kubo•chasm
Lafi•to indulge, or pamper (spoil)
Lam•book
Loshai•sky
Maht•dead
Maht'tu hala•death-lock key
Mohim•love
Mosh•delicious
Mulhi•ugly/bad
Nabi• grain or food in general
Nabi'usha•meat
Nabiya•to eat
Nahara•stop
Niru•hot
Nur•road
Parh•rain
Pashim•friend
Pelima•snow
Pesha•white
Pivan•meadow
Polima•cold
Pom•lazy
Ra•to spill or overturn

Rashiya•to kill
Rathal•mountain
Ratim•harm
Ratimya•to harm
Renma•exhausted
Ro•similar
Rousma•hill
Sabir•wolf or wild dog
Sam•fast
Sango•run
Shir•an animal
Sho•best
Sira•water or beverages in general
Siraya•to drink
Sumah•bone
Tahjid•witch
Tahldi•deer (mount)
Tamur•city
Tash•still, motionless
Taye•a grain
Tehji•terrible
Tu•lock
Tumah•peace
Umbhra•orchard
Usha•blood
Ushmana•holy
Ushmana'lam•sacred books
Ushmura•monastery
Vass•speak
Vishan•wine
Vun•man/male
Vur•woman/female
Wahbai•asshole
Yasi•black
Yasistana•a kind of medicinal tree

Ad•future tense
Ah•past tense
Al•adverb
An•adjective
At•possible or speculative
Atdou•hoped for (future)
Ati•source of action
Atiss•hoped against(future)
Dou•positive
Hi•command form
Hir•object of action
Hlil•one who does
Im•plural
Iss•negative
Sa•question
Um•possessive (singular)
Un•possessive (plural)
Ya•present tense
(Ya literally means "to do" or "to be.")
Yas•gerund

Pronouns

Li• I/me
Li'um •mine
Li'im •we/us
Lim'un• ours

Yura •you
Yura'um• yours
Yura'im •you (plural)
Yura'un• yours (plural)

Pun •a person (not gendered)
Pun'im •they (not gendered)
Pun'un •theirs (not gendered)

Vur •she/her
Vur'um •hers
Vur'im• they (all female)
Vur'un• theirs (all female)

Vun• he/him
Vun'um •his
Vun'im •they(all male)
Vun'un •theirs(all male)

Shir •it (animal/ object)
Shir'um •its (animal/ object)
Shir'im • they (animals/ objects)
Shir'un• theirs (animals/ objects)

OTHER PUBLICATIONS FROM GINN HALE

Novels

Wicked Gentlemen
Lord of the White Hell Book One
Lord of the White Hell Book Two
Champion of the Scarlet Wolf Book One
Champion of the Scarlet Wolf Book Two
Master of Restless Shadows Book One
Master of Restless Shadows Book Two
Price of a Thousand Blessings Volume One
Price of a Thousand Blessings Volume Two
Price of a Thousand Blessings Volume Three
Price of a Thousand Blessings Volume Four

Novellas

Feral Machines—Tangle (Anthology)
Touching Sparks—Hell Cop (Anthology)
Such Heights— Hell Cop Two (Anthology)
Things Unseen and Deadly—Irregulars (Anthology)
Swift and the Black Dog—Charmed and Dangerous (Anthology)
The Long Past—The Long Past and other stories (Anthology)
Get Lucky—The Long Past and Other Stories (Anthology)
Counterfeit Viscount—Devil Take Me (Anthology)

Short Stories

"Shy Hunter"—Queer Wolf
"Blood Beneath the Throne"—Icarus Magazine
"Seed Stitch Solution"—Once Upon A Fact
"Treasured Island"—Scourges of the Seas of Time (and Space)
"The Hollow History of Professor Perfectus"—The Long Past & Other Stories

About the Author

Ginn Hale is a multi-award-winning author of fantasy and science fiction. She lives in the Pacific Northwest with her wife of over thirty years and their indulged cat. There, she spends the cloudy days and rainy evenings drinking coffee and writing books featuring LGBTQ+ characters.

Her most recent publications include the Cadelonians series: *Lord of the White Hell*, *Champion of the Scarlet Wolf* and *Master of Restless Shadows.*

She can be reached on Patreon as well as through her website www.ginnhale.com Her Instagram account, however, is largely a collection of botanical photos . . . so be warned.

Content Warning

Characters in this series face physical and mental hardship, which includes starvation, warfare, torture, political oppression, religious oppression, grief, guilt, and death. Sexual assault and child abuse occur but are not explicitly depicted. None of these subjects are meant to be glorified or romanticized.